TO
DEAR PETER,
MOST FAITHFUL OF FRIENDS
AND DEAREST OF COMPANIONS,
A DOG IN A THOUSAND

Agatha Christie®

Dumb Witness

HarperCollins*Publishers*

HarperCollins*Publishers* Ltd
1 London Bridge Street
London SE1 9GF
www.harpercollins.co.uk

This paperback edition 2015

First published in Great Britain by
Collins 1937

A catalogue record for this book is
available from the British Library

ISBN 978-0-00-812956-9 (PB)
ISBN 978-0-00-825601-2 (POD PB)

Find out more about HarperCollins and the environment at
www.harpercollins.co.uk/green

Contents

CHAPTER 1

The Mistress of Littlegreen House

Miss Arundell died on May 1st. Though her illness was short her death did not occasion much surprise in the little country town of Market Basing where she had lived since she was a girl of sixteen. For Emily Arundell was well over seventy, the last of a family of five, and she had been known to be in delicate health for many years and had indeed nearly died of a similar attack to the one that killed her some eighteen months before.

But though Miss Arundell's death surprised no one, something else did. The provisions of her will gave rise to varying emotions, astonishment, pleasurable excitement, deep condemnation, fury, despair, anger and general gossip. For weeks and even months Market Basing was to talk of nothing else! Everyone had their own contribution to make to the subject from Mr Jones the grocer, who held that 'blood was thicker than water', to Mrs Lamphrey at the post office, who repeated *ad nauseam* that 'there's something behind it, depend upon it! You mark my words.'

What added zest to the speculations on the subject was the fact that the will had been made as lately as April 21st. Add to this the further fact that Emily Arundell's near relations had been staying with her just before that date over Easter Bank Holiday and it will be realized that the most scandalous theories could be propounded, pleasurably relieving the monotony of everyday life in Market Basing.

There was one person who was shrewdly suspected of knowing more about the matter than she was willing to admit. That was Miss Wilhelmina Lawson, Miss Arundell's companion. Miss Lawson, however, professed herself just as much in the dark as everyone else. She, too, she declared, had been dumbfounded when the will was read out.

A lot of people, of course, did not believe this. Nevertheless, whether Miss Lawson was or was not as ignorant as she declared herself to be, only one person really knew the true facts. That person was the dead woman herself. Emily Arundell had kept her own counsel as she was in the habit of doing. Even to her lawyer she had said nothing of the motives underlying her action. She was content with making her wishes clear.

In that reticence could be found the keynote of Emily Arundell's character. She was, in every respect, a typical product of her generation. She had both its virtues and its vices. She was autocratic and often overbearing, but she was also intensely warm-hearted. Her tongue was sharp but her actions were kind. She was outwardly sentimental but inwardly shrewd. She had a succession of companions whom she bullied unmercifully, but treated with great generosity. She had a great sense of family obligation.

On the Friday before Easter Emily Arundell was standing in the hall of Littlegreen House giving various directions to Miss Lawson.

Emily Arundell had been a handsome girl and she was now a well-preserved handsome old lady with a straight back and a brisk manner. A faint yellowness in her skin was a warning that she could not eat rich food with impunity.

Miss Arundell was saying:

'Now then, Minnie, where have you put them all?'

'Well, I thought—I hope I've done right—Dr and Mrs Tanios in the Oak room and Theresa in the Blue room and Mr Charles in the Old Nursery—'

Miss Arundell interrupted:

'Theresa can have the Old Nursery and Charles will have the Blue room.'

'Oh, yes—I'm sorry—I thought the Old Nursery being rather more inconvenient—'

'It will do very nicely for Theresa.'

In Miss Arundell's day, women took second place. Men were the important members of society.

'I'm so sorry the dear little children aren't coming,' murmured Miss Lawson, sentimentally.

She loved children and was quite incapable of managing them.

'Four visitors will be quite enough,' said Miss Arundell. 'In any case Bella spoils her children abominably. They never dream of doing what they are told.'

Minnie Lawson murmured:

'Mrs Tanios is a very devoted mother.'

Miss Arundell said with grave approval:

'Bella is a good woman.'

Miss Lawson sighed and said:

'It must be very hard for her sometimes—living in an outlandish place like Smyrna.'

Emily Arundell replied:

'She has made her bed and she must lie on it.'

And having uttered this final Victorian pronouncement she went on:

'I am going to the village now to speak about the orders for the weekend.'

'Oh, Miss Arundell, do let me. I mean—'

'Nonsense. I prefer to go myself. Rogers needs a sharp word. The trouble with you is, Minnie, that you're not *emphatic* enough. Bob! Bob! Where *is* the dog?'

A wire-haired terrier came tearing down the stairs. He circled round and round his mistress uttering short staccato barks of delight and expectation.

Together mistress and dog passed out of the front door and down the short path to the gate.

Miss Lawson stood in the doorway smiling rather foolishly after them, her mouth a little open. Behind her a voice said tartly:

'Them pillowcases you gave me, miss, isn't a pair.'

'What? How stupid of me…'

Minnie Lawson plunged once more into household routine.

Emily Arundell, attended by Bob, made a royal progress down the main street of Market Basing.

It was very much of a royal progress. In each shop she entered the proprietor always hurried forward to attend to her.

She was Miss Arundell of Littlegreen House. She was 'one of our oldest customers'. She was 'one of the old school. Not many about like her nowadays'.

'Good morning, miss. What can I have the pleasure of doing for you—Not tender? Well, I'm sorry to hear that. I thought myself it was as nice a little saddle—Yes, of course, Miss Arundell. If you say so, it is so—No, indeed I wouldn't think of sending Canterbury to *you*, Miss Arundell—Yes, I'll see to it myself, Miss Arundell.'

Bob and Spot, the butcher's dog, circled slowly round each other, hackles raised, growling gently. Spot was a stout dog of nondescript breed. He knew that he must not fight with customers' dogs, but he permitted himself to tell them, by subtle indication, just exactly what mincemeat he would make of them were he free to do so.

Bob, a dog of spirit, replied in kind.

Emily Arundell said 'Bob!' sharply and passed on.

In the greengrocer's there was a meeting of heavenly bodies. Another old lady, spherical in outline, but equally distinguished by that air of royalty, said:

'Mornin', Emily.'

'Good morning, Caroline.'

Caroline Peabody said:

'Expecting any of your young people down?'

'Yes, all of them. Theresa, Charles and Bella.'

'So Bella's home, is she? Husband too?'

'Yes.'

Agatha Christie

It was a simple monosyllable, but underlying it was knowledge common to both ladies.

For Bella Biggs, Emily Arundell's niece, had married a Greek. And Emily Arundell's people, who were what is known as 'all service people', simply did not marry Greeks.

By way of being obscurely comforting (for of course such a matter could not be referred to openly) Miss Peabody said:

'Bella's husband's got brains. *And* charming manners!'

'His manners are delightful,' agreed Miss Arundell.

Moving out into the street Miss Peabody asked:

'What's this about Theresa being engaged to young Donaldson?'

Miss Arundell shrugged her shoulders.

'Young people are so casual nowadays. I'm afraid it will have to be a rather long engagement—that is, if anything comes of it. He has no money.'

'Of course Theresa has her own money,' said Miss Peabody.

Miss Arundell said stiffly:

'A man could not possibly wish to live on his wife's money.'

Miss Peabody gave a rich, throaty chuckle.

'They don't seem to mind doing it, nowadays. You and I are out of date, Emily. What I can't understand is what the child *sees* in him. Of all the namby-pamby young men!'

'He's a clever doctor, I believe.'

'Those *pince-nez*—and that stiff way of talking! In my young days we'd have called him a poor stick!'

There was a pause while Miss Peabody's memory, diving into the past, conjured up visions of dashing, bewhiskered young men...

6

She said with a sigh:

'Send that young dog Charles along to see me—if he'll come.'

'Of course. I'll tell him.'

The two ladies parted.

They had known each other for considerably over fifty years. Miss Peabody knew of certain regrettable lapses in the life of General Arundell, Emily's father. She knew just precisely what a shock Thomas Arundell's marriage had been to his sisters. She had a very shrewd idea of certain troubles connected with the younger generation.

But no word had ever passed between the two ladies on any of these subjects. They were both upholders of family dignity, family solidarity, and complete reticence on family matters.

Miss Arundell walked home, Bob trotting sedately at her heels. To herself, Emily Arundell admitted what she would never have admitted to another human being, her dissatisfaction with the younger generation of her family.

Theresa, for instance. She had no control over Theresa since the latter had come into her own money at the age of twenty-one. Since then the girl had achieved a certain notoriety. Her picture was often in the papers. She belonged to a young, bright, go-ahead set in London—a set that had freak parties and occasionally ended up in the police courts. It was not the kind of notoriety that Emily Arundell approved of for an Arundell. In fact, she disapproved very much of Theresa's way of living. As regards the girl's engagement, her feelings were slightly confused. On the one

7

hand she did not consider an upstart Dr Donaldson good enough for an Arundell. On the other she was uneasily conscious that Theresa was a most unsuitable wife for a quiet country doctor.

With a sigh her thoughts passed on to Bella. There was no fault to find with Bella. She was a good woman—a devoted wife and mother, quite exemplary in behaviour—and extremely dull! But even Bella could not be regarded with complete approval. For Bella had married a foreigner—and not only a foreigner—but a Greek. In Miss Arundell's prejudiced mind a Greek was almost as bad as an Argentine or a Turk. The fact that Dr Tanios had a charming manner and was said to be extremely able in his profession only prejudiced the old lady slightly more against him. She distrusted charm and easy compliments. For this reason, too, she found it difficult to be fond of the two children. They had both taken after their father in looks—there was really nothing English about them.

And then Charles...

Yes, Charles...

It was no use blinding one's eyes to facts. Charles, charming though he was, was not to be trusted...

Emily Arundell sighed. She felt suddenly tired, old, depressed...

She supposed that she couldn't last much longer...

Her mind reverted to the will she had made some years ago.

Legacies to the servants—to charities—and the main bulk of her considerable fortune to be divided equally between these, her three surviving relations...

It still seemed to her that she had done the right and equitable thing. It just crossed her mind to wonder whether there might not be some way of securing Bella's share of the money so that her husband could not touch it... She must ask Mr Purvis.

She turned in at the gate of Littlegreen House.

Charles and Theresa Arundell arrived by car—the Tanioses, by train.

The brother and sister arrived first. Charles, tall and good-looking, with his slightly mocking manner, said:

'Hullo, Aunt Emily, how's the girl? You look fine.'

And he kissed her.

Theresa put an indifferent young cheek against her withered one.

'How are you, Aunt Emily?'

Theresa, her aunt thought, was looking far from well. Her face, beneath its plentiful make-up, was slightly haggard and there were lines round her eyes.

They had tea in the drawing-room. Bella Tanios, her hair inclined to straggle in wisps from below the fashionable hat that she wore at the wrong angle, stared at her cousin Theresa with a pathetic eagerness to assimilate and memorize her clothes. It was poor Bella's fate in life to be passionately fond of clothes without having any clothes sense. Theresa's clothes were expensive, slightly bizarre, and she herself had an exquisite figure.

Bella, when she arrived in England from Smyrna, had tried earnestly to copy Theresa's elegance at an inferior price and cut.

Dr Tanios, who was a big bearded jolly looking man, was talking to Miss Arundell. His voice was warm and full—an attractive voice that charmed a listener almost against his or her will. Almost in spite of herself, it charmed Miss Arundell.

Miss Lawson was fidgeting a good deal. She jumped up and down, handing plates, fussing over the tea-table. Charles, whose manners were excellent, rose more than once to help her, but she expressed no gratitude.

When, after tea, the party went out to make a tour of the garden Charles murmured to his sister:

'Lawson doesn't like me. Odd, isn't it?'

Theresa said, mockingly:

'Very odd. So there *is* one person who can withstand your fatal fascination?'

Charles grinned—an engaging grin—and said:

'Lucky it's only Lawson...'

In the garden Miss Lawson walked with Mrs Tanios and asked her questions about the children. Bella Tanios' rather drab face lighted up. She forgot to watch Theresa. She talked eagerly and animatedly. Mary had said such a *quaint* thing on the boat...

She found Minnie Lawson a most sympathetic listener.

Presently a fair-haired young man with a solemn face and *pince-nez* was shown into the garden from the house. He looked rather embarrassed. Miss Arundell greeted him politely.

Theresa said:

'Hullo, Rex!'

She slipped an arm through his. They wandered away.

Charles made a face. He slipped away to have a word with the gardener, an ally of his from old days.

When Miss Arundell re-entered the house Charles was playing with Bob. The dog stood at the top of the stairs, his ball in his mouth, his tail gently wagging.

'Come on, old man,' said Charles.

Bob sank down on his haunches, nosed his ball slowly and slowly nearer the edge. As he finally bunted it over he sprang to his feet in great excitement. The ball bumped slowly down the stairs. Charles caught it and tossed it up to him. Bob caught it neatly in his mouth. The performance was repeated.

'Regular game of his, this,' said Charles.

Emily Arundell smiled.

'He'll go on for hours,' she said.

She turned into the drawing-room and Charles followed her. Bob gave a disappointed bark.

Glancing through the window Charles said:

'Look at Theresa and her young man. They *are* an odd couple!'

'You think Theresa is really serious over this?'

'Oh, she's crazy about him!' said Charles with confidence. 'Odd taste, but there it is. I think it must be the way he looks at her as though she were a scientific specimen and not a live woman. That's rather a novelty for Theresa. Pity the fellow's so poor. Theresa's got expensive tastes.'

Miss Arundell said drily:

'I've no doubt she can change her way of living—if she wants to! And after all she has her own income.'

'Eh? Oh yes, yes, of course.'

Charles shot an almost guilty look at her.

That evening, as the others were assembled in the drawing-room waiting to go in to dinner, there was a scurry and a burst of profanity on the stairs. Charles entered with his face rather red.

'Sorry, Aunt Emily, am I late? That dog of yours nearly made me take the most frightful toss. He'd left that ball of his on the top of the stairs.'

'Careless little doggie,' cried Miss Lawson, bending down to Bob.

Bob looked at her contemptuously and turned his head away.

'I know,' said Miss Arundell. 'It's most dangerous. Minnie, fetch the ball and put it away.'

Miss Lawson hurried out.

Dr Tanios monopolized the conversation at the dinner-table most of the time. He told amusing stories of his life in Smyrna.

The party went to bed early. Miss Lawson carrying wool, spectacles, a large velvet bag and a book accompanied her employer to her bedroom chattering happily.

'Really *most* amusing, Dr Tanios. He is such *good* company! Not that I should care for that kind of life myself... One would have to boil the water, I expect... And goat's milk, perhaps—such a disagreeable taste—'

Miss Arundell snapped:

'Don't be a fool, Minnie. You told Ellen to call me at half-past six?'

'Oh, yes, Miss Arundell. I said no tea, but don't you think it might be wiser—You know, the vicar at Southbridge—a

12

most conscientious man, told me distinctly that there was no obligation to come fasting—'

Once more Miss Arundell cut her short.

'I've never yet taken anything before Early Service and I'm not going to begin now. *You* can do as you like.'

'Oh, no—I didn't mean—I'm sure—'

Miss Lawson was flustered and upset.

'Take Bob's collar off,' said Miss Arundell.

The slave hastened to obey.

Still trying to please she said:

'Such a *pleasant* evening. They all seem so *pleased* to be here.'

'Hmph,' said Emily Arundell. 'All here for what they can get.'

'Oh, dear Miss Arundell—'

'My good Minnie, I'm not a fool whatever else I am! I just wonder which of them will open the subject first.'

She was not long left in doubt on that point. She and Miss Lawson returned from attending Early Service just after nine. Dr and Mrs Tanios were in the dining-room, but there were no signs of the two Arundells. After breakfast, when the others had left, Miss Arundell sat on, entering up some accounts in a little book.

Charles entered the room about ten.

'Sorry I'm late, Aunt Emily. But Theresa's worse. She's not unclosed an eyelid yet.'

'At half-past ten breakfast will be cleared away,' said Miss Arundell. 'I know it is the fashion not to consider servants nowadays, but that is not the case in *my* house.'

'Good. That's the true diehard spirit!'

Charles helped himself to kidneys and sat down beside her.

His grin, as always, was very attractive. Emily Arundell soon found herself smiling indulgently at him. Emboldened by this sign of favour, Charles plunged.

'Look here, Aunt Emily, sorry to bother you, but I'm in the devil of a hole. Can you possibly help me out? A hundred would do it.'

His aunt's face was not encouraging. A certain grimness showed itself in her expression.

Emily Arundell was not afraid of speaking her mind. She spoke it.

Miss Lawson hustling across the hall almost collided with Charles as he left the dining-room. She glanced at him curiously. She entered the dining-room to find Miss Arundell sitting very upright with a flushed face.

CHAPTER 2

The Relations

Charles ran lightly up the stairs and tapped on his sister's door. Her answering 'Come in' came promptly and he entered.

Theresa was sitting up in bed yawning.

Charles took a seat on the bed.

'What a decorative female you are, Theresa,' he remarked appreciatively.

Theresa said sharply:

'What's the matter?'

Charles grinned.

'Sharp, aren't you? Well, I stole a march on you, my girl! Thought I'd make my touch before *you* got to work.'

'Well?'

Charles spread his hands downwards in negation.

'Nothing doing! Aunt Emily ticked me off good and proper. She intimated that she was under no illusions as to why her affectionate family had gathered round her! And she also intimated that the said affectionate family would be disappointed. Nothing being handed out but affection—and not so much of that.'

'You might have waited a bit,' said Theresa drily.

Charles grinned again.

'I was afraid you or Tanios might get in ahead of me. I'm sadly afraid, Theresa my sweet, that there'll be nothing doing this time. Old Emily is by no means a fool.'

'I never thought she was.'

'I even tried to put the wind up her.'

'What d'you mean?' asked his sister sharply.

'Told her she was going about it the right way to get bumped off. After all she can't take the dibs to heaven with her. Why not loosen up a bit?'

'Charles, you are a fool!'

'No, I'm not. I'm a bit of a psychologist in my way. It's never a bit of good sucking up to the old girl. She much prefers you to stand up to her. And after all, I was only talking sense. We get the money when she dies—she might just as well part with a little beforehand! Otherwise the temptation to help her out of the way might become overwhelming.'

'Did she see your point?' asked Theresa, her delicate mouth curling up scornfully.

'I'm not sure. She didn't admit it. Just thanked me rather nastily for my advice and said she was perfectly capable of taking care of herself. "Well," I said, "I've warned you." "I'll remember it," she said.'

Theresa said angrily:

'Really, Charles, you are an utter fool.'

'Damn it all, Theresa, I was a bit ratty myself! The old girl's rolling—simply rolling. I bet she doesn't spend a tenth part of her income—what has she got to spend it on, anyway? And here we are—young, able to enjoy life—and to spite us she's capable of living to a hundred... I want my fun now... So do you...'

Theresa nodded.

She said in a low, breathless voice:

'They don't understand—old people don't...they can't... They don't know what it is to *live*!'

Brother and sister were silent for some minutes.

Charles got up.

'Well, my love, I wish you better success than I've had. But I rather doubt it.'

Theresa said:

'I'm rather counting on Rex to do the trick. If I can make old Emily realize how brilliant he is, and how it matters terrifically that he should have his chance and not have to sink into a rut as a general practitioner... Oh, Charles, a few thousand of capital just at this minute would make all the difference in the world to our lives!'

'Hope you get it, but I don't think you will. You've got through a bit too much capital in riotous living in your time. I say, Theresa, you don't think the dreary Bella or the dubious Tanios will get anything, do you?'

'I don't see that money would be any good to Bella. She goes about looking like a rag-bag and her tastes are purely domestic.'

'Oh, well,' said Charles, vaguely. 'I expect she wants things for those unprepossessing children of hers, schools, and plates for their front teeth and music lessons. And

Agatha Christie

anyway it isn't Bella—it's Tanios. I bet *he's* got a nose for money all right! Trust a Greek for that. You know he's got through most of Bella's? Speculated with it and lost it all.'

'Do you think he'll get something out of old Emily?'

'He won't if I can prevent him,' said Charles, grimly.

He left the room and wandered downstairs. Bob was in the hall. He fussed up to Charles agreeably. Dogs liked Charles.

He ran towards the drawing-room door and looked back at Charles.

'What's the matter?' said Charles, strolling after him.

Bob hurried into the drawing-room and sat down expectantly by a small bureau.

Charles strolled over to him.

'What's it all about?'

Bob wagged his tail, looked hard at the drawers of the bureau and uttered an appealing squeak.

'Want something that's in here?'

Charles pulled open the top drawer. His eyebrows rose. 'Dear, dear,' he said.

At one side of the drawer was a little pile of treasury notes.

Charles picked up the bundle and counted them. With a grin he removed three one pound notes and two ten shilling ones and put them in his pocket. He replaced the rest of the notes carefully in the drawer where he had found them.

'That was a good idea, Bob,' he said. 'Your Uncle Charles will be able at any rate to cover expenses. A little ready cash always comes in handy.'

Bob uttered a faint reproachful bark as Charles shut the drawer.

'Sorry old man,' Charles apologized. He opened the next drawer. Bob's ball was in the corner of it. He took it out.

'Here you are. Enjoy yourself with it.' Bob caught the ball, trotted out of the room and presently bump, bump, bump, was heard down the stairs.

Charles strolled out into the garden. It was a fine sunny morning with a scent of lilac.

Miss Arundell had Dr Tanios by her side. He was speaking of the advantage of an English education—a good education—for children and how deeply he regretted that he could not afford such a luxury for his own children.

Charles smiled with satisfied malice. He joined in the conversation in a light-hearted manner, turning it adroitly into entirely different channels.

Emily Arundell smiled at him quite amiably. He even fancied that she was amused by his tactics and was subtly encouraging them.

Charles' spirits rose. Perhaps, after all, before he left—

Charles was an incurable optimist.

Dr Donaldson called for Theresa in his car that afternoon and drove her to Worthem Abbey, one of the local beauty spots. They wandered away from the Abbey itself into the woods.

There Rex Donaldson told Theresa at length about his theories and some of his recent experiments. She understood very little but listened in a spellbound manner, thinking to herself:

'How clever Rex is—and how absolutely adorable!'

Her fiancé paused once and said rather doubtfully:

'I'm afraid this is dull stuff for you, Theresa.'

'Darling, it's too thrilling,' said Theresa, firmly. 'Go on. You take some of the blood of the infected rabbit—?'

Presently Theresa said with a sigh:

'Your work means a terrible lot to you, my sweet.'

'Naturally,' said Dr Donaldson.

It did not seem at all natural to Theresa. Very few of her friends did any work at all, and if they did they made extremely heavy weather about it.

She thought as she had thought once or twice before, how singularly unsuitable it was that she should have fallen in love with Rex Donaldson. Why did these things, these ludicrous and amazing madnesses, happen to one? A profit-less question. This had happened to her.

She frowned, wondered at herself. Her crowd had been so gay—so cynical. Love affairs were necessary to life, of course, but why take them seriously? One loved and passed on.

But this feeling of hers for Rex Donaldson was different, it went deeper. She felt instinctively that here there would be no passing on... Her need of him was simple and profound. Everything about him fascinated her. His calmness and detachment, so different from her own hectic, grasping life, the clear, logical coldness of his scientific mind, and something else, imperfectly understood, a secret force in the man masked by his unassuming slightly pedantic manner, but which she nevertheless felt and sensed instinctively.

In Rex Donaldson there was genius—and the fact that his profession was the main preoccupation of his life and that she was only a part—though a necessary part—of existence to him only heightened his attraction for her. She found herself for the first time in her selfish pleasure-loving life content to take second place. The prospect fascinated her. For Rex she would do anything—anything!

'What a damned nuisance money is,' she said, petulantly. 'If only Aunt Emily were to die we could get married at once, and you could come to London and have a laboratory full of test tubes and guinea pigs, and never bother any more about children with mumps and old ladies with livers.'

Donaldson said:

'There's no reason why your aunt shouldn't live for many years to come—if she's careful.'

Theresa said despondently:

'I know that...'

In the big double-bedded room with the old-fashioned oak furniture, Dr Tanios said to his wife:

'I think that I have prepared the ground sufficiently. It is now your turn, my dear.'

He was pouring water from the old-fashioned copper can into the rose-patterned china basin.

Bella Tanios sat in front of the dressing-table wondering why, when she combed her hair as Theresa did, it should not look like Theresa's!

There was a moment before she replied. Then she said:

'I don't think I want—to ask Aunt Emily for money.'

'It's not for yourself, Bella, it's for the sake of the children. Our investments have been so unlucky.'

His back was turned, he did not see the swift glance she gave him—a furtive, shrinking glance.

She said with mild obstinacy:

'All the same, I think I'd rather not… Aunt Emily is rather difficult. She can be generous but she doesn't like being asked.'

Drying his hands, Tanios came across from the washstand.

'Really, Bella, it isn't like you to be so obstinate. After all, what have we come down here for?'

She murmured:

'I didn't—I never meant—it wasn't to ask for money…'

'Yet you agreed that the only hope if we are to educate the children properly is for your aunt to come to the rescue.'

Bella Tanios did not answer. She moved uneasily.

But her face bore the mild mulish look that many clever husbands of stupid wives know to their cost.

She said:

'Perhaps Aunt Emily herself may suggest—'

'It is possible, but I've seen no signs of it so far.'

Bella said:

'If we could have brought the children with us. Aunt Emily couldn't have helped loving Mary. And Edward is *so* intelligent.'

Tanios said, drily:

'I don't think your aunt is a great child lover. It is probably just as well the children aren't here.'

'Oh, Jacob, but—'

'Yes, yes, my dear. I know your feelings. But these desiccated English spinsters—bah, they are not human. We want to do the best we can, do we not, for our Mary and our Edward? To help us a little would involve no hardship to Miss Arundell.'

Mrs Tanios turned, there was a flush in her cheeks.

'Oh, please, please, Jacob, not this time. I'm sure it would be unwise. I would so very very much rather not.'

Tanios stood close behind her, his arm encircled her shoulders. She trembled a little and then was still—almost rigid.

He said and his voice was still pleasant:

'All the same, Bella, I think—I think you will do what I ask... You usually do, you know—in the end... Yes, I think you will do what I say...'

CHAPTER 3

The Accident

It was Tuesday afternoon. The side door to the garden was open. Miss Arundell stood on the threshold and threw Bob's ball the length of the garden path. The terrier rushed after it.

'Just once more, Bob,' said Emily Arundell. 'A good one.'

Once again the ball sped along the ground with Bob racing at full speed in pursuit.

Miss Arundell stooped down, picked up the ball from where Bob laid it at her feet and went into the house, Bob following her closely. She shut the side door, went into the drawing-room, Bob still at her heels, and put the ball away in the drawer.

She glanced at the clock on the mantelpiece. It was half-past six.

'A little rest before dinner, I think, Bob.'

She ascended the stairs to her bedroom. Bob accompanied her. Lying on the big chintz-covered couch with Bob at her feet, Miss Arundell sighed. She was glad that it was Tuesday and that her guests would be going tomorrow. It was not that this weekend had disclosed anything to her that she had not known before. It was more the fact that it had not permitted her to forget her own knowledge.

She said to herself:

'I'm getting old, I suppose...' And then, with a little shock of surprise: 'I *am* old...'

She lay with her eyes closed for half an hour, then the elderly house-parlourmaid, Ellen, brought hot water and she rose and prepared for dinner.

Dr Donaldson was to dine with them that night. Emily Arundell wished to have an opportunity of studying him at close quarters. It still seemed to her a little incredible that the exotic Theresa should want to marry this rather stiff and pedantic young man. It also seemed a little odd that this stiff and pedantic young man should want to marry Theresa.

She did not feel as the evening progressed that she was getting to know Dr Donaldson any better. He was very polite, very formal and, to her mind, intensely boring. In her own mind she agreed with Miss Peabody's judgement. The thought flashed across her brain, 'Better stuff in our young days.'

Dr Donaldson did not stay late. He rose to go at ten o'clock. After he had taken his departure Emily Arundell herself announced that she was going to bed. She went upstairs and her young relations went up also. They all seemed somewhat subdued tonight. Miss Lawson remained downstairs performing her final duties, letting Bob out for his run, poking down the fire, putting the guard up and rolling back the hearthrug in case of fire.

She arrived rather breathless in her employer's room about five minutes later.

'I think I've got everything,' she said, putting down wool, work-bag, and a library book. 'I do hope the book will be all right. She hadn't got any of the ones on your list but she said she was sure you'd like this one.'

'That girl's a fool,' said Emily Arundell. 'Her taste in books is the worst I've ever come across.'

'Oh, dear. I'm so sorry—Perhaps I ought—'

'Nonsense, it's not your fault.' Emily Arundell added kindly, 'I hope you enjoyed yourself this afternoon.'

Miss Lawson's face lighted up. She looked eager and almost youthful.

'Oh, yes, thank you very much. So *kind* of you to spare me. I had the most interesting time. We had the Planchette and really—it wrote the most *interesting* things. There were several messages... Of course it's not *quite* the same thing as the sittings... Julia Tripp has been having a lot of success with the automatic writing. Several messages from Those who have Passed Over. It—it really makes one feel so grateful—that such things should be permitted...'

Miss Arundell said with a slight smile:

'Better not let the vicar hear you.'

'Oh, but indeed, dear Miss Arundell, I am convinced—quite convinced—there can be *nothing* wrong about it. I only wish dear Mr Lonsdale would *examine* the subject. It seems to me so narrow-minded to condemn a thing that you have not even *investigated*. Both Julia and Isabel Tripp are such truly *spiritual* women.'

'Almost too spiritual to be alive,' said Miss Arundell.

She did not care much for Julia and Isabel Tripp. She thought their clothes ridiculous, their vegetarian and uncooked fruit meals absurd, and their manner affected. They were women of no traditions, no roots—in fact—no breeding! But she got a certain amount of amusement out of their earnestness and she was at bottom kind-hearted enough not to grudge the pleasure that their friendship obviously gave to poor Minnie.

Poor Minnie! Emily Arundell looked at her companion with mingled affection and contempt. She had had so many of these foolish, middle-aged women to minister to her—all much the same, kind, fussy, subservient and almost entirely mindless.

Really poor Minnie was looking quite excited tonight. Her eyes were shining. She fussed about the room vaguely touching things here and there without the least idea of what she was doing, her eyes all bright and shining.

She stammered out rather nervously:

'I—I do wish you'd been there... I feel, you know, that you're not quite a believer yet. But tonight there was a message—for E.A., the initials came *quite* definitely. It was from a man who had passed over many years ago—a very good-looking military man—Isabel saw him quite distinctly. It must have been dear General Arundell. Such a beautiful message, so full of love and comfort, and how through patience all could be attained.'

'Those sentiments sound very unlike papa,' said Miss Arundell.

'Oh, but our Dear Ones change so—on the other side. Everything is love and understanding. And then the Planchette spelt out something about a *key*—I think it was the key of the Boule cabinet—could that be it?'

'The key of the Boule cabinet?' Emily Arundell's voice sounded sharp and interested.

'I think that was it. I thought perhaps it might be important papers—something of the kind. There was a well-authenticated case where a message came to look in a certain piece of furniture and actually a *will* was discovered there.'

'There wasn't a will in the Boule cabinet,' said Miss Arundell. She added abruptly: 'Go to bed, Minnie. You're tired. So am I. We'll ask the Tripps in for an evening soon.'

'Oh, that *will* be nice! Good night, dear. Sure you've got everything? I hope you haven't been tired with so many people here. I must tell Ellen to air the drawing-room *very well* tomorrow, and shake out the curtains—all this smoking leaves such a smell. I must say I think it's very good of you to let them all smoke in the drawing-room!'

'I must make some concessions to modernity,' said Emily Arundell. 'Good night, Minnie.'

As the other woman left the room, Emily Arundell wondered if this spiritualistic business was really good for Minnie. Her eyes had been popping out of her head, and she had looked so restless and excited.

Odd about the Boule cabinet, thought Emily Arundell as she got into bed. She smiled grimly as she remembered the scene of long ago. The key that had come to light after papa's death, and the cascade of empty brandy bottles that had tumbled out when the cabinet had been unlocked! It was little things like that, things that surely neither Minnie Lawson nor Isabel and Julia Tripp could possibly know, which made one wonder whether, after all, there wasn't something in this spiritualistic business...

She felt wakeful lying on her big four-poster bed. Nowadays she found it increasingly difficult to sleep. But she scorned Dr Grainger's tentative suggestion of a sleeping draught. Sleeping draughts were for weaklings, for people who couldn't bear a finger-ache, or a little toothache, or the tedium of a sleepless night.

Often she would get up and wander noiselessly round the house, picking up a book, fingering an ornament, rearranging a vase of flowers, writing a letter or two. In those midnight hours she had a feeling of the equal liveliness of the house through which she wandered. They were not disagreeable, those nocturnal wanderings. It was as though ghosts walked beside her, the ghosts of her sisters, Arabella, Matilda and Agnes, the ghost of her brother Thomas, the dear fellow as he was before That Woman got hold of him! Even the ghost of General Charles Laverton Arundell, that domestic tyrant with the charming manners who shouted and bullied his daughters but who nevertheless was an object of pride to them with his experiences in the Indian Mutiny and his knowledge of the world. What if there were days when he was 'not quite so well' as his daughters put it evasively?

Her mind reverting to her niece's fiancé, Miss Arundell thought, 'I don't suppose *he'll* ever take to drink! Calls himself a *man* and drank *barley water* this evening! Barley water! And I opened papa's special port.'

Charles had done justice to the port all right. Oh! if only Charles were to be trusted. If only one didn't know that with him—

Her thoughts broke off... Her mind ranged over the events of the weekend...

Everything seemed vaguely disquieting...

She tried to put worrying thoughts out of her mind.

It was no good.

She raised herself on her elbow and by the light of the night-light that always burned in a little saucer she looked at the time.

One o'clock and she had never felt less like sleep.

She got out of bed and put on her slippers and her warm dressing-gown. She would go downstairs and just check over the weekly books ready for the paying of them the following morning.

Like a shadow she slipped from her room and along the corridor where one small electric bulb was allowed to burn all night.

She came to the head of the stairs, stretched out one hand to the baluster rail and then, unaccountably, she stumbled, tried to recover her balance, failed and went headlong down the stairs.

The sound of her fall, the cry she gave, stirred the sleeping house to wakefulness. Doors opened, lights flashed on.

Miss Lawson popped out of her room at the head of the staircase.

Uttering little cries of distress she pattered down the stairs. One by one the others arrived—Charles, yawning, in a resplendent dressing-gown. Theresa, wrapped in dark silk. Bella in a navy-blue kimono, her hair bristling with combs to 'set the wave'.

Dazed and confused Emily Arundell lay in a crushed heap. Her shoulder hurt her and her ankle—her whole body was a confused mass of pain. She was conscious of people standing over her, of that fool Minnie Lawson crying and making ineffectual gestures with her hands, of Theresa with a startled look in her dark eyes, of Bella standing with her mouth open looking expectant, of the voice of Charles saying from somewhere—very far away so it seemed—

'It's that damned dog's ball! He must have left it here and she tripped over it. See? Here it is!'

And then she was conscious of authority, putting the others aside, kneeling beside her, touching her with hands that did not fumble but *knew*.

A feeling of relief swept over her. It would be all right now. Dr Tanios was saying in firm, reassuring tones:

'No, it's all right. No bones broken… Just badly shaken and bruised—and of course she's had a bad shock. But she's been very lucky that it's no worse.'

Then he cleared the others off a little and picked her up quite easily and carried her up to her bedroom, where he had held her wrist for a minute, counting, then nodded his head, sent Minnie (who was still crying and being generally a nuisance) out of the room to fetch brandy and to heat water for a hot bottle.

Confused, shaken, and racked with pain, she felt acutely grateful to Jacob Tanios in that moment. The relief of feeling oneself in capable hands. He gave you just that feeling of assurance—of confidence—that a doctor ought to give.

There was something—something she couldn't quite get hold of—something vaguely disquieting—but she wouldn't think of it now. She would drink this and go to sleep as they told her.

But surely there was something missing—someone.

Oh well, she wouldn't think... Her shoulder hurt her— She drank down what she was given.

She heard Dr Tanios say—and in what a comfortable assured voice—'She'll be all right, now.'

She closed her eyes.

She awoke to a sound that she knew—a soft, muffled bark.

She was wide awake in a minute.

Bob—naughty Bob! He was barking outside the front door—his own particular 'out all night very ashamed of himself' bark, pitched in a subdued key but repeated hopefully.

Miss Arundell strained her ears. Ah, yes, that was all right. She could hear Minnie going down to let him in. She heard the creak of the opening front door, a confused low murmur—Minnie's futile reproaches—'Oh, you naughty little doggie—a very naughty little Bobsie—' She heard the pantry door open. Bob's bed was under the pantry table.

And at that moment Emily realized what it was she had subconsciously missed at the moment of her accident. It was Bob. All that commotion—her fall, people running—normally

Bob would have responded by a crescendo of barking from inside the pantry.

So *that* was what had been worrying her at the back of her mind. But it was explained now—Bob, when he had been let out last night, had shamelessly and deliberately gone off on pleasure bent. From time to time he had these lapses from virtue—though his apologies afterwards were always all that could be desired.

So that was all right. But was it? What else was there worrying her, nagging at the back of her head? Her accident—something to do with her accident.

Ah, yes, somebody had said—Charles—that she had slipped on Bob's ball which he had left on the top of the stairs...

The ball had been there—he had held it up in his hand...

Emily Arundell's head ached. Her shoulder throbbed. Her bruised body suffered...

But in the midst of her suffering her mind was clear and lucid. She was no longer confused by shock. Her memory was perfectly clear.

She went over in her mind all the events from six o'clock yesterday evening... She retraced every step...till she came to the moment when she arrived at the stairhead and started to descend the stairs...

A thrill of incredulous horror shot through her...

Surely—surely, she must be mistaken... One often had queer fancies after an event had happened. She tried—earnestly she tried—to recall the slippery roundness of Bob's ball under her foot...

But she could recall nothing of the kind.

Instead—

'Sheer nerves,' said Emily Arundell. 'Ridiculous fancies.'

But her sensible, shrewd, Victorian mind would not admit that for a moment. There was no foolish optimism about the Victorians. They could believe the worst with the utmost ease.

Emily Arundell believed the worst.

CHAPTER 4

Miss Arundell Writes a Letter

It was Friday.

The relations had left.

They left on the Wednesday as originally planned. One and all, they had offered to stay on. One and all they had been steadfastly refused. Miss Arundell explained that she preferred to be 'quite quiet'.

During the two days that had elapsed since their departure, Emily Arundell had been alarmingly meditative. Often she did not hear what Minnie Lawson said to her. She would stare at her and curtly order her to begin all over again.

'It's the *shock*, poor dear,' said Miss Lawson.

And she added with the kind of gloomy relish in disaster which brightens so many otherwise drab lives:

'I dare say she'll never be quite herself again.'

Dr Grainger, on the other hand, rallied her heartily.

He told her that she'd be downstairs again by the end of the week, that it was a positive disgrace she had no bones broken, and what kind of patient was she for a struggling medical man? If all his patients were like her, he might as well take down his plate straight away.

Emily Arundell replied with spirit—she and old Dr Grainger were allies of long standing. He bullied and she defied—they always got a good deal of pleasure out of each other's company!

But now, after the doctor had stumped away, the old lady lay with a frown on her face, thinking—thinking—responding absent-mindedly to Minnie Lawson's well-meant fussing—and then suddenly coming back to consciousness and rending her with a vitriolic tongue.

'Poor little Bobsie,' twittered Miss Lawson, bending over Bob who had a rug spread on the corner of his mistress's bed. 'Wouldn't little Bobsie be unhappy if he knew what he'd done to his poor, poor Missus?'

Miss Arundell snapped:

'Don't be idiotic, Minnie. And where's your English sense of justice? Don't you know that everyone in this country is accounted innocent until he or she is proved guilty?'

'Oh, but we do know—'

Emily snapped:

'We don't know anything at all. Do stop fidgeting, Minnie. Pulling this and pulling that. Haven't you any idea how to behave in a sick-room? Go away and send Ellen to me.'

Meekly Miss Lawson crept away.

Emily Arundell looked after her with a slight feeling of self-reproach. Maddening as Minnie was, she did her best.

Then the frown settled down again on her face.

She was desperately unhappy. She had all a vigorous strong-minded old lady's dislike of inaction in any given situation. But in this particular situation she could not decide upon her line of action.

There were moments when she distrusted her own faculties, her own memory of events. And there was no-one, absolutely no-one in whom she could confide.

Half an hour later, when Miss Lawson tiptoed creakingly into the room, carrying a cup of beef-tea, and then paused irresolute at the view of her employer lying with closed eyes, Emily Arundell suddenly spoke two words with such force and decision that Miss Lawson nearly dropped the cup.

'Mary Fox,' said Miss Arundell.

'A box, dear?' said Miss Lawson. 'Did you say you wanted a box?'

'You're getting deaf, Minnie. I didn't say anything about a box. I said Mary Fox. The woman I met at Cheltenham last year. She was the sister of one of the Canons of Exeter Cathedral. Give me that cup. You've spilt it into the saucer. And don't tiptoe when you come into a room. You don't know how irritating it is. Now go downstairs and get me the London telephone book.'

'Can I find the number for you, dear? Or the address?'

'If I'd wanted you to do that I'd have told you so. Do what I tell you. Bring it here, and put my writing things by the bed.'

Miss Lawson obeyed orders.

As she was going out of the room after having done everything required of her, Emily Arundell said unexpectedly:

'You're a good, faithful creature, Minnie. Don't mind my bark. It's a good deal worse than my bite. You're very patient and good to me.'

Miss Lawson went out of the room with her face pink and incoherent words burbling from her lips.

Sitting up in bed, Miss Arundell wrote a letter. She wrote it slowly and carefully, with numerous pauses for thought and copious underlining. She crossed and recrossed the page—for she had been brought up in a school that was taught never to waste notepaper. Finally, with a sigh of satisfaction, she signed her name and put it into an envelope. She wrote a name upon the envelope. Then she took a fresh sheet of paper. This time she made a rough draft and after having reread it and made certain alterations and erasures, she wrote out a fair copy. She read the whole thing through very carefully, then satisfied that she had expressed her meaning she enclosed it in an envelope and addressed it to William Purvis, Esq., Messrs Purvis, Purvis, Charlesworth and Purvis, Solicitors, Harchester.

She took up the first envelope again, which was addressed to M. Hercule Poirot, and opened the telephone directory. Having found the address she added it.

A tap sounded at the door.

Miss Arundell hastily thrust the letter she had just finished addressing—the letter to Hercule Poirot—inside the flap of her writing-case.

She had no intention of rousing Minnie's curiosity. Minnie was a great deal too inquisitive.

She called 'Come in' and lay back on her pillows with a sigh of relief.

She had taken steps to deal with the situation.

CHAPTER 5

Hercule Poirot Receives a Letter

The events which I have just narrated were not, of course, known to me until a long time afterwards. But by questioning various members of the family in detail, I have, I think, set them down accurately enough.

Poirot and I were only drawn into the affair when we received Miss Arundell's letter.

I remember the day well. It was a hot, airless morning towards the end of June.

Poirot had a particular routine when opening his morning correspondence. He picked up each letter, scrutinized it carefully and neatly slit the envelope open with his paper-cutter. Its contents were perused and then placed in one of four piles beyond the chocolate-pot. (Poirot always drank chocolate for breakfast—a revolting habit.) All this with a machine-like regularity!

So much was this the case that the least interruption of the rhythm attracted one's attention.

I was sitting by the window, looking out at the passing

traffic. I had recently returned from the Argentine and there was something particularly exciting to me in being once more in the roar of London.

Turning my head, I said with a smile:

'Poirot, I—the humble Watson—am going to hazard a deduction.'

'Enchanted, my friend. What is it?'

I struck an attitude and said pompously:

'You have received this morning *one* letter of particular interest!'

'You are indeed the Sherlock Holmes! Yes, you are perfectly right.'

I laughed.

'You see, *I know your methods*, Poirot. If you read a letter through twice it must mean that it is of special interest.'

'You shall judge for yourself, Hastings.'

With a smile my friend tendered me the letter in question.

I took it with no little interest, but immediately made a slight grimace. It was written in one of those old-fashioned spidery handwritings, and it was, moreover, crossed on two pages.

'Must I read this, Poirot?' I complained.

'Ah, no, there is no compulsion. Assuredly not.'

'Can't you tell me what it says?'

'I would prefer you to form your own judgement. But do not trouble if it bores you.'

'No, no, I want to know what it's all about,' I protested.

My friend remarked drily:

'You can hardly do *that*. In effect, the letter says nothing at all.'

Taking this as an exaggeration I plunged without more ado into the letter.

'M. Hercule Poirot.
   Dear Sir,
      After much doubt and indecision, I am writing (the last word was crossed out and the letter went on) I am emboldened to write to you in the hope that you may be able to assist me in a matter of a strictly private nature. (The words *strictly private* were underlined three times.) I may say that your name is not unknown to me. It was mentioned to me by a Miss Fox of Exeter, and although Miss Fox was not herself acquainted with you, she mentioned that her brother-in-law's sister (whose name I cannot, I am sorry to say, recall) had spoken of your kindness and discretion in the highest terms (highest terms underlined once). I did not inquire, of course, as to the nature (nature underlined) of the inquiry you had conducted on her behalf, but I understood from Miss Fox that it was of a painful and confidential nature (last four words underlined heavily).'

I broke off my difficult task of spelling out the spidery words.
   'Poirot,' I said. 'Must I go on? Does she ever get to the point?'
   'Continue, my friend. Patience.'
   'Patience!' I grumbled. 'It's exactly as though a spider had got into an inkpot and was walking over a sheet of notepaper! I remember my Great-Aunt Mary's writing used to be much the same!'

Once more I plunged into the epistle.

'In my present dilemma, it occurs to me that you might undertake the necessary investigations on my behalf. The matter is such, as you will readily understand, as calls for the utmost discretion and I may, in fact—and I need hardly say how sincerely I hope and pray (pray underlined twice) that this may be the case—I may, in fact, be completely mistaken. One is apt sometimes to attribute too much significance to facts capable of a natural explanation.'

'I haven't left out a sheet?' I murmured in some perplexity. Poirot chuckled.

'No, no.'

'Because this doesn't seem to make sense. What is it she is talking about?'

'*Continuez toujours.*'

'The matter is such, as you will readily understand—No, I'd got past that. Oh! here we are. In the circumstances as I am sure you will be the first to appreciate, it is quite impossible for me to consult anyone in Market Basing (I glanced back at the heading of the letter. Littlegreen House, Market Basing, Berks), *but at the same time you will naturally understand that I feel uneasy (uneasy underlined). During the last few days I have reproached myself with being unduly fanciful (fanciful underlined three times) but have only felt increasingly perturbed. I may be attaching undue*

importance to what is, after all, a trifle (trifle underlined twice) but my uneasiness remains. I feel definitely that my mind must be set at rest on the matter. It is actually preying on my mind and affecting my health, and naturally I am in a difficult position as I can say nothing to anyone (nothing to anyone underlined with heavy lines). In your wisdom you may say, of course, that the whole thing is nothing but a mare's nest. The facts may be capable of a perfectly innocent explanation (innocent underlined). Nevertheless, however trivial it may seem, ever since the incident of the dog's ball, I have felt increasingly doubtful and alarmed. I should therefore welcome your views and counsel on the matter. It would, I feel sure, take a great weight off my mind. Perhaps you would kindly let me know what your fees are and what you advise me to do in the matter?

'I must impress on you again that nobody here knows anything at all. The facts are, I know, very trivial and unimportant, but my health is not too good and my nerves (nerves underlined three times) are not what they used to be. Worry of this kind, I am convinced, is very bad for me, and the more I think over the matter, the more I am convinced that I was quite right and no mistake was possible. Of course, I shall not dream of saying anything (underlined) to anyone (underlined).

Hoping to have your advice in the matter at an early date.

*I remain, Yours faithfully,
Emily Arundell.*'

I turned the letter over and scanned each page closely. 'But, Poirot,' I expostulated, 'what is it all *about*?'

My friend shrugged his shoulders.

'What indeed?'

I tapped the sheets with some impatience.

'What a woman! Why can't Mrs—or Miss Arundell—'

'Miss, I think. It is typically the letter of a spinster.'

'Yes,' I said. 'A real, fussy old maid. Why can't she say what she's talking about?'

Poirot sighed.

'As you say—a regrettable failure to employ order and method in the mental processes, and without order and method, Hastings—'

'Quite so,' I interrupted hastily. 'Little grey cells practically non-existent.'

'I would not say that, my friend.'

'I would. What's the *sense* of writing a letter like that?'

'Very little—that is true,' Poirot admitted.

'A long rigmarole all about nothing,' I went on. 'Probably some upset to her fat lapdog—an asthmatic pug or a yapping Pekinese!' I looked at my friend curiously. 'And yet you read that letter through twice. I do not understand you, Poirot.'

Poirot smiled.

'You, Hastings, you would have put it straight in the waste-paper basket?'

'I'm afraid I should.' I frowned down on the letter. 'I suppose I'm being dense, as usual, but *I* can't see anything of interest in this letter!'

'Yet there is one point in it of great interest—a point that struck me at once.'

'Wait,' I cried. 'Don't tell me. Let me see if I can't discover it for myself.'

It was childish of me, perhaps. I examined the letter very thoroughly. Then I shook my head.

'No, I don't see it. The old lady's got the wind up, I realize that—but then, old ladies often do! It may be about nothing—it may conceivably be about something, but I don't see that you can tell that that is so. Unless your instinct—'

Poirot raised an offended hand.

'Instinct! You know how I dislike that word. "Something seems to tell me"—that is what you infer. *Jamais de la vie!* Me, I *reason*. I employ the little grey cells. There is one interesting point about that letter which you have overlooked utterly, Hastings.'

'Oh, well,' I said wearily. 'I'll buy it.'

'Buy it? Buy what?'

'An expression. Meaning that I will permit you to enjoy yourself by telling me just where I have been a fool.'

'Not a fool, Hastings, merely unobservant.'

'Well, out with it. What's the interesting point? I suppose, like the "incident of the dog's ball," the point *is* that there is no interesting point!'

Poirot disregarded this sally on my part. He said quietly and calmly:

'The interesting point is the *date*.'

'The date?'

I picked up the letter. On the top left-hand corner was written April 17th.

'Yes,' I said slowly. 'That *is* odd. April 17th.'

'And we are today June 28th. *C'est curieux, n'est ce pas?* Over two months ago.'

I shook my head doubtfully.

'It probably doesn't mean anything. A slip. She meant to put June and wrote April instead.'

'Even then it would be ten or eleven days old—an odd fact. But actually you are in error. Look at the colour of the ink. That letter was written more than ten or eleven days ago. No, April 17th is the date assuredly. But why was the letter not sent?'

I shrugged my shoulders.

'That's easy. The old pussy changed her mind.'

'Then why did she not destroy the letter? Why keep it over two months and post it now?'

I had to admit that that was harder to answer. In fact I couldn't think of a really satisfactory answer. I merely shook my head and said nothing.

Poirot nodded.

'You see—it is a point! Yes, decidedly a curious point.'

'You are answering the letter?' I asked.

'*Oui, mon ami.*'

The room was silent except for the scratching of Poirot's pen. It was a hot, airless morning. A smell of dust and tar came in through the window.

Poirot rose from his desk, the completed letter in his hand. He opened a drawer and drew out a little square box. From this he took out a stamp. Moistening this with a little sponge he prepared to affix it to the letter.

Then suddenly he paused, stamp in hand, shaking his head with vigour.

'*Non!*' he exclaimed. 'That is the wrong thing I do.' He tore the letter across and threw it into the waste-paper basket.

'Not so must we tackle this matter! We will *go*, my friend.'

'You mean to go down to Market Basing?'

'Precisely. Why not? Does not one stifle in London today? Would not the country air be agreeable?'

'Well, if you put it like that,' I said. 'Shall we go in the car?'

I had acquired a second-hand Austin.

'Excellent. A very pleasant day for motoring. One will hardly need the muffler. A light overcoat, a silk scarf—'

'My dear fellow, you're not going to the North Pole!' I protested.

'One must be careful of catching the chill,' said Poirot sententiously.

'On a day like this?'

Disregarding my protests, Poirot proceeded to don a fawn-coloured overcoat and wrap his neck up with a white silk handkerchief. Having carefully placed the wetted stamp face downwards on the blotting-paper to dry, we left the room together.

CHAPTER 6

We Go to Littlegreen House

I don't know what Poirot felt like in his coat and muffler but I myself felt roasted before we got out of London. An open car in traffic is far from being a refreshing place on a hot summer's day.

Once we were outside London, however, and getting a bit of pace on the Great West Road my spirits rose.

Our drive took us about an hour and a half, and it was close upon twelve o'clock when we came into the little town of Market Basing. Originally on the main road, a modern by-pass now left it some three miles to the north of the main stream of traffic and in consequence it had kept an air of old-fashioned dignity and quietude about it. Its one wide street and ample market square seemed to say, 'I was a place of importance once and to any person of sense and breeding I am still the same. Let this modern speeding world dash along their new-fangled road; I was built to endure in a day when solidarity and beauty went hand in hand.'

There was a parking area in the middle of the big square, though there were only a few cars occupying it. I duly parked the Austin, Poirot divested himself of his superfluous garments, assured himself that his moustaches were in their proper condition of symmetrical flamboyance and we were then ready to proceed.

For once in a way our first tentative inquiry did not meet with the usual response, 'Sorry, but I'm a stranger in these parts.' It would seem indeed probable that there were no strangers in Market Basing! It had that effect! Already, I felt, Poirot and myself (and especially Poirot) were somewhat noticeable. We tended to stick out from the mellow background of an English market town secure in its traditions.

'Littlegreen House?' The man, a burly, ox-eyed fellow, looked us over thoughtfully. 'You go straight up the High Street and you can't miss it. On your left. There's no name on the gate, but it's the first big house after the bank.' He repeated again, 'You can't miss it.'

His eyes followed us as we started on our course.

'Dear me,' I complained. 'There is something about this place that makes me feel extremely conspicuous. As for you, Poirot, you look positively exotic.'

'You think it is noticed that I am a foreigner—yes?'

'The fact cries aloud to heaven,' I assured him.

'And yet my clothes are made by an English tailor,' mused Poirot.

'Clothes are not everything,' I said. 'It cannot be denied, Poirot, that you have a noticeable personality. I have often wondered that it has not hindered you in your career.'

Poirot sighed.

'That is because you have the mistaken idea implanted in your head that a detective is necessarily a man who puts on a false beard and hides behind a pillar! The false beard, it is *vieux jeu*, and shadowing is only done by the lowest branch of my profession. The Hercule Poirots, my friend, need only to sit back in a chair and think.'

'Which explains why we are walking along this exceedingly hot street on an exceedingly hot morning.'

'That is very neatly replied, Hastings. For once, I admit, you have made the score off me.'

We found Littlegreen House easily enough, but a shock awaited us—a house-agent's board.

As we were staring at it, a dog's bark attracted my attention.

The bushes were thin at that point and the dog could be easily seen. He was a wire-haired terrier, somewhat shaggy as to coat. His feet were planted wide apart, slightly to one side, and he barked with an obvious enjoyment of his own performance that showed him to be actuated by the most amiable motives.

'Good watchdog, aren't I?' he seemed to be saying. 'Don't mind me! This is just my fun! My duty too, of course. Just have to let 'em know there's a dog about the place! Deadly dull morning. Quite a blessing to have something to do. Coming into our place? Hope so. It's darned dull. I could do with a little conversation.'

'Hallo, old man,' I said and shoved forward a fist.

Craning his neck through the railings he sniffed suspiciously, then gently wagged his tail, uttering a few short staccato barks.

'Not been properly introduced, of course, have to keep this up! But I see you know the proper advances to make.'

'Good old boy,' I said.

'Wuff,' said the terrier amiably.

'Well, Poirot?' I said, desisting from this conversation and turning to my friend.

There was an odd expression on his face—one that I could not quite fathom. A kind of deliberately suppressed excitement seems to describe it best.

'The Incident of the Dog's Ball,' he murmured. 'Well, at least, we have here a dog.'

'Wuff,' observed our new friend. Then he sat down, yawned widely and looked at us hopefully.

'What next?' I asked.

The dog seemed to be asking the same question.

'*Parbleu*, to Messrs—what is it—Messrs Gabler and Stretcher.'

'That does seem indicated,' I agreed.

We turned and retraced our steps, our canine acquaintance sending a few disgusted barks after us.

The premises of Messrs Gabler and Stretcher were situated in the Market Square. We entered a dim outer office where we were received by a young woman with adenoids and a lack-lustre eye.

'Good morning,' said Poirot politely.

The young woman was at the moment speaking into a telephone but she indicated a chair and Poirot sat down. I found another and brought it forward.

'I couldn't say, I'm sure,' said the young woman into the telephone vacantly. 'No, I don't know what the rates would be... Pardon? Oh, main water, I think, but, of course, I couldn't be certain... I'm very sorry, I'm sure... No, he's out... No, I couldn't say... Yes, of course I'll ask him... Yes...8135? I'm afraid I haven't quite got it. Oh...8935...39... Oh, 5135... Yes, I'll ask him to ring you...after six... Oh, pardon, before six... Thank you so much.'

She replaced the receiver, scribbled 5319 on the blotting-pad and turned a mildly inquiring but uninterested gaze on Poirot.

Poirot began briskly.

'I observe that there is a house to be sold just on the outskirts of this town. Littlegreen House, I think is the name.'

'Pardon?'

'A house to be let or sold,' said Poirot slowly and distinctly. 'Littlegreen House.'

'Oh, Littlegreen House,' said the young woman vaguely. '*Littlegreen* House, did you say?'

'That is what I said.'

'Littlegreen *House*,' said the young woman, making a tremendous mental effort. 'Oh, well, I expect Mr Gabler would know about that.'

'Can I see Mr Gabler?'

'He's out,' said the young woman with a kind of faint, anaemic satisfaction as of one who says, 'A point to me.'

'Do you know when he will be in?'

'I couldn't say, I'm sure,' said the young woman.

'You comprehend, I am looking for a house in this neighbourhood,' said Poirot.

'Oh, yes,' said the young woman, uninterested.

'And Littlegreen House seems to me just what I am looking for. Can you give me particulars?'

'Particulars?' The young woman seemed startled.

'Particulars of Littlegreen House.'

Unwillingly she opened a drawer and took out an untidy file of papers.

Then she called, 'John.'

A lanky youth sitting in a corner looked up.

'Yes, miss.'

'Have we got any particulars of—what did you say?'

'Littlegreen House,' said Poirot distinctly.

'You've got a large bill of it here,' I remarked, pointing to the wall.

She looked at me coldly. Two to one, she seemed to think, was an unfair way of playing the game. She called up her own reinforcements.

'You don't know anything about Littlegreen House, do you, John?'

'No, miss. Should be in the file.'

'I'm sorry,' said the young woman without looking so in the least. 'I rather fancy we must have sent all the particulars out.'

'*C'est dommage.*'

'Pardon?'

'A pity.'

'We've a nice bungalow at Hemel End, two bed., one sitt.'

She spoke without enthusiasm, but with the air of one willing to do her duty by her employer.

'I thank you, no.'

'And a semi-detached with small conservatory. I could give you particulars of that.'

'No, thank you. I desired to know what rent you were asking for Littlegreen House.'

'It's not to be rented,' said the young woman, abandoning her position of complete ignorance of anything to do with Littlegreen House in the pleasure of scoring a point. 'Only to be sold outright.'

'The board says, "To be Let or Sold."'

'I couldn't say as to that, but it's for sale only.'

At this stage in the battle the door opened and a grey-haired, middle-aged man entered with a rush. His eye, a militant one, swept over us with a gleam. His eyebrows asked a question of his employee.

'This is Mr Gabler,' said the young woman.

Mr Gabler opened the door of an inner sanctum with a flourish.

'Step in here, gentlemen.' He ushered us in, an ample gesture swept us into chairs and he himself was facing us across a flat-topped desk.

'And now what can I do for you?'

Poirot began again perseveringly.

'I desired a few particulars of Littlegreen House—'

He got no further. Mr Gabler took command.

'Ah! Littlegreen House—*there's* a property! An absolute bargain. Only just come into the market. I can tell you gentlemen, we don't often get a house of that class going at the price. Taste's swinging round. People are fed up with jerry-building. They want sound stuff. Good,

honest building. A beautiful property—character—feeling—
Georgian throughout. That's what people want nowadays—
there's a feeling for period houses if you understand what
I mean. Ah, yes, Littlegreen House won't be long in the
market. It'll be snapped up. Snapped up! A member of
Parliament came to look at it only last Saturday. Liked it
so much he's coming down again this weekend. And there's
a stock exchange gentleman after it too. People want quiet
nowadays when they come to the country, want to be well
away from main roads. That's all very well for some people,
but we attract class here. And that's what that house has
got. Class! You've got to admit, they knew how to build
for gentlemen in those days. Yes, we shan't have Littlegreen
long on our books.'

Mr Gabler, who, it occurred to me, lived up to his name
very happily, paused for breath.

'Has it changed hands often in the last few years?' inquired
Poirot.

'On the contrary. Been in one family over fifty years.
Name of Arundell. Very much respected in the town. Ladies
of the old school.'

He shot up, opened the door and called:

'Particulars of Littlegreen House, Miss Jenkins. Quickly now.'

He returned to the desk.

'I require a house about this distance from London,' said
Poirot. 'In the country, but not in the dead country, if you
understand me—'

'Perfectly—perfectly. Too much in the country doesn't
do. Servants don't like it for one thing. Here, you have the

advantages of the country but not the disadvantages.' Miss Jenkins flitted in with a typewritten sheet of paper which she placed in front of her employer who dismissed her with a nod.

'Here we are,' said Mr Gabler, reading with practised rapidity. 'Period House of character: four recep., eight bed and dressing, usual offices, commodious kitchen premises, ample outbuildings, stables, etc. Main water, old-world gardens, inexpensive upkeep, amounting in all to three acres, two summer-houses, etc., etc. Price £2,850 or near offer.'

'You can give me an order to view?'

'Certainly, my dear sir.' Mr Gabler began writing in a flourishing fashion. 'Your name and address?'

Slightly to my surprise, Poirot gave his name as Mr Parotti.

'We have one or two other properties on our books which might interest you,' Mr Gabler went on.

Poirot allowed him to add two further additions.

'Littlegreen House can be viewed any time?' he inquired.

'Certainly, my dear sir. There are servants in residence. I might perhaps ring up to make certain. You will be going there immediately? Or after lunch?'

'Perhaps after lunch would be better.'

'Certainly—certainly. I'll ring up and tell them to expect you about two o'clock—eh? Is that right?'

'Thank you. Did you say the owner of the house—a Miss Arundell, I think you said?'

'Lawson. Miss Lawson. That is the name of the present owner. Miss Arundell, I am sorry to say, died a short time ago. That is how the place has come into the market. And I can assure you it will be snapped up. Not a doubt of it.

Between you and me, just in confidence, if you do think of making an offer I should make it quickly. As I've told you, there are two gentlemen after it already, and I shouldn't be surprised to get an offer for it any day from one or other of them. Each of them knows the other's after it, you see. And there's no doubt that competition spurs a man on. Ha, ha! I shouldn't like you to be disappointed.'

'Miss Lawson is anxious to sell, I gather.'

Mr Gabler lowered his voice confidentially.

'That's just it. The place is larger than she wants—one middle-aged lady living by herself. She wants to get rid of this and take a house in London. Quite understandable. That's why the place is going so ridiculously cheap.'

'She would be open, perhaps, to an offer?'

'That's the idea, sir. Make an offer and set the ball rolling. But you can take it from me that there will be no difficulty in getting a price very near the figure named. Why, it's ridiculous! To build a house like that nowadays would cost every penny of six thousand, let alone the land value and the valuable frontages.'

'Miss Arundell died very suddenly, didn't she?'

'Oh, I wouldn't say that. Anno domini—anno domini. She had passed her three-score and ten some time ago. And she'd been ailing for a long time. The last of her family—you know something about the family, perhaps?'

'I know some people of the same name who have relations in this part of the world. I fancy it must be the same family.'

'Very likely. Four sisters there were. One married fairly late in life and the other three lived on here. Ladies of the old school. Miss Emily was the last of them. Very highly thought of in the town.'

He leant forward and handed Poirot the orders.

'You'll drop in again and let me know what you think of it, eh? Of course, it may need a little modernizing here and there. That's only to be expected. But I always say, "What's a bathroom or two? That's easily done."'

We took our leave and the last thing we heard was the vacant voice of Miss Jenkins saying:

'Mrs Samuels rang up, sir. She'd like you to ring her—Holland 5391.'

As far as I could remember that was neither the number Miss Jenkins had scribbled on her pad nor the number finally arrived at through the telephone.

I felt convinced that Miss Jenkins was having her revenge for having been forced to find the particulars of Littlegreen House.

CHAPTER 7

Lunch at the George

As we emerged into the market square, I remarked that Mr Gabler lived up to his name! Poirot assented with a smile.

'He'll be rather disappointed when you don't return,' I said. 'I think he feels he has as good as sold you that house already.'

'Indeed, yes, I fear there is a deception in store for him.'

'I suppose we might as well have lunch here before returning to London, or shall we lunch at some more likely spot on our way back?'

'My dear Hastings, I am not proposing to leave Market Basing so quickly. We have not yet accomplished that which we came to do.'

I stared.

'Do you mean—but, my dear fellow, that's all a wash-out. The old lady is dead.'

'Exactly.'

The tone of that one word made me stare at him harder than ever. It was evident that he had some bee in his bonnet over this incoherent letter.

'But if she's dead, Poirot,' I said gently, 'what's the use? She can't tell you anything now. Whatever the trouble was, it's over and finished with.'

'How lightly and easily you put the matter aside! Let me tell you that *no* matter is finished with until Hercule Poirot ceases to concern himself with it!'

I should have known from experience that to argue with Poirot is quite useless. Unwarily I proceeded.

'But since she is dead—'

'Exactly, Hastings. Exactly—exactly—exactly… You keep repeating the significant point with a magnificently obtuse disregard of its significance. Do you not see the importance of the point? Miss Arundell is *dead*.'

'But my dear Poirot, her death was perfectly natural and ordinary! There wasn't anything odd or unexplained about it. We have old Gabler's word for that.'

'We have his word that Littlegreen House is a bargain at £2,850. Do you accept that as gospel also?'

'No, indeed. It struck me that Gabler was all out to get the place sold—it probably needs modernizing from top to toe. I'd swear he—or rather his client—will be willing to accept a very much lower figure than that. These large Georgian houses fronting right on the street must be the devil to get rid of.'

'*Eh bien*, then,' said Poirot. 'Do not say, "But Gabler says so!" as though he were an inspired prophet who could not lie.'

I was about to protest further, but at this minute we passed the threshold of the George and with an emphatic 'Chut!' Poirot put a damper on further conversation.

We were directed to the coffee-room, a room of fine proportions, tightly-shut windows and an odour of stale food. An elderly waiter attended to us, a slow, heavy-breathing man. We appeared to be the only lunchers. We had some excellent mutton, large slabs of watery cabbage and some dispirited potatoes. Some rather tasteless stewed fruit and custard followed. After gorgonzola and biscuits the waiter brought us two cups of a doubtful fluid called coffee.

At this point Poirot produced his orders to view and invited the waiter's aid.

'Yes, sir. I know where most of these are. Hemel Down is three miles away—on the Much Benham road—quite a little place. Naylor's Farm is about a mile away. There's a kind of lane goes off to it not long after the King's Head. Bisset Grange? No, I've never heard of that. Littlegreen House is just close by, not more than a few minutes' walk.'

'Ah, I think I have already seen it from the outside. That is the most possible one, I think. It is in good repair—yes?'

'Oh, yes, sir. It's in good condition—roof and drains and all that. Old-fashioned, of course. It's never been modern-ized in any way. The gardens are a picture. Very fond of her garden Miss Arundell was.'

'It belongs, I see, to a Miss Lawson.'

'That's right, sir. Miss Lawson, she was Miss Arundell's companion and when the old lady died everything was left to her—house and all.'

'Indeed? I suppose she had no relations to whom to leave it?'

'Well, it was not quite like that, sir. She *had* nieces and nephews living. But, of course, Miss Lawson was with her all the time. And, of course, she was an old lady and—well—that's how it was.'

'In any case I suppose there was just the house and not much money?'

I have often had occasion to notice how, where a direct question would fail to elicit a response, a false assumption brings instant information in the form of a contradiction.

'Very far from that, sir. Very far indeed. Everyone was surprised at the amount the old lady left. The will was in the paper and the amount and everything. It seems she hadn't lived up to her income for many a long year. Something like three or four hundred thousand pounds she left.'

'You astonish me,' cried Poirot. 'It is like a fairy tale—eh? The poor companion suddenly becomes unbelievably wealthy. Is she still young, this Miss Lawson? Can she enjoy her newfound wealth?'

'Oh, no, sir, she's a middle-aged person, sir.'

His enunciation of the word person was quite an artistic performance. It was clear that Miss Lawson, ex-companion, had cut no kind of a figure in Market Basing.

'It must have been disappointing for the nephews and nieces,' mused Poirot.

'Yes, sir, I believe it came as somewhat of a shock to them. Very unexpected. There's been feeling over it here in Market Basing. There are those who hold it isn't right to leave things away from your own flesh and blood. But, of course, there's others as hold that everyone's got a right to do as they like with their own. There's something to be said for both points of view, of course.'

'Miss Arundell had lived for many years here, had she not?'

'Yes, sir. She and her sisters and old General Arundell, their father, before them. Not that I remember him, naturally, but I believe he was quite a character. Was in the Indian Mutiny.'

'There were several daughters?'

'Three of them that I remember, and I believe there was one that married. Yes, Miss Matilda, Miss Agnes, and Miss Emily. Miss Matilda, she died first, and then Miss Agnes, and finally Miss Emily.'

'That was quite recently?'

'Beginning of May—or it may have been the end of April.'

'Had she been ill some time?'

'On and off—on and off. She was on the sickly side. Nearly went off a year ago with that there jaundice. Yellow as an orange she was for some time after. Yes, she'd had poor health for the last five years of her life.'

'I suppose you have some good doctors down here?'

'Well, there's Dr Grainger. Been here close on forty years, he has, and folks mostly go to him. He's a bit crotchety and he has his fancies but he's a good doctor, none better. He's got a young partner, Dr Donaldson. He's more the new-fangled kind. Some folk prefer him. Then, of course, there's Dr Harding, but he doesn't do much.'

'Dr Grainger was Miss Arundell's doctor, I suppose?'

'Oh, yes. He's pulled her through many a bad turn. He's the kind that fair bullies you into living whether you want to or not.'

Poirot nodded.

'One should learn a little about a place before one comes to settle in it,' he remarked. 'A good doctor is one of the most important people.'

'That's very true, sir.'

Poirot then asked for his bill to which he added a substantial tip.

'Thank you, sir. Thank you very much, sir. I'm sure I hope you'll settle here, sir.'

'I hope so, too,' said Poirot mendaciously.

We set forth from the George.

'Satisfied yet, Poirot?' I asked as we emerged into the street.

'Not in the least, my friend.'

He turned in an unexpected direction.

'Where are you off to now, Poirot?'

'The church, my friend. It may be interesting. Some brasses—an old monument.'

I shook my head doubtfully.

Poirot's scrutiny of the interior of the church was brief. Though an attractive specimen of what the guidebook calls Early Perp., it had been so conscientiously restored in Victorian vandal days that little of interest remained.

Poirot next wandered seemingly aimlessly about the churchyard reading some of the epitaphs, commenting on the number of deaths in certain families, occasionally exclaiming over the quaintness of a name.

I was not surprised, however, when he finally halted before what I was pretty sure had been his objective from the beginning.

An imposing marble slab bore a partly-effaced inscription:

SACRED

TO THE MEMORY OF

JOHN LAVERTON ARUNDELL

GENERAL 24TH SIKHS

WHO FELL ASLEEP IN CHRIST MAY 19TH 1888

AGED 69

'FIGHT THE GOOD FIGHT WITH ALL THY MIGHT'

ALSO OF

MATILDA ANN ARUNDELL

DIED MARCH 10TH 1912

'I WILL ARISE AND GO TO MY FATHER'

ALSO OF

AGNES GEORGINA MARY ARUNDELL

DIED NOVEMBER 20TH 1921

'ASK AND YE SHALL RECEIVE'

Then came a brand new piece of lettering, evidently just done:

ALSO OF

EMILY HARRIET LAVERTON ARUNDELL

DIED MAY 1ST 1936

'THY WILL BE DONE'

Poirot stood looking for some time.

He murmured softly:

'May 1st... May 1st... And today, June 28th, I receive

her letter. You see, do you not, Hastings, that that fact has got to be explained?'

I saw that it had.

That is to say, I saw that Poirot was determined that it should be explained.

CHAPTER 8

Interior of Littlegreen House

On leaving the churchyard, Poirot led the way briskly in
the direction of Littlegreen House. I gathered that his role
was still that of the prospective purchaser. Carefully holding
the various orders to view in his hand, with the Littlegreen
House one uppermost, he pushed open the gate and walked
up the path to the front door.

On this occasion our friend the terrier was not to be seen,
but the sound of barking could be heard inside the house,
though at some distance—I guessed in the kitchen quarters.

Presently we heard footsteps crossing the hall and the
door was opened by a pleasant-faced woman of between
fifty and sixty, clearly the old-fashioned type of servant
seldom seen nowadays.

Poirot presented his credentials.

'Yes, sir, the house-agent telephoned. Will you step this
way, sir?'

The shutters which I had noticed were closed on our
first visit to spy out the land, were now all thrown open

in preparation for our visit. Everything, I observed, was spotlessly clean and well kept. Clearly our guide was a thoroughly conscientious woman.

'This is the morning-room, sir.'

I glanced round approvingly. A pleasant room with its long windows giving on the street. It was furnished with good, solid, old-fashioned furniture, mostly Victorian, but there was a Chippendale bookcase and a set of attractive Hepplewhite chairs.

Poirot and I behaved in the customary fashion of people being shown over houses. We stood stock still, looking a little ill at ease, murmuring remarks such as 'very nice.' 'A very pleasant room.' 'The morning-room, you say?'

The maid conducted us across the hall and into the corresponding room on the other side. This was much larger.

'The dining-room, sir.'

This room was definitely Victorian. A heavy mahogany dining-table, a massive sideboard of almost purplish mahogany with great clusters of carved fruit, solid leather-covered dining-room chairs. On the wall hung what were obviously family portraits.

The terrier had continued to bark in some sequestered spot. Now the sound suddenly increased in volume. With a crescendo of barking he could be heard galloping across the hall.

'*Who's* come into the house? *I'll* tear him limb from limb,' was clearly the 'burden of his song'.

He arrived in the doorway, sniffing violently.

'Oh, Bob, you naughty dog,' exclaimed our conductress. 'Don't mind him, sir. He won't do you no harm.'

Bob, indeed, having discovered the intruders, completely changed his manner. He fussed in and introduced himself to us in an agreeable manner.

'Pleased to meet you, I'm sure,' he observed as he sniffed round our ankles. 'Excuse the noise, won't you, but I have my job to do. Got to be careful who we let in, you know. But it's a dull life and I'm really quite pleased to see a visitor. Dogs of your own, I fancy?'

This last was addressed to me as I stooped and patted him.

'Nice little fellow,' I said to the woman. 'Needs plucking a bit, though.'

'Yes, sir, he's usually plucked three times a year.'

'Is he an old dog?'

Oh, no, sir. Bob's not more than six. And sometimes he behaves just like a puppy. Gets hold of cook's slippers and prances about with them. And he's very gentle though you wouldn't believe it to hear the noise he makes sometimes. The only person he goes for is the postman. Downright scared of him the postman is.'

Bob was now investigating the legs of Poirot's trousers. Having learned all he could he gave vent to a prolonged sniff ('H'm, not too bad, but not really a doggy person') and returned to me cocking his head on one side and looking at me expectantly.

'I don't know why dogs always go for postmen, I'm sure,' continued our guide.

'It's a matter of reasoning,' said Poirot. 'The dog, he argues from reason. He is intelligent, he makes his deductions according to his point of view. There are people who may enter a house and there are people who may not—that a dog soon learns. *Eh bien*, who is the person who most persistently tries to gain admission, rattling on the door twice or three times a day—and who is never by any chance admitted? The postman. Clearly, then, an undesirable guest from the point of view of the master of the house. He is always sent about his business, but he persistently returns and tries again. Then a dog's duty is clear, to aid in driving this undesirable man away, and to bite him if possible. A most reasonable proceeding.'

He beamed on Bob.

'And a most intelligent person, I fancy.'

'Oh, he is, sir. He's almost human, Bob is.'

She flung open another door.

'The drawing-room, sir.'

The drawing-room conjured up memories of the past. A faint fragrance of potpourri hung about it. The chintzes were worn, their pattern faded garlands of roses. On the walls were prints and water-colour drawings. There was a good deal of china—fragile shepherds and shepherdesses. There were cushions worked in crewel stitch. There were faded photographs in handsome silver frames. There were many inlaid work-boxes and tea caddies. Most fascinating of all to me were two exquisitely cut tissue-paper ladies under glass stands. One with a spinning-wheel, one with a cat on her knee.

The atmosphere of a bygone day, a day of leisure, of refinement, of 'ladies and gentlemen' closed round me. This was indeed a 'withdrawing-room'. Here ladies sat and did their fancy-work, and if a cigarette was ever smoked by a favoured member of the male sex, what a shaking out of curtains and general airing of the room there would be afterwards!

My attention was drawn by Bob. He was sitting in an attitude of rapt attention close beside an elegant little table with two drawers in it.

As he saw that I was noticing him, he gave a short, plaintive yelp, looking from me to the table.

'What does he want?' I asked.

Our interest in Bob was clearly pleasing to the maid, who obviously was very fond of him.

'It's his ball, sir. It was always kept in that drawer. That's why he sits there and asks.'

Her voice changed. She addressed Bob in a high falsetto.

'It isn't there any longer, beautiful. Bob's ball is in the kitchen. In the kitchen, Bobsie.'

Bob shifted his gaze impatiently to Poirot.

'This woman's a fool,' he seemed to be saying. 'You look a brainy sort of chap. Balls are kept in certain places—this drawer is one of those places. There always has been a ball here. Therefore there should be a ball there now. That's obvious dog-logic, isn't it?'

'It's not there now, boy,' I said.

He looked at me doubtfully. then, as we went out of the room he followed slowly in an unconvinced manner.

We were shown various cupboards, a downstairs cloak-room, and a small pantry place, 'where the mistress used to do the flowers, sir'.

'You were with your mistress a long time?' asked Poirot.

'Twenty-two years, sir.'

'You are alone here caretaking?'

'Me and cook, sir.'

'She was also a long time with Miss Arundell?'

'Four years, sir. The old cook died.'

'Supposing I were to buy the house, would you be prepared to stay on?'

She blushed a little.

'It's very kind of you, sir, I'm sure, but I'm going to retire from service. The mistress left me a nice little sum, you see, and I'm going to my brother. I'm only remaining here as a convenience to Miss Lawson until the place is sold—to look after everything.'

Poirot nodded.

In the momentary silence a new sound was heard.

'Bump, bump, BUMP.'

A monotonous sound increasing in volume and seeming to descend from above.

'It's Bob, sir.' She was smiling. 'He's got hold of his ball and he's bumping it down the stairs. It's a little game of his.'

As we reached the bottom of the stairs a black rubber ball arrived with a thud on the last step. I caught it and looked up. Bob was lying on the top step, his paws splayed out, his tail gently wagging. I threw it up to him. He caught it neatly, chewed it for a minute or two with evident relish, then laid it between his paws and gently edged it forward with his nose till he finally bunted it over and it bumped once more down the stairs, Bob wagging his tail furiously as he watched its progress.

'He'll stay like that for hours, sir. Regular game of his. He'd go on all day at it. That'll do now, Bob. The gentlemen have got something else to do than play with you.'

A dog is a great promoter of friendly intercourse. Our interest and liking for Bob had quite broken down the natural stiffness of the good servant. As we went up to the bedroom floors, our guide was talking quite garrulously as she gave us accounts of Bob's wonderful sagacity. The ball had been left at the foot of the stairs. As we passed him, Bob gave us a look of deep disgust and stalked down in a dignified fashion to retrieve it. As we turned to the right I saw him slowly coming up again with it in his mouth, his gait that of an extremely old man forced by unthinking persons to exert himself unduly.

As we went round the bedrooms, Poirot began gradually to draw our conductress out.

'There were four Miss Arundells lived here, did they not?' he asked.

'Originally, yes, sir, but that was before my time. There was only Miss Agnes and Miss Emily when I came and Miss Agnes died soon afterwards. She was the youngest of the family. It seemed odd she should go before her sister.'

'I suppose she was not so strong as her sister?'

'No, sir, it's odd that. My Miss Arundell, Miss Emily, she was always the delicate one. She'd had a lot to do with doctors all her life. Miss Agnes was always strong and robust and yet she went first and Miss Emily who'd been delicate from a child outlived all the family. Very odd the way things happen.'

'Astonishing how often that is the case.'

Poirot plunged into (I feel sure) a wholly mendacious story of an invalid uncle which I will not trouble to repeat here. It suffices to say that it had its effect. Discussions of death and such matters do more to unlock the human tongue than any other subject. Poirot was in a position to ask questions that would have been regarded with suspicious hostility twenty minutes earlier.

'Was Miss Arundell's illness a long and painful one?'

'No, I wouldn't say that, sir. She'd been ailing, if you know what I mean, for a long time—ever since two winters before. Very bad she was then—this here jaundice. Yellow in the face they go and the whites of their eyes—'

'Ah, yes, indeed—' (Anecdote of Poirot's cousin who appeared to have been the Yellow Peril in person.)

'That's right—just as you say, sir. Terribly ill she was, poor dear. Couldn't keep anything down. If you ask me, Dr Grainger hardly thought she'd pull through. But he'd a wonderful way with her—bullying, you know. "Made up your mind to lie back and order your tombstone?" he'd say. And she'd say, "I've a bit of fight in me still, doctor," and he'd say, "That's right—that's what I like to hear." A hospital nurse we had, and she made up her mind that it was all over—even said to the doctor once that she supposed she'd better not worry the old lady too much by forcing her to take food—but the doctor rounded on her. "Nonsense," he said, "Worry her? You've got to bully her into taking nourishment." Valentine's beef juice at such and such a time, Brand's essence—teaspoonfuls of brandy. And at the end he said something that I've never forgotten. "You're young, my girl," he said to her, "you don't realize what fine fighting material there is in age. It's young people who turn up their toes and die because they're not interested enough to live. You show me anyone who's lived to over seventy and you show me a fighter—someone who's got the will to live." And it's true, sir—we're always saying how wonderful old people are—their vitality and the way they've kept their faculties—but as the doctor put it that's just *why* they've lived so long and got to be so old.'

'But it is profound what you say there—very profound! And Miss Arundell was like that? Very alive. Very interested in life?'

'Oh, yes, indeed, sir. Her health was poor, but her brain was as keen as anything. And as I was saying, she got over that illness of hers—surprised the nurse, it did. A stuck-up young thing she was, all starched collars and cuffs and the waiting on she had to have and tea at all hours.'

'A fine recovery.'

'Yes, indeed, sir. Of course, the mistress had to be very careful as to diet at first, everything boiled and steamed, no grease in the cooking, and she wasn't allowed to eat eggs either. Very monotonous it was for her.'

'Still the main thing is she got well.'

'Yes, sir. Of course, she had her little turns. What I'd call bilious attacks. She wasn't always very careful about her food after a time—but still they weren't very serious until the last attack.'

'Was it like her illness of two years before?'

75

'Yes, just the same sort of thing, sir. That nasty jaundice—an awful yellow colour again—and the terrible sickness and all the rest of it. Brought it on herself I'm afraid she did, poor dear. Ate a lot of things she shouldn't have done. That very evening she was took bad she'd had curry for supper and as you know, sir, curry's rich and a bit oily.'

'Her illness came on suddenly, did it?'

'Well, it seemed so, sir, but Dr Grainger he said it had been working up for some time. A chill—the weather had been very changeable—and too rich feeding.'

'Surely her companion—Miss Lawson was her companion was she not—could have dissuaded her from rich dishes?'

'Oh, I don't think Miss Lawson would have much say. Miss Arundell wasn't one to take orders from anyone.'

'Had Miss Lawson been with her during her previous illness?'

'No, she came after that. She'd been with her about a year.'

'I suppose she'd had companions before that?'

'Oh, quite a number, sir.'

'Her companions didn't stay as long as her servants,' said Poirot, smiling.

The woman flushed.

'Well, you see, sir, it was different. Miss Arundell didn't get out much and what with one thing and another—' she paused.

Poirot eyed her for a minute then he said:

'I understand a little the mentality of elderly ladies. They crave, do they not, for novelty. They get, perhaps, to the end of a person.'

'Well, now, that's very clever of you, sir. You've hit it exactly. When a new lady came Miss Arundell was always interested to start with—about her life and her childhood and where she'd been and what she thought about things, and then, when she knew all about her, well, she'd get— well, I suppose bored is the real word.'

'Exactly. And between you and me, these ladies who go as companions, they are not usually very interesting—very amusing, eh?'

'No, indeed, sir. They're poor-spirited creatures, most of them. Downright foolish, now and then. Miss Arundell soon got through with them, so to speak. And then she'd make a change and have someone else.'

'She must have been unusually attached to Miss Lawson, though.'

'Oh, I don't think so, sir.'

'Miss Lawson was not in any way a remarkable woman?'

'I shouldn't have said so, sir. Quite an ordinary person.'

'You liked her, yes?'

The woman shrugged her shoulders slightly.

'There wasn't anything to like or dislike. Fussy she was—a regular old maid and full of this nonsense about spirits.'

'*Spirits?*' Poirot looked alert.

'Yes, sir, spirits. Sitting in the dark round a table and dead people came back and spoke to you. Downright irreligious I call it—as if we didn't know departed souls had their rightful place and aren't likely to leave it.'

'So Miss Lawson was a spiritualist! Was Miss Arundell a believer too?'

'Miss Lawson would have liked her to be!' snapped the other. There was a spice of satisfied malice in her tone.

'But she wasn't?' Poirot persisted.

'The mistress had too much sense.' She snorted. 'Mind you, I don't say it didn't *amuse* her. "I'm willing to be convinced," she'd say. But she'd often look at Miss Lawson as much as to say, "My poor dear, what a fool you are to be so taken in!"'

'I comprehend. She did not believe in it, but it was a source of amusement to her.'

'That's right, sir. I sometimes wondered if she didn't—well have a bit of quiet fun, so to speak, pushing the table and that sort of thing. And the others all as serious as death.'

'The others?'

'Miss Lawson and the two Miss Tripps.'

'Miss Lawson was a very convinced spiritualist?'

'Took it all for gospel, sir.'

'And Miss Arundell was very attached to Miss Lawson, of course.'

It was the second time Poirot had made this certain remark and he got the same response.

'Well, hardly that, sir.'

'But surely,' said Poirot. 'If she left her everything. She did, did she not?'

The change was immediate. The human being vanished. The correct maid-servant returned. The woman drew herself up and said in a colourless voice that held reproof for familiarity in it:

'The way the mistress left her money is hardly my business, sir.'

I felt that Poirot had bungled the job. Having got the woman in a friendly mood, he was now proceeding to throw away his advantage. He was wise enough to make no immediate attempt to recover lost ground. After a commonplace remark about the size and number of the bedrooms he went towards the head of the stairs.

Bob had disappeared, but as I came to the stair-head, I stumbled and nearly fell. Catching at the baluster to steady myself I looked down and saw that I had inadvertently placed my foot on Bob's ball which he had left lying on the top of the stairs.

The woman apologized quickly.

'I'm sorry, sir. It's Bob's fault. He leaves his ball there. And you can't see it against the dark carpet. Death of someone some day it'll be. The poor mistress had a nasty fall through it. Might easily have been the death of her.'

Poirot stopped suddenly on the stairs.

'She had an accident you say?'

'Yes, sir. Bob left his ball there, as he often did, and the mistress came out of her room and fell over it and went right down the stairs. Might have been killed.'

'Was she much hurt?'

'Not as much as you'd think. Very lucky she was, Dr Grainger said. Cut her head a little, and strained her back, and of course there were bruises and it was a nasty shock. She was in bed for about a week, but it wasn't serious.'

'Was this long ago?'

'Just a week or two before she died.'

Poirot stooped to recover something he had dropped.

'Pardon—my fountain pen—ah, yes, there it is.'

He stood up again.

'He is careless, this Master Bob,' he observed.

'Ah well, he don't know no better, sir,' said the woman in an indulgent voice. 'Nearly human he may be, but you can't have everything. The mistress, you see, usedn't to sleep well at night and often she'd get up and wander downstairs and round and about the house.'

'She did that often?'

'Most nights. But she wouldn't have Miss Lawson or anyone fussing after her.'

Poirot had turned into the drawing-room again.

'A beautiful room this,' he observed. 'I wonder, would there be space in this recess for my bookcase? What do you think, Hastings?'

Quite fogged I remarked cautiously that it would be difficult to say.

'Yes, sizes are so deceptive. Take, I pray you, my little rule and measure the width of it and I will write it down.'

Obediently I took the folding rule that Poirot handed me and took various measurements under his direction whilst he wrote on the back of an envelope.

I was just wondering why he adopted such an untidy and uncharacteristic method instead of making a neat entry in his little pocket-book when he handed the envelope to me, saying:

'That is right, is it not? Perhaps you had better verify it.'

There were no figures on the envelope. Instead was written: 'When we go upstairs again, pretend to remember an appointment and ask if you can telephone. Let the woman come with you and delay her as long as you can.'

'That's all right,' I said, pocketing the envelope. 'I should say both bookcases would go in perfectly.'

'It is as well to be sure though. I think, if it is not too much trouble, I would like to look at the principal bedroom again. I am not quite sure of the wall space there.'

'Certainly, sir. It's no trouble.'

We went up again. Poirot measured a portion of wall, and was just commenting aloud on the respective possible positions of bed, wardrobe and writing table, when I looked at my watch, gave a somewhat exaggerated start and exclaimed:

'By Jove, do you know it's three o'clock already? What will Anderson think? I ought to telephone to him.' I turned to the woman. 'I wonder if I might use your telephone if you have one.'

'Why, certainly, sir. It's in the little room off the hall. I'll show you.'

She bustled down with me, indicating the instrument, and then I got her to help me in finding a number in the telephone directory. In the end I made a call—to a Mr Anderson in the neighbouring town of Harchester. Fortunately he was out and I was able to leave a message saying it was unimportant and that I would ring up later!

When I emerged Poirot had descended the staircase and was standing in the hall. His eyes had a slightly green tinge. I had no clue to his excitement but I realized that he *was* excited.

Poirot said:

'That fall from the top of the stairs must have given your mistress a great shock. Did she seem perturbed about Bob and his ball after it?'

'It's funny your saying that, sir. It worried her a lot. Why, just as she was dying, she was delirious and she rambled on a lot about Bob and his ball and something about a picture that was ajar.'

'A picture that was ajar,' said Poirot thoughtfully.

'Of course, it didn't make sense, sir, but she was rambling, you see.'

'One moment—I must just go into the drawing-room once more.'

He wandered round the room examining the ornaments. In especial, one big jar with a lid on it seemed to attract him. It was not, I fancy, a particularly good bit of china. A piece of Victorian humour—it had on it a rather crude picture of a bulldog sitting outside a front door with a mournful expression on its face. Below was written: *Out all night and no key.*

Poirot, whose taste I have always been convinced, is hopelessly Bourgeois, seemed lost in admiration.

'*Out all night and no key*,' he murmured. 'It is amusing, that! Is that true of our Master Bob? Does he sometimes stay out all night?'

'Very occasional, sir. Oh, very occasional. He's a very good dog, Bob is.'

'I am sure he is. But even the best of dogs—'

'Oh, it's quite true, sir. Once or twice he's gone off and come home perhaps at four in the morning. Then he sits down on the step and barks till he's let in.'

'Who lets him in—Miss Lawson?'

'Well, anyone who hears him, sir. It was Miss Lawson, sir, last time. It was the night of the mistress's accident. And Bob came home about five. Miss Lawson hurried down to let him in before he could make a noise. She was afraid of waking up the mistress and hadn't told her Bob was missing for fear of worrying her.'

'I see. She thought it was better Miss Arundell shouldn't be told?'

'That's what she said, sir. She said, "He's sure to come back. He always does, but she might worry and that would never do." So we didn't say anything.'

'Was Bob fond of Miss Lawson?'

'Well, he was rather contemptuous of her if you know what I mean, sir. Dogs can be. She was kind to him. Called him a good doggie and a nice doggie, but he used to look at her kind of scornful like and he didn't pay any attention at all to what she told him to do.'

Poirot nodded. 'I see,' he said.

Suddenly he did something which startled me.

He pulled a letter from his pocket—the letter he had received this morning.

'Ellen,' he said, 'do you know anything about this?'

The change that came over Ellen's face was remarkable.

Her jaw dropped and she stared at Poirot with an almost comical expression of bewilderment.

'Well,' she ejaculated. 'I never did!'

The observation lacked coherency, perhaps, but it left no doubt of Ellen's meaning.

Gathering her wits about her she said slowly:

'Are you the gentleman that letter was written to then?'

'I am. I am Hercule Poirot.'

Like most people, Ellen had not glanced at the name on the order Poirot had held out to her on his arrival. She nodded her head slowly.

'That was it,' she said. 'Hercules Poirot.' She added an S to the Christian name and sounded the T of the surname.

'My word!' she exclaimed. 'Cook *will* be surprised.'

Poirot said, quickly:

'Would it not be advisable, perhaps, for us to go to the kitchen and there in company with your friend, we could talk this matter over?'

'Well—if you don't mind, sir.'

Ellen sounded just a little doubtful. This particular social dilemma was clearly new to her. But Poirot's matter of fact manner reassured her and we departed forthwith to the kitchen, Ellen elucidating the situation to a large, pleasant-faced woman who was just lifting a kettle from a gas ring.

'You'll never believe it, Annie. This is actually the gentleman that letter was to. You know, the one I found in the blotter.'

'You must remember I am in the dark,' said Poirot. 'Perhaps you will tell me how the letter came to be posted so late in the day?'

'Well, sir, to tell the truth I didn't know what to do. Neither of us did, did we?'

'Indeed, we didn't,' the cook confirmed.

'You see, sir, when Miss Lawson was turning out things after the mistress's death a good lot of things were given away or thrown away. Among them was a little papier-mâché, I think they call it, blotter. Very pretty it was, with a lily of the valley on it. The mistress always used it when she wrote in bed. Well, Miss Lawson didn't want it so she gave it to me along with a lot of other little odds and ends that had belonged to the mistress. I put it away in a drawer, and it wasn't till yesterday that I took it out. I was going to put some new blotting-paper in it so that it was ready for me to use. There was a sort of pocket inside and I just slipped my hand in it when what should I find but a letter in the mistress's handwriting, tucked away.

'Well, as I say I didn't know rightly what to do about it. It was the mistress's hand all right, and I saw as she'd written it and slipped it in there waiting to post it the next day and then she'd forgot, which is the kind of thing she did many a time, poor dear. Once it was a dividend warrant to her bank and no one could think where it had got to, and at last it was found pushed right back in the pigeon-holes of the desk.'

'Was she untidy?'

'Oh, no, sir, just the opposite. She was always putting things away and clearing them up. That was half the trouble. If she'd left things about it would really have been better. It was their being tidied away and then forgotten that was always happening.'

'Things like Bob's ball, for instance?' asked Poirot with a smile.

The sagacious terrier had just trotted in from outdoors and greeted us anew in a very friendly manner.

'Yes, indeed, sir. As soon as Bob finished playing with his ball she'd put it away. But that was all right because it had its own place—in the drawer I showed you.'

'I see. But I interrupted you. Pray go on. You discovered the letter in the blotter?'

'Yes, sir, that was the way of it, and I asked Annie what she thought I'd better do. I didn't like to put it in the fire— and of course, I couldn't take upon myself to open it, and neither Annie nor I could see that it was any business of Miss Lawson's so after we'd talked it over a bit, I just put a stamp on it and ran out to the post box and posted it.'

Poirot turned slightly to me.

'*Voilà*,' he murmured.

I could not help saying, maliciously:

'Amazing how simple an explanation can be!'

I thought he looked a little crestfallen, and rather wished I hadn't been so quick to try and rub it in.

He turned again to Ellen.

'As my friend says: How simple an explanation can be! You understand, when I received a letter dated over two months ago, I was somewhat surprised.'

'Yes, I suppose you must have been, sir. We didn't think of that.'

'Also—' Poirot coughed. 'I am in a little dilemma. That letter, you see—it was a commission with which Miss Arundell wished to entrust me. A matter of a somewhat private character.' He cleared his throat importantly. 'Now that Miss Arundell is dead I am in some doubt how to act. Would Miss Arundell have wished me to undertake the commission in these circumstances or not? It is difficult—very difficult.'

Both women were looking at him respectfully.

'I shall have, I think, to consult Miss Arundell's lawyer. She had a lawyer, did she not?'

Ellen answered, quickly.

'Oh, yes, sir. Mr Purvis from Harchester.'

'He knew all her affairs?'

'I think so, sir. He's done everything for her ever since I can remember. It was him she sent for after the fall she had.'

'The fall down the stairs?'

'Yes, sir.'

'Now let me see when was that exactly?'

The cook broke in.

'Day after Bank Holiday it was. I remember that well. I stayed in to oblige on Bank Holiday seeing she had all those people staying and I had the day on Wednesday instead.'

Poirot whipped out his pocket almanac.

'Precisely—precisely. Easter Bank Holiday, I see, fell on the thirteenth this year. Then Miss Arundell had her accident on the fourteenth. This letter to me was written three days later. A pity it was never sent. However, it may still not be too late—' he paused. 'I rather fancy that the—er—commission she wished me to perform was connected with one of the—er—guests you mentioned just now.'

This remark, which could only have been a pure shot in the dark, met with immediate response. A quick look of intelligence passed across Ellen's face. She turned to the cook who gave her back an answering glance.

'That'll be Mr Charles,' she said.

'If you would tell me just who was there—' Poirot suggested.

'Dr Tanios and his wife, Miss Bella that was, and Miss Theresa and Mr Charles.'

'They were all nephews and nieces?'

'That's right, sir. Dr Tanios, of course, is no relation. In fact he's a foreigner, a Greek or something of the sort, I believe. He married Miss Bella, Miss Arundell's niece, her sister's child. Mr Charles and Miss Theresa are brother and sister.'

'Ah, yes, I see. A family party. And when did they leave?'

'On the Wednesday morning, sir. And Dr Tanios and Miss Bella came down again the next weekend because they were worried about Miss Arundell.'

'And Mr Charles and Miss Theresa?'

'They came the weekend after. The weekend before she died.'

Poirot's curiosity, I felt, was quite insatiable. I could see no point in these continued questions. He got the explanation of his mystery, and in my opinion the sooner he retired with dignity the better.

The thought seemed to go from my brain to his.

'*Eh bien*,' he said. 'This information you have given me is very helpful. I must consult this Mr Purvis, I think you said? Thank you very much for all your help.'

He stooped and patted Bob.

'*Brave chien, va!* You loved your mistress.'

Bob responded amiably to these overtures and, hopeful of a little play, went and fetched a large piece of coal. For this he was reproved and the coal removed from him. He sent me a glance in search of sympathy.

'These women,' he seemed to say. 'Generous with the food, but not really sportsmen!'

CHAPTER 9

Reconstruction of the Dog's Ball Incident

'Well, Poirot,' I said, as the gate of Littlegreen House closed behind us. 'You are satisfied now, I hope!'

'Yes, my friend. I am satisfied.'

'Thank heavens for that! All the mysteries explained! The Wicked Companion and the Rich Old Lady myth exploded. The delayed letter and even the famous incident of the dog's ball shown in their true colours. Everything settled satisfactorily and according to Cocker!'

Poirot gave a dry little cough and said:

'I would not use the word *satisfactorily*, Hastings.'

'You did a minute ago.'

'No, no. I did not say the matter was *satisfactory*. I said that, personally, my curiosity was *satisfied*. I know the truth of the Dog's Ball incident.'

'And very simple it was too!'

'Not quite so simple as you think.' He nodded his head several times. Then he went on: 'You see, I know one little thing which you do not.'

'And what is that?' I asked somewhat sceptically.

'*I know that there is a nail driven into the skirting board at the top of the stairs.*'

I stared at him. His face was quite grave.

'Well,' I said after a minute or two. 'Why shouldn't there be?'

'The question is, Hastings, why should there be.'

'How do I know. Some household reason, perhaps. Does it matter?'

'Certainly it matters. And I think of no household reason for a nail to be driven in at the top of the skirting board in that particular place. It was carefully varnished, too, so as not to show.'

'What are you driving at, Poirot? Do *you* know the reason?'

'I can imagine it quite easily. If you wanted to stretch a piece of strong thread or wire across the top of the stairs about a foot from the ground, you could tie it on one side to the balusters, but on the inner wall side you would need something like a nail to attach the thread to.'

'Poirot!' I cried. 'What on earth are you driving at?'

'*Mon cher ami*, I am reconstructing *the incident of the Dog's Ball*! Would you like to hear my reconstruction?'

'Go ahead.'

'*Eh bien*, here it is. Someone had noticed the habit Bob had of leaving his ball at the top of the stairs. A dangerous thing to do—it might lead to an accident.' Poirot paused a minute, then said in a slightly different tone. 'If you wished to kill someone, Hastings, how would you set about it?'

'I—well really—I don't know. Fake up some *alibi* or something, I suppose.'

'A proceeding, I assure you, both difficult and dangerous. But then you are not the type of a cold-blooded cautious murderer. Does it not strike you that the *easiest* way of removing someone you want to remove from your path is to take advantage of *accident*? Accidents are happening all the time. And sometimes—Hastings—they *can be helped to happen*!'

He paused a minute then went on:

'I think the dog's ball left so fortuitously at the top of the stairs gave our murderer an idea. Miss Arundell was in the habit of coming out of her room in the night and wandering about—her eyesight was not good, it was quite within the bounds of probability that she might stumble over it and fall headlong down those stairs. But a careful murderer does not leave things to chance. A *thread* stretched across the top of the stairs would be a much better way. It would send her pitching head foremost. Then, when the household come rushing out—there, plain to see, is the *cause* of the accident—*Bob's ball*!'

'How horrible!' I cried.

Poirot said, gravely:

'Yes, it was horrible... It was also unsuccessful... Miss Arundell was very little hurt though she might easily have broken her neck. Very disappointing for our unknown friend! But Miss Arundell was a sharp-witted old lady. Everyone told her she had slipped on the ball, and there the ball was in evidence, but she herself recalling the happening felt that the accident had arisen differently. She had *not* slipped on the ball. And in addition she remembered something else.

She remembered hearing Bob barking for admission at five o'clock the next morning.

'This, I admit, is something in the way of guess-work but I believe I am right. *Miss Arundell had put away Bob's ball herself* the evening before in its drawer. After that he went out *and did not return.* In that case *it was not Bob* who put that ball on the top of the stairs.'

'That is pure guess-work, Poirot,' I objected.

He demurred.

'Not quite, my friend. There are the significant words uttered by Miss Arundell when she was delirious—something about Bob's ball and a "picture ajar." You see the point, do you not?'

'Not in the least.'

'Curious. I know your language well enough to realize that one does not talk of a picture being *ajar.* A *door* is *ajar.* A picture is *awry.*'

'Or simply crooked.'

'Or simply crooked, as you say. So I realized at once that Ellen has mistaken the meaning of the words she heard. It is not ajar—but a or the jar that was meant. Now in the drawing-room there is a rather noticeable china jar. There, I have already observed a picture of a dog on it. With the remembrance of these delirious ravings in my mind I go up and examine it more closely. I find that it deals with the subject of a *dog who has been out all night.* You see the trend of the feverish woman's thoughts? Bob was like the dog in the picture on the jar—out all night—*so it was not he who left the ball on the stairs.*'

I cried out, feeling some admiration in spite of myself.

'You're an ingenious devil, Poirot! How you think of these things beats me!'

'I do not "think of them". They are *there*—plain—for anyone to see. *Eh bien*, you realize the position? Miss Arundell, lying in bed after her fall, becomes suspicious. That suspicion she feels is perhaps fanciful and absurd but there it is. "*Since the incident of the dog's ball I have been increasingly uneasy.*" And so—and so she writes to me, and by a piece of bad luck her letter does not reach me until over two months have gone by. Tell me, does her letter not fit in *perfectly* with these facts?'

'Yes,' I admitted. 'It does.'

Poirot went on:

'There is another point worthy of consideration. Miss Lawson was exceedingly anxious that the fact of Bob's being out all night should not get to Miss Arundell's ears.'

'You think that she—'

'I think that the fact should be noted very carefully.'

I turned the thing over in my mind for a minute or two.

'Well,' I said at last with a sigh. 'It's all very interesting—as a mental exercise that is. And I take off my hat to you. It's been a masterful piece of reconstruction. It's almost a pity really that the old lady has died.'

'A pity—yes. She wrote to me that someone had attempted to murder her (that is what it amounts to, after all) and a very short time after, she was dead.'

'Yes,' I said. 'And it's a grand disappointment to you that she died a natural death, isn't it? Come, admit it.'

Poirot shrugged his shoulders.

'Or perhaps you think she was poisoned,' I said maliciously.

Poirot shook his head somewhat despondently.

'It certainly seems,' he admitted, 'as though Miss Arundell died from natural causes.'

'And therefore,' I said, 'we return to London with our tail between our legs.'

'*Pardon*, my friend, but we do *not* return to London.'

'What do you mean, Poirot?' I cried.

'If you show the dog the rabbit, my friend, does he return to London? No, he goes into the rabbit hole.'

'What do you mean?'

'The dog hunts rabbits. Hercule Poirot hunts murderers. We have here a murderer—a murderer whose crime failed, yes, perhaps, but nevertheless a murderer. And I, my friend, am going into the burrow after him—or her as the case may be.'

He turned sharply in at the gate.

'Where are you off to, Poirot?'

'Into the burrow, my friend. This is the house of Dr Grainger who attended Miss Arundell in her last illness.'

Dr Grainger was a man of sixty odd. His face was thin and bony with an aggressive chin, bushy eyebrows, and a pair of very shrewd eyes. He looked keenly from me to Poirot.

'Well, what can I do for you?' he asked abruptly.

Poirot swept into speech in the most flamboyant manner.

'I must apologize, Dr Grainger, for this intrusion. I must confess straightaway that I do not come to consult you professionally.'

Dr Grainger said drily:

'Glad to hear it. You look healthy enough!'

'I must explain the purpose of my visit,' went on Poirot. 'The truth of the matter is that I am writing a book—the life of the late General Arundell who I understand lived in Market Basing for some years before his death.'

The doctor looked rather surprised.

'Yes, General Arundell lived here till his death. At Little-green House—just up the road past the Bank—you've been there, perhaps?' Poirot nodded assent. 'But you understand that was a good bit before my time. I came here in 1919.'

'You knew his daughter, however, the late Miss Arundell?'

'I knew Emily Arundell well.'

'You comprehend, it has been a severe blow to me to find that Miss Arundell has recently died.'

'End of April.'

'So I discovered. I counted, you see, on her giving me various personal details and reminiscences of her father.'

'Quite—quite. But I don't see what I can do about it.'

Poirot asked:

'General Arundell has no other sons or daughters living?'

'No. All dead, the lot of them.'

'How many were there?'

'Five. Four daughters, one son.'

'And in the next generation?'

'Charles Arundell and his sister Theresa. You could get on to them. I doubt, though, if it would be much use to you. The younger generation doesn't take much interest in its grandfathers. And there's a Mrs Tanios, but I doubt if you'd get much there either.'

'They might have family papers—documents?'

'They might have. Doubt it, though. A lot of stuff was cleared out and burnt after Miss Emily's death, I know.'

Poirot uttered a groan of anguish.

Grainger looked at him curiously.

'What's the interest in old Arundell? I never heard he was a big pot in any way?'

'My dear sir.' Poirot's eyes gleamed with the excitement of the fanatic. 'Is there not a saying that History knows nothing of its greatest men? Recently certain papers have come to light which throw an entirely different light on the whole subject of the Indian Mutiny. There is secret history there. And in that secret history John Arundell played a big part. The whole thing is fascinating—fascinating! And let me tell you, my dear sir, it is of especial interest at the present time. India—the English policy in regard to it—is the burning question of the hour.'

'H'm,' said the doctor. 'I have heard that old General Arundell used to hold forth a good deal on the subject of the Mutiny. As a matter of fact, he was considered a prize bore on the subject.'

'Who told you that?'

'A Miss Peabody. You might call on her, by the way. She's our oldest inhabitant—knew the Arundells intimately. And gossip is her chief recreation. She's worth seeing for her own sake—a character.'

'Thank you. That is an excellent idea. Perhaps, too, you would give me the address of young Mr Arundell, the grandson of the late General Arundell.'

'Charles? Yes, I can put you on to him. But he's an irreverent young devil. Family history means nothing to him.'

'He is quite young?'

'He's what an old fogy like me calls young,' said the doctor with a twinkle. 'Early thirties. The kind of young man that's born to be a trouble and responsibility to their families. Charm of personality and nothing else. He's been shipped about all over the world and done no good anywhere.'

'His aunt was doubtless fond of him?' ventured Poirot. 'It is often that way.'

'H'm—I don't know. Emily Arundell was no fool. As far as I know he never succeeded in getting any money out of her. Bit of a tartar that old lady. I liked her. Respected her too. An old soldier every inch of her.'

'Was her death sudden?'

'Yes, in a way. Mind you, she'd been in poor health for some years. But she'd pulled through some narrow squeaks.'

'There was some story—I apologize for repeating gossip—' Poirot spread out his hands deprecatingly—'that she had quarrelled with her family?'

'She didn't exactly *quarrel* with them,' said Dr Grainger slowly. 'No, there was no open quarrel as far as I know.'

'I beg your pardon. I am, perhaps, being indiscreet.'

'No, no. After all, the information's public property.'

'She left her money away from her family, I understand?'

'Yes, left it all to a frightened, fluttering hen of a companion. Odd thing to do. Can't understand it myself. Not like her.'

'Ah, well,' said Poirot thoughtfully. 'One can imagine such a thing happening. An old lady, frail and in ill-health.

Very dependent on the person who attends and cares for her. A clever woman with a certain amount of personality could gain a great ascendency that way.'

The word ascendency seemed to act like a red rag to a bull.

Dr Grainger snorted out:

'Ascendency? Ascendency? Nothing of the kind! Emily Arundell treated Minnie Lawson worse than a dog. Characteristic of that generation! Anyway, women who earn their living as companions are usually fools. If they've got brains they're earning a better living some other way. Emily Arundell didn't suffer fools gladly. She usually wore out one poor devil a year. Ascendency? Nothing of the sort!'

Poirot hastened off the treacherous ground.

'It is possible, perhaps,' he suggested, 'that there are old family letters and documents in this Miss—er—Lawson's possession?'

'Might be,' agreed Grainger. 'Usually are a lot of things tucked away in an old maid's house. I don't suppose Miss Lawson's been through half of it yet.'

Poirot rose.

'Thank you very much, Dr Grainger. You have been most kind.'

'Don't thank me,' said the doctor. 'Sorry I can't do anything helpful. Miss Peabody's your best chance. Lives at Morton Manor—about a mile out.'

Poirot was sniffing at a large bouquet of roses on the doctor's table.

'Delicious,' he murmured.

'Yes, I suppose so. Can't smell 'em myself. Lost my sense of smell when I had flu four years ago. Nice admission for a doctor, eh? "Physician, heal thyself." Damned nuisance. Can't enjoy a smoke as I used to.'

'Unfortunate, yes. By the way, you *will* give me young Arundell's address?'

'I can get it for you, yes.' He ushered us out into the hall and called: 'Donaldson.'

'My partner,' he explained. 'He should have it all right. He's by way of being engaged to Charles's sister, Theresa.'

He called again: 'Donaldson.'

A young man came out from a room at the back of the house. He was of medium height and of rather colourless appearance. His manner was precise. A greater contrast to Dr Grainger could not be imagined.

The latter explained what he wanted.

Dr Donaldson's eyes, very pale blue eyes slightly prominent, swept over us appraisingly. When he spoke it was in a dry, precise manner.

'I don't know exactly where Charles is to be found,' he said. 'I can give you Miss Theresa Arundell's address. Doubtless she will be able to put you in touch with her brother.'

Poirot assured him that that would do perfectly.

The doctor wrote down an address on a page of his notebook, tore it out and handed it to Poirot.

Poirot thanked him and said goodbye to both doctors. As we went out of the door I was conscious of Dr Donaldson standing in the hall peering after us with a slightly startled look on his face.

CHAPTER 10

Visit to Miss Peabody

'Is it really necessary to tell such elaborate lies, Poirot?' I asked as we walked away.

Poirot shrugged his shoulders.

'If one is going to tell a lie at all—and I notice, by the way, that your nature is very much averse to lying—now, me, it does not trouble at all—'

'So I've noticed,' I interjected.

'—As I was remarking, *if* one is going to tell a lie at all, it might as well be an artistic lie, a romantic lie, a convincing lie!'

'Do you consider this a convincing lie? Do you think Dr Donaldson was convinced?'

'That young man is of a sceptical nature,' admitted Poirot, thoughtfully.

'He looked definitely suspicious to me.'

'I do not see why he should be so. Imbeciles are writing the lives of other imbeciles every day. It is as you say, done.'

'First time I've heard you call yourself an imbecile,' I said, grinning.

'I can adopt a rôle, I hope, as well as anyone,' said Poirot coldly. 'I am sorry you do not think my little fiction well imagined. I was rather pleased with it myself.'

I changed the subject.

'What do we do next?'

'That is easy. We get into your car and pay a visit to Morton Manor.'

Morton Manor proved to be an ugly substantial house of the Victorian period. A decrepit butler received us somewhat doubtfully and presently returned to ask if 'we had an appointment'.

'Please tell Miss Peabody that we come from Dr Grainger,' said Poirot.

After a wait of a few minutes the door opened and a short, fat woman waddled into the room. Her sparse, white hair was neatly parted in the middle. She wore a black velvet dress, the nap of which was completely rubbed off in various places, and some really beautiful fine point lace was fastened at her neck with a large cameo brooch.

She came across the room peering at us short-sightedly. Her first words were somewhat of a surprise.

'Got anything to sell?'

'Nothing, madame,' said Poirot.

'Sure?'

'But absolutely.'

'No vacuum cleaners?'

'No.'

'No stockings?'

'No.'

'No rugs?'

'No.'

'Oh, well,' said Miss Peabody, settling herself in a chair. 'I suppose it's all right. You'd better sit down then.'

We sat obediently.

'You'll excuse my asking,' said Miss Peabody with a trace of apology in her manner. 'Got to be careful. You wouldn't believe the people who come along. Servants are no good. They can't tell. Can't blame 'em either. Right voices, right clothes, right names. How are they to tell? Commander Ridgeway, Mr Scot Edgerton, Captain d'Arcy Fitzherbert. Nice-looking fellows, some of 'em. But before you know where you are they've shoved a cream-making machine under your nose.'

Poirot said earnestly:

'I assure you, madame, that we have nothing whatever of that kind.'

'Well, you should know,' said Miss Peabody.

Poirot plunged into his story. Miss Peabody heard him out without comment, blinking once or twice out of her small eyes. At the end she said:

'Goin' to write a book, eh?'

'Yes.'

'In English?'

'Certainly—in English.'

'But you're a foreigner. Eh? Come now, you're a foreigner, aren't you?'

'That is true.'

She transferred her gaze to me.

'You are his secretary, I suppose?'

'Er—yes,' I said doubtfully.

'Can you write decent English?'

'I hope so.'

'H'm—where did you go to school?'

'Eton.'

'Then you can't.'

I was forced to let this sweeping charge against an old and venerable centre of education pass unchallenged as Miss Peabody turned her attention once more to Poirot.

'Goin' to write a life of General Arundell, eh?'

'Yes. You knew him, I think.'

'Yes, I knew John Arundell. He drank.'

There was a momentary pause. Then Miss Peabody went on musingly:

'Indian Mutiny, eh? Seems a bit like flogging a dead horse to me. But that's your business.'

'You know, madame, there is a fashion in these things. At the moment India is the mode.'

'Something in that. Things do come round. Look at sleeves.'

We maintained a respectful silence.

'Leg o' muttons were always ugly,' said Miss Peabody. 'But I always looked well in Bishops.' She fixed a bright eye on Poirot. 'Now then, what do you want to know?'

Poirot spread out his hands.

'Anything! Family history. Gossip. Home life.'

'Can't tell you anything about India,' said Miss Peabody. 'Truth is, I didn't listen. Rather boring these old men and their anecdotes. He was a very stupid man—but I dare say none the worse General for that. I've always heard that intelligence didn't get you far in the army. Pay attention to your Colonel's wife and listen respectfully to your superior officers and you'll get on—that's what my father used to say.'

Treating this dictum respectfully, Poirot allowed a moment or two to elapse before he said:

'You knew the Arundell family intimately, did you not?'

'Knew 'em all,' said Miss Peabody. 'Matilda, she was the eldest. A spotty girl. Used to teach in Sunday School. Was sweet on one of the curates. Then there was Emily. Good seat on a horse, she had. She was the only one who could do anything with her father when he had one of his bouts on. Cartloads of bottles used to be taken out of that house. Buried them at night, they did. Then, let me see, who came next, Arabella or Thomas? Thomas, I think. Always felt sorry for Thomas. One man and four women. Makes a man look a fool. He was a bit of an old woman himself, Thomas was. Nobody thought he'd ever marry. Bit of a shock when he did.'

She chuckled—a rich Victorian fruity chuckle.

It was clear that Miss Peabody was enjoying herself. As an audience we were almost forgotten. Miss Peabody was well away in the past.

'Then came Arabella. Plain girl. Face like a scone. She married all right though, even if she were the plainest of the family. Professor at Cambridge. Quite an old man. Must have been sixty if he was a day. He gave a series of lectures here—on the wonders of Modern Chemistry I think it was. I went to 'em. He mumbled, I remember. Had a beard.

Couldn't hear much of what he said. Arabella used to stay behind and ask questions. She wasn't a chicken herself. Must have been getting on for forty. Ah well, they're both dead now. Quite a happy marriage it was. There's something to be said for marrying a plain woman—you know the worst at once and she's not so likely to be flighty. Then there was Agnes. She was the youngest—the pretty one. Rather gay we used to think her. Almost fast! Odd, you'd think if any of them had married it would have been Agnes, but she didn't. She died not long after the war.'

Poirot murmured:

'You said that Mr Thomas's marriage was rather unexpected.'

Again Miss Peabody produced that rich, throaty chuckle.

'Unexpected? I should say it was! Made a nine days' scandal. You'd never have thought it of him—such a quiet, timid, retiring man and devoted to his sisters.'

She paused a minute.

'Remember a case that made rather a stir in the late nineties? Mrs Varley? Supposed to have poisoned her husband with arsenic. Good-looking woman. Made a big do, that case. She was acquitted. Well, Thomas Arundell quite lost his head. Used to get all the papers and read about the case and cut out the photographs of Mrs Varley. And would you believe it, when the trial was over, off he went to London and asked her to marry him? Thomas! Quiet, stay at home Thomas! Never can tell with men, can you? They're always liable to break out.'

'And what happened?'

'Oh, she married him all right.'

'It was a great shock to his sisters?'

'I should think so! They wouldn't receive her. I don't know that I blame them, all things considered. Thomas was mortally offended. He went off to live in the Channel Islands and nobody heard any more of him. Don't know whether his wife poisoned her first husband. She didn't poison Thomas. He survived her by three years. There were two children, boy and girl. Good-looking pair—took after their mother.'

'I suppose they came here to their aunt a good deal?'

'Not till after their parents died. They were at school and almost grown-up by then. They used to come for holidays. Emily was alone in the world then and they and Bella Biggs were the only kith and kin she had.'

'Biggs?'

'Arabella's daughter. Dull girl—some years older than Theresa. Made a fool of herself though. Married some Dago who was over at the University. A Greek doctor. Dreadful-looking man—got rather a charming manner, though, I must admit. Well, I don't suppose poor Bella had many chances. Spent her time helping her father or holding wool for her mother. This fellow was exotic. It appealed to her.'

'Has it been a happy marriage?'

Miss Peabody snapped out:

'I wouldn't like to say for certain about *any* marriage! They *seem* quite happy. Two rather yellow-looking children. They live in Smyrna.'

'But they are now in England, are they not?'

'Yes, they came over in March. I rather fancy they'll be going back soon.'

'Was Miss Emily Arundell fond of her niece?'

'Fond of Bella? Oh, quite. She's a dull woman—wrapped up in her children and that sort of thing.'

'Did she approve of the husband?'

Miss Peabody chuckled.

'She didn't *approve* of him, but I think she rather liked the rascal. He's got brains, you know. If you ask me, he was jockeying her along very nicely. Got a nose for money that man.'

Poirot coughed.

'I understand Miss Arundell died a rich woman?' he murmured.

Miss Peabody settled herself more comfortably in her chair.

'Yes, that's what made all the pother! Nobody dreamed she was quite as well off as she was. How it came about was this way. Old General Arundell left quite a nice little income—divided equally among his son and daughters. Some of it was reinvested, and I think every investment has done well. There were some original shares of Mortauld. Now, of course, Thomas and Arabella took their shares with them when they married. The other three sisters lived here, and they didn't spend a tenth part of their joint income, it all went back and was reinvested. When Matilda died, she left her money to be divided between Emily and Agnes, and when Agnes died she left hers to Emily. And Emily still went on spending very little. Result, she died a rich woman—and the Lawson woman gets it all!'

Miss Peabody brought out the last sentence as a kind of triumphal climax.

'Did that come as a surprise to you, Miss Peabody?'

'To tell you the truth, it did! Emily had always given out quite openly that at her death her money was to be divided between her nieces and her nephew. And as a matter of fact that was the way it was in the original will. Legacies to the servants and so on and then to be divided between Theresa, Charles and Bella. My goodness, there *was* a to do when, after her death, it was found she'd made a new will leaving it all to poor Miss Lawson!'

'Was the will made just before her death?'

Miss Peabody directed a sharp glance at him.

'Thinking of undue influence. No, I'm afraid that's no use. And I shouldn't think poor Lawson had the brains or the nerve to attempt anything of the sort. To tell you the truth, she seemed as much surprised as anybody—or said she was!'

Poirot smiled at the addition.

'The will was made about ten days before her death,' went on Miss Peabody. 'Lawyer says it's all right. Well—it may be.'

'You mean—' Poirot leaned forward.

'Hanky panky, that's what I say,' said Miss Peabody. 'Something fishy somewhere.'

'Just what exactly is your idea?'

'Haven't got one! How should I know where the hanky panky comes in? I'm not a lawyer. But there's something queer about it, mark my words.'

Poirot said, slowly:

'Has there been any question of contesting the will?'

'Theresa's taken counsel's opinion, I believe. A lot of good that'll do her! What's a lawyer's opinion nine times out of ten? "Don't!" Five lawyers advised me once against bringing an action. What did I do? Paid no attention. Won my case too. They had me in the witness-box and a clever young whipper-snapper from London tried to make me contradict myself. But he didn't manage it. "You can hardly identify these furs positively, Miss Peabody," he said. "There is no furrier's mark on them."

'"That may be," I said. "But there's a darn on the lining and if anyone can do a darn like that nowadays I'll eat my umbrella." Collapsed utterly, he did.'

Miss Peabody chuckled heartily.

'I suppose,' said Poirot cautiously, 'that—er—feeling—runs rather high between Miss Lawson and members of Miss Arundell's family?'

'What do you expect? You know what human nature is. Always trouble after a death, anyway. A man or woman is hardly cold in their coffin before most of the mourners are scratching each other's eyes out.'

Poirot sighed.

'Too true.'

'That's human nature,' said Miss Peabody tolerantly.

Poirot changed to another subject.

'Is it true that Miss Arundell dabbled in spiritualism?'

Miss Peabody's penetrating eye observed him very acutely.

'If you think,' she said, 'that the spirit of John Arundell came back and ordered Emily to leave her money to Minnie Lawson and that Emily obeyed, I can tell you that you're

110

very much mistaken. Emily wouldn't be that kind of fool. If you ask me, she found spiritualism one degree better than playing patience or cribbage. Seen the Tripps?'

'No.'

'If you had, you'd realize just the sort of silliness it was. Irritating women. Always giving you messages from one or other of your relations—and always totally incongruous ones. They believe it all. So did Minnie Lawson. Oh, well, one way of passing your evenings is as good as another, I suppose.'

Poirot tried yet another tack.

'You know young Charles Arundell, I presume? What kind of person is he?'

'He's no good. Charmin' fellow. Always hard up—always in debt—always returning like a bad penny from all over the world. Knows how to get round women all right.' She chuckled. 'I've seen too many like him to be taken in! Funny son for Thomas to have had, I must say. He was a staid old fogy if you like. Model of rectitude. Ah, well, bad blood somewhere. Mind you, I *like* the rascal—but he's the kind who would murder his grandmother for a shilling or two quite cheerfully. No moral sense. Odd the way some people seem to be born without it.'

'And his sister?'

'Theresa?' Miss Peabody shook her head and said slowly: 'I don't know. She's an exotic creature. Not usual. She's engaged to that namby-pamby doctor down here. You've seen him, perhaps?'

'Dr Donaldson.'

111

'Yes. Clever in his profession, they say. But he's a poor stick in other ways. Not the sort of young man I'd fancy if I were a young girl. Well, Theresa should know her mind. She's had her experiences, I'll be bound.'

'Dr Donaldson did not attend Miss Arundell?'

'He used to when Grainger was away on holiday.'

'But not in her last illness.'

'Don't think so.'

Poirot said, smiling:

'I gather, Miss Peabody, that you don't think much of him as a doctor?'

'Never said so. As a matter of fact you're wrong. He's sharp enough, and clever enough in his way—but it's not *my* way. Take an instance. In the old days when a child ate too many green apples it had a bilious attack and the doctor called it a bilious attack and went home and sent you along a few pills from the surgery. Nowadays, you're told the child suffers from pronounced acidosis, that its diet must be supervised and you get the same medicine, only it's in nice little white tablets put up by manufacturing chemists and costs you about three times as much! Donaldson belongs to that school, and mind you, most young mothers prefer it. It *sounds* better. Not that that young man will be in this place long ministering to measles and bilious attacks. He's got his eye on London. He's ambitious. He means to specialize.'

'In any particular line?'

'Serum therapeutics. I think I've got it right. The idea being that you get one of these nasty hypodermic needles stuck into you no matter how well you feel, just in case you should catch something. I don't hold with all these messy injections myself.'

'Is Dr Donaldson experimenting with any particular disease?'

'Don't ask me. All I know is a G.P.'s practice isn't good enough for him. He wants to set up in London. But to do that he's got to have money and he's as poor as a church mouse, whatever a church mouse may be.'

Poirot murmured:

'Sad that real ability is so often baulked by lack of money. And yet there are people who do not spend a quarter of their incomes.'

'Emily Arundell didn't,' said Miss Peabody. 'It was quite a surprise to some people when that will was read. The amount, I mean, not the way it was left.'

'Was it a surprise, do you think, to the members of her own family?'

'That's telling,' said Miss Peabody screwing up her eyes with a good deal of enjoyment. 'I wouldn't say yes, and I wouldn't say no. One of 'em had a pretty shrewd idea.'

'Which one?'

'Master Charles. He'd done a bit of calculation on his own account. He's no fool, Charles.'

'But a little bit of a rogue, eh?'

'At any rate, he isn't a namby-pamby stick,' said Miss Peabody viciously.

She paused a minute and then asked:

'Going to get in touch with him?'

'That was my intention.' Poirot went on solemnly. 'It seems to me possible that he might have certain family papers relating to his grandfather?'

'More likely to have made a bonfire of them. No respect for his elders, that young man.'

'One must try all avenues,' said Poirot sententiously.

'So it seems,' said Miss Peabody drily.

There was a momentary glint in her blue eye that seemed to affect Poirot disagreeably. He rose.

'I must not trespass any longer on your time, madame. I am most grateful for what you have been able to tell me.'

'I've done my best,' said Miss Peabody. 'Seem to have got rather a long way from the Indian Mutiny, don't we?'

She shook hands with us both.

'Let me know when the book comes out,' was her parting remark. 'I shall be *so* interested.'

And the last thing we heard as we left the room was a rich, throaty chuckle.

CHAPTER 11

Visit to the Misses Tripp

'And now,' said Poirot as we re-entered the car. 'What do we do next?'

Warned by experience I did not this time suggest a return to town. After all, if Poirot was enjoying himself in his own fashion why should I object?

I suggested some tea.

'Tea, Hastings? What an idea! Regard the time.'

'I have regarded it—looked at it, I mean. It's half-past five. Tea is clearly indicated.'

Poirot sighed.

'Always the afternoon tea with you English! No, *mon ami*, no tea for us. In a book of etiquette I read the other day that one must not make the afternoon call after six o'clock. To do so is to commit the solecism. We have, therefore, but half an hour in which to accomplish our purpose.'

'How social you are today, Poirot! On whom are we calling now?'

'*Les demoiselles* Tripp.'

'Are you writing a book on spiritualism now? Or is it still the life of General Arundell?'

'It will be simpler than that, my friend. But we must inquire where these ladies live.'

Directions were forthcoming readily enough, but of a somewhat confused nature involving as they did a series of lanes. The abode of the Misses Tripp turned out to be a picturesque cottage—so extremely old-world and pictur-esque that it looked as though it might collapse any minute.

A child of fourteen or thereabouts opened the door and with difficulty squeezed herself against the wall sufficiently to allow us to pass inside.

The interior was very rich in old oak beams—there was a big open fireplace and such very small windows that it was difficult to see clearly. All the furniture was of pseudo simplicity—ye olde oake for ye cottage dweller—there was a good deal of fruit in wooden bowls and large numbers of photographs—most of them, I noticed, of the same two people represented in different poses—usually with bunches of flowers clasped to their breasts or clutching large leghorn picture-hats.

The child who had admitted us had murmured something and disappeared, but her voice was clearly audible in an upper storey.

'Two gentlemen to see you, Miss.'

A sort of twitter of female voices arose and presently with a good deal of creaking and rustling a lady descended the staircase and came graciously towards us.

She was nearer fifty than forty, her hair was parted in the middle in Madonna fashion, her eyes were brown and slightly prominent. She wore a sprigged muslin dress that conveyed an odd suggestion of fancy dress.

Poirot stepped forward and started the conversation in his most flourishing manner.

'I must apologize for intruding upon you, mademoiselle, but I am in somewhat of a predicament. I came here to find a certain lady, but she has left Market Basing and I was told that you would certainly have her address.'

'Really? Who was that?'

'Miss Lawson.'

'Oh, Minnie Lawson. Of *course*! We are the *greatest* friends. Do sit down, Mr—er—?'

'Parotti—my friend, Captain Hastings.'

Miss Tripp acknowledged the introductions and began to fuss a little.

'Sit here, won't you—no, please—really, I always prefer an *upright* chair myself. Now, are you sure you are comfortable there? Dear Minnie Lawson—oh, here is my sister.'

More creaking and rustling and we were joined by a second lady, dressed in green gingham that would have been suitable for a girl of sixteen.

'My sister Isabel—Mr—er—Parrot—and—er—Captain Hawkins. Isabel dear, these gentlemen are friends of Minnie Lawson's.'

Miss Isabel Tripp was less buxom than her sister. She might indeed have been described as scraggy. She had very fair hair done up into a large quantity of rather messy curls. She cultivated a girlish manner and was easily recognizable as the subject of most of the flower poses

117

in the photography. She clasped her hands now in girlish excitement.

'How delightful! Dear Minnie! You have seen her lately?'

'Not for some years,' explained Poirot. 'We have quite lost touch with each other. I have been travelling. That is why I was so astonished and delighted to hear of the good fortune that had befallen my old friend.'

'Yes, indeed. And so *well* deserved! Minnie is such a rare soul. So simple—so earnest.'

'Julia,' cried Isabel.

'Yes, Isabel?'

'How remarkable. *P.* You remember the planchette distinctly insisted on *P.* last night. A visitor from over the water and the initial *P.*'

'So it did,' agreed Julia.

Both ladies looked at Poirot in rapt and delighted surprise.

'It never lies,' said Miss Julia softly.

'Are you interested at all in the occult, Mr Parrot?'

'I have little experience, mademoiselle, but—like anyone who has travelled much in the East, I am bound to admit that there is much one does not understand and that cannot be explained by natural means.'

'So true,' said Julia. 'Profoundly true.'

'The East,' murmured Isabel. 'The home of mysticism and the occult.'

Poirot's travellings in the East, as far as I knew, consisted of one journey to Syria extended to Iraq, and which occupied perhaps a few weeks. To judge by his present conversation one would swear that he had spent most of his life in jungles and bazaars and in intimate converse with fakirs, dervishes, and mahatmas.

As far as I could make out the Misses Tripp were vegetarians, theosophists, British Israelites, Christian Scientists, spiritualists and enthusiastic amateur photographers.

'One sometimes feels,' said Julia with a sigh, 'that Market Basing is an impossible place to live. There is no beauty here—no *soul*. One must have soul, don't you think so, Captain Hawkins?'

'Quite,' I said slightly embarrassed. 'Oh, quite.'

'*Where there is no vision the people perish*,' quoted Isabel with a sigh. 'I have often tried to discuss things with the vicar, but find him painfully *narrow*. Don't you think, Mr Parrot, that any definite creed is bound to be *narrowing*?'

'And everything is so simple, really,' put in her sister. 'As we know so well, everything is joy and love!'

'As you say, as you say,' said Poirot. 'What a pity it seems that misunderstandings and quarrels should arise—especially over money.'

'Money is so sordid,' sighed Julia.

'I gather that the late Miss Arundell was one of your converts?' said Poirot.

The two sisters looked at each other.

'I wonder,' said Isabel.

'We were never quite sure,' breathed Julia. 'One minute she seemed to be convinced and then she would say something—so—so ribald.'

'Ah, but you remember that last manifestation,' said Julia. 'That was really most remarkable.' She turned to Poirot. 'It was the night dear Miss Arundell was taken ill. My sister and I went round after dinner and we had a sitting—just the four of us. And you know we saw—we all three saw—*most* distinctly, a kind of *halo* round Miss Arundell's head.'

'*Comment?*'

'Yes. It was a kind of luminous haze.' She turned to her sister. 'Isn't that how you would describe it, Isabel?'

'Yes. Yes, just that. A luminous haze gradually surrounding Miss Arundell's head—an aureole of faint light. It was a *sign*—we know that now—a sign that she was about to pass over to the other side.'

'Remarkable,' said Poirot in a suitably impressed voice. 'It was dark in the room, yes?'

'Oh, yes, we always get better results in the dark, and it was quite a warm evening so we didn't even have the fire on.'

'A most interesting spirit spoke to us,' said Isabel. 'Fatima, her name was. She told us she had passed over in the time of the Crusades. She gave us a most beautiful message.'

'She actually spoke to you?'

'No, not direct voice. She rapped it out. Love. Hope. Life. Beautiful words.'

'And Miss Arundell was actually taken ill at the seance?'

'It was just after. Some sandwiches and port wine were brought in, and dear Miss Arundell said she wouldn't have any as she wasn't feeling very well. That was the beginning of her illness. Mercifully, she did not have to endure much suffering.'

'She passed over four days later,' said Isabel.

'And we have already had messages from her,' said Julia eagerly. 'Saying that she is very happy and that everything is beautiful and that she hopes that there is love and peace among all her dear ones.'

Poirot coughed.

'That—er—is hardly the case, I fear?'

'The relations have behaved *disgracefully* to poor Minnie,' said Isabel. Her face flushed with indignation.

'Minnie is the most *unworldly* soul,' chimed in Julia.

'People have gone about saying the *unkindest* things— that she *schemed* for this money to be left her!'

'When really it was the *greatest* surprise to her—'

'She could hardly believe her *ears* when the lawyer read the will—'

'She told us so herself. "Julia," she said to me. "My dear, you could have knocked me over with a feather. Just a few bequests to the servants and then Littlegreen House and the residue of my estate to Wilhelmina Lawson." She was so flabbergasted she could hardly speak. And when she could she asked how much it would be—thinking perhaps it would be a few thousand pounds—and Mr Purvis, after humming and hawing and talking about confusing things like gross and net personalities, said it would be in the neighbourhood of three hundred and seventy-five thousand pounds. Poor Minnie nearly fainted, she told us.'

'She had no *idea*,' the other sister reiterated. 'She never thought of such a thing happening!'

'That is what she told you, yes?'

'Oh, yes, she repeated it several times. And that's what makes it so *wicked* of the Arundell family to go on as they have done—cold-shouldering her and treating her with suspicion. After all, this is a free country—'

'English people seem to labour under that misapprehension,' murmured Poirot.

'And I should hope *anyone* can leave their money exactly as they choose! *I* think Miss Arundell acted very *wisely*. Obviously she *mistrusted* her own relatives and I dare say she had her reasons.'

'Ah?' Poirot leant forward with interest. 'Indeed?'

This flattering attention encouraged Isabel to proceed.

'Yes, indeed. Mr Charles Arundell, her nephew, is a thoroughly bad lot. That's well known! I believe he's even wanted by the police in some foreign country. Not at all a desirable character. As for his sister, well, I've not actually *spoken* to her, but she's a very queer-looking girl. Ultra modern, of course, and terribly made-up. Really, the sight of her mouth made me quite *ill*. It looked like *blood*. And I rather suspect she takes drugs—her manner was so *odd* sometimes. She's by way of being engaged to that nice young Dr Donaldson, but I fancy even *he* looked disgusted sometimes. Of course, she is attractive in her way, but I hope that he will come to his senses in time and marry some nice English girl who is fond of country life and outdoor pursuits.'

'And the other relations?'

'Well, there you are again. Very undesirable. Not that I've anything to say against Mrs Tanios—she's quite a nice woman—but absolutely stupid and completely under her husband's thumb. Of course, he's really a Turk, I believe— rather dreadful for an English girl to marry a *Turk*, I think, don't you? It shows a certain lack of *fastidiousness*. Of course, Mrs Tanios is a very good mother, though the children are singularly unattractive, poor little things.'

'So altogether you think Miss Lawson was a more worthy recipient of Miss Arundell's fortune?'

Julia said serenely:

'Minnie Lawson is a thoroughly *good* woman. And so *unworldly*. It isn't as though she had ever *thought* about money. She was *never* grasping.'

'Still, she has never thought of refusing to accept the legacy?'

Isabel drew back a little.

'Oh, well—one would hardly do *that*.'

Poirot smiled.

'No, perhaps not...'

'You see, Mr Parrot,' put in Julia. 'She regards it as a *trust*—a sacred *trust*.'

'And she is quite willing to do something for Mrs Tanios or for the Tanios children,' went on Isabel. 'Only she doesn't want *him* to get hold of it.'

'She even said she would consider making Theresa an allowance.'

'And that, I think, was very generous of her—considering the off-hand way that girl has always treated her.'

'Indeed, Mr Parrot, Minnie is the most *generous* of creatures. But there now, you know her, of course!'

'Yes,' said Poirot. 'I know her. But I still do not know—her address.'

'Of course! How stupid of me! Shall I write it down for you?'

123

'I can write it down.'

Poirot produced the invariable notebook.

'17, Clanroyden Mansions, W.2. Not very far from Whiteleys. You'll give her our love, won't you? We haven't heard from her just lately.'

Poirot rose and I followed suit.

'I have to thank you both very much,' he declared, 'for a most charming talk as well as for your kindness in supplying me with my friend's address.'

'I wonder they didn't give it to you at the house,' exclaimed Isabel. 'It must be that Ellen! Servants are so *jealous* and *so small minded*. They used to be quite rude to Minnie sometimes.'

Julia shook hands in a *grande dame* manner.

'We have enjoyed your visit,' she declared graciously. 'I wonder—'

She flashed a glance of inquiry at her sister.

'You would, perhaps—' Isabel flushed a little. 'Would you, that is to say, stay and share our evening meal? A very simple one—some shredded raw vegetables, brown bread and butter, fruit.'

'It sounds delicious,' Poirot said hastily. 'But alas! my friend and I have to return to London.'

With renewed handshaking and messages to be delivered to Miss Lawson, we at last made our exit.

CHAPTER 12

Poirot Discusses the Case

'Thank goodness, Poirot,' I said with fervour, 'you got us out of those raw carrots! What awful women!'

'*Pour nous, un bon bifteck*—with the fried potatoes—and a good bottle of wine. What should we have had to drink there, I wonder?'

'Well, water, I should think,' I replied with a shudder. 'Or non-alcoholic cider. It was that kind of place! I bet there's no bath and no sanitation except an E.C. in the garden!'

'Strange how women enjoy living an uncomfortable life,' said Poirot thoughtfully. 'It is not always poverty, though they are good at making the best of straitened circumstances.'

'What orders for the chauffeur now?' I asked, as I nego-tiated the last bend of the winding lanes, and we emerged on the road to Market Basing. 'On what local light do we call next? Or do we return to the George and interrogate the asthmatic waiter once more?'

'You will be glad to hear, Hastings, that we have finished with Market Basing—'

'Splendid.'

'For the moment only. I shall return!'

'Still on the track of your unsuccessful murderer?'

'Exactly.'

'Did you learn anything from the fandango of nonsense we've just been listening to?'

Poirot said precisely:

'There were certain points deserving of attention. The various characters in our drama begin to emerge more clearly. In some ways it resembles, does it not, a novelette of older days? The humble companion, once despised, is raised to affluence and now plays the part of lady bountiful.'

'I should imagine that such a patronage must be very galling to people who regard themselves as the rightful heirs!'

'As you say, Hastings. Yes, that is very true.'

We drove on in silence for some minutes. We had passed through Market Basing and were now once more on the main road. I hummed to myself softly the tune of 'Little Man, You've had a Busy Day.'

'Enjoyed yourself, Poirot?' I asked at last.

Poirot said coldly:

'I do not know quite what you mean by "enjoyed myself", Hastings.'

'Well,' I said, 'it seemed to me you've been treating yourself to a busman's holiday!'

'You do not think that I am serious?'

'Oh, you're *serious* enough. But this business seems to be of the academic kind. You're tackling it for your own mental satisfaction. What I mean is—it's not *real*.'

'*Au contraire*, it is intensely real.'

'I express myself badly. What I mean is, if there were a question of *helping* our old lady, or protecting her against further attack—well, there would be some excitement then. But as it is, I can't help feeling that as she is dead, why worry?'

'In that case, *mon ami*, one would not investigate a murder case at all!'

'No, no, no. That's quite different. I mean, then you have a *body*... Oh, dash it all!'

'Do not enrage yourself. I comprehend perfectly. You make a distinction between a *body* and a mere *decease*. Supposing, for instance, that Miss Arundell had died with sudden and alarming violence instead of respectably of a long-standing illness—then you would not remain indifferent to my efforts to discover the truth?'

'Of course I wouldn't.'

'But all the same, someone did attempt to murder her?'

'Yes, but they didn't *succeed*. That makes all the difference.'

'It does not intrigue you at all to know *who* attempted to kill her?'

'Well, yes, it does in a way.'

'We have a very restricted circle,' said Poirot musingly. 'That thread—'

'The thread which you merely deduce from a nail in the skirting-board!' I interrupted. 'Why, that nail may have been there for years!'

'No. The varnish was quite fresh.'

'Well, I still think there might be all sorts of explanations of it.'

Agatha Christie

'Give me one.'

At the moment I could not think of anything sufficiently plausible. Poirot took advantage of my silence to sweep on with his discourse.

'Yes, a restricted circle. That thread could only have been stretched across the top of the stairs after everyone had gone to bed. Therefore we have *only the occupants of the house to consider*. That is to say, the guilt lies between seven people. Dr Tanios. Mrs Tanios. Theresa Arundell. Charles Arundell. Miss Lawson. Ellen. Cook.'

'Surely you can leave the servants out of it.'

'They received legacies, *mon cher*. And there *might* have been other reasons—spite—a quarrel—dishonesty—one cannot be *certain*.'

'It seems to me very unlikely.'

'Unlikely, I agree. But one must take all possibilities into consideration.'

'In that case, you must allow for eight people, not seven.'

'How so?'

I felt I was about to score a point.

'You must include *Miss Arundell* herself. How do you know she may not have stretched that thread across the stairs in order to trip up some other members of the house-party?'

Poirot shrugged his shoulders.

'It is a *bêtise* you say there, my friend. If Miss Arundell laid a trap, she would be careful not to fall into it herself. It was *she* who fell down the stairs, remember.'

I retired crestfallen.

Poirot went on in a thoughtful voice:

'The sequence of events is quite clear—the fall—the letter to me—the visit of the lawyer—but there is one doubtful point. Did Miss Arundell deliberately hold back the letter to me, hesitating to post it? Or did she, once having written it, assume it *was* posted?'

'That we can't possibly tell,' I said. 'No. We can only *guess*. Personally, I fancy that she assumed it had been posted. She must have been surprised at getting no reply...'

My thoughts had been busy in another direction.

'Do you think this spiritualistic nonsense counted at all?' I asked. 'I mean, do you think, in spite of Miss Peabody's ridiculing of the suggestion, that a command was given at one of these *séances* that she should alter her will and leave her money to the Lawson woman?'

Poirot shook his head doubtfully.

'That does not seem to fit in with the general impression I have formed of Miss Arundell's character.'

'The Tripp women say that Miss Lawson was completely taken aback when the will was read,' I said thoughtfully.

'That is what she told them, yes,' agreed Poirot.

'But you don't believe it?'

'*Mon ami*—you know my suspicious nature! I believe nothing that anyone says unless it can be confirmed or corroborated.'

'That's right, old boy,' I said affectionately. 'A thoroughly nice, trustful nature.'

'"He says," "she says," "they say"—Bah! what does that mean? Nothing at all. It may be absolute truth. It may be useful falsehood. Me, I deal only with *facts*.'

'And the facts are?'

'Miss Arundell had a fall. That, nobody disputes. The fall was not a natural one—it was contrived.'

'The evidence for that being that Hercule Poirot says so!'

'Not at all. There is the evidence of the nail. The evidence of Miss Arundell's letter to me. The evidence of the dog having been out that night. The evidence of Miss Arundell's words about the jar and the picture and Bob's ball. All these things are *facts*.'

'And the next fact, please?'

'The next fact is the answer to our usual question. Who benefits by Miss Arundell's death? Answer—Miss Lawson.'

'The wicked companion! On the other hand, the others thought they were going to benefit. And at the time of the accident they *would* have benefited.'

'Exactly, Hastings. That is why they all lie equally under suspicion. There is also the little fact that Miss Lawson took pains to prevent Miss Arundell learning that Bob had been out all night.'

'You call that suspicious?'

'Not at all. I merely note it. It may have been natural concern for the old lady's peace of mind. That is by far the most likely explanation.'

I looked at Poirot sideways. He is so confoundedly slippery.

'Miss Peabody expressed the opinion that there was "hanky-panky" about the will,' I said. 'What do you suppose she meant by that?'

'It was, I think, her way of expressing various nebulous and unformulated suspicions.'

'Undue influence, it seems, can be washed out,' I said thoughtfully. 'And it certainly looks as though Emily Arundell was much too sensible to believe in any tomfoolery like spiritualism.'

'What makes you say that spiritualism is tomfoolery, Hastings?'

I stared at him in astonishment.

'My dear Poirot—those appalling women—'

He smiled.

'I quite agree with your estimate of the Misses Tripp. But the mere fact that the Misses Tripp have adopted with enthusiasm Christian Science, vegetarianism, theosophy and spiritualism does not really constitute a damning indictment of those subjects! Because a foolish woman will tell you a lot of nonsense about a fake scarab which she has bought from a rascal dealer, that does not necessarily bring discredit on the general subject of Egyptology!'

'Do you mean you *believe* in spiritualism, Poirot?'

'I have an open mind on the subject. I have never studied any of its manifestations myself, but it must be accepted that many men of science and learning have pronounced themselves satisfied that there are phenomena which cannot be accounted for by—shall we say the credulity of a Miss Tripp?'

'Then you believe in this rigmarole of an aureole of light surrounding Miss Arundell's head?'

Poirot waved a hand.

'I was speaking generally—rebuking your attitude of quite unreasoning scepticism. I may say that, having formed a certain opinion of Miss Tripp and her sister, I should examine very carefully any fact they presented for my notice.

Agatha Christie

Foolish women, *mon ami*, are foolish women, whether they are talking about spiritualism or politics or the relation of the sexes or the tenets of the Budhist faith.'

'Yet you listened to what they had to say very carefully.'

'That has been my task today—to listen. To hear what everyone has got to tell me about these seven people—and mainly, of course, the five people primarily concerned. Already we know certain aspects of these people. Take Miss Lawson. From the Misses Tripp we learn she was devoted, unselfish, unworldly and altogether a beautiful character. From Miss Peabody we learn that she was credulous, stupid, without the nerve or the brains to attempt anything criminal. From Dr Grainger we learn that she was down-trodden, that her position was precarious, and that she was a poor "frightened, fluttering hen", were, I think, the words he used. From our waiter we learned that Miss Lawson was "a person", and from Ellen that Bob, the dog, despised her! Everyone, you see, saw her from a slightly different angle. That is the same with the others. Nobody's opinion of Charles Arundell's morals seems to have been high, but nevertheless they vary in their manner of speaking of him. Dr Grainger calls him indulgently "an irreverent young devil". Miss Peabody says he would murder his grandmother for twopence but clearly prefers a rascal to a "stick". Miss Tripp hints not only that he would do a criminal action but that he has done one—or more. These side-lights are all very useful and interesting. They lead to the next thing.'

'Which is?'

'To see for ourselves, my friend.'

CHAPTER 13

Theresa Arundell

On the following morning we made our way to the address given us by Dr Donaldson.

I suggested to Poirot that a visit to the lawyer, Mr Purvis, might be a good thing, but Poirot negatived the idea strongly.

'No, indeed, my friend. What could we say—what reason could we advance for seeking information?'

'You're usually pretty ready with reasons, Poirot! Any old lie would do, wouldn't it?'

'On the contrary, my friend, "any old lie," as you put it, would *not* do. Not with a lawyer. We should be—how do you say it—thrown out with the flea upon the ear.'

'Oh, well,' I said. 'Don't let us risk *that*!'

So, as I have said, we set out for the flat occupied by Theresa Arundell.

The flat in question was situated in a block at Chelsea overlooking the river. It was furnished expensively in the modern style, with gleaming chromium and thick rugs with geometric designs upon them.

We were kept waiting a few minutes and then a girl entered the room and looked at us inquiringly.

Theresa Arundell looked about twenty-eight or nine. She was tall and very slender, and she looked rather like an exaggerated drawing in black and white. Her hair was jet black—her face heavily made-up, dead pale. Her eyebrows, freakishly plucked, gave her an air of mocking irony. Her lips were the only spot of colour, a brilliant gash of scarlet in a white face. She also conveyed the impression—how I do not quite know, for her manner was almost wearily indifferent—of being at least twice as much alive as most people. There hung about her the restrained energy of a whip-lash.

With an air of cool inquiry she looked from me to Poirot.

Wearied (I hoped) of deceit, Poirot had on this occasion sent in his own card. She was holding it now in her fingers, twirling it to and fro.

'I suppose,' she said, 'you're M. Poirot?'

Poirot bowed in his best manner.

'At your service, mademoiselle. You permit me to trespass for a few moments of your valuable time?'

With a faint imitation of Poirot's manner she replied:

'Enchanted, M. Poirot. Pray sit down.'

Poirot sat, rather gingerly, on a low square easy-chair. I took an upright one of webbing and chromium. Theresa sat negligently on a low stool in front of the fireplace. She offered us both cigarettes. We refused and she lighted one herself.

'You know my name perhaps, mademoiselle?'

She nodded.

'Little friend of Scotland Yard. That's right, isn't it?'

Poirot, I think, did not much relish this description. He said with some importance:

'I concern myself with problems of crime, mademoiselle.'

'How frightfully thrilling,' said Theresa Arundell in a bored voice. 'And to think I've lost my autograph book!'

'The matter with which I concern myself is this,' continued Poirot. 'Yesterday I received a letter from your aunt.'

Her eyes—very long, almond-shaped eyes—opened a little. She puffed smoke in a cloud.

'From my *aunt*, M. Poirot?'

'That is what I said, mademoiselle.'

She murmured:

'I'm sorry if I'm spoiling sport in any way, but really, you know, there isn't any such person! All my aunts are mercifully dead. The last died two months ago.'

'Miss Emily Arundell?'

'Yes, Miss Emily Arundell. You don't receive letters from corpses, do you, M. Poirot?'

'Sometimes I do, mademoiselle.'

'How *macabre*!'

But there was a new note in her voice—a note suddenly alert and watchful.

'And what did my aunt say, M. Poirot?'

'That, mademoiselle, I can hardly tell you just at present. It was, you see, a somewhat'—he coughed—'delicate matter.'

There was silence for a minute or two. Theresa Arundell smoked. Then she said:

'It all sounds delightfully hush-hush. But where exactly do I come in?'

'I hoped, mademoiselle, that you might consent to answer a few questions.'

'Questions? What about?'

'Questions of a family nature.'

Again I saw her eyes widen.

'That sounds rather pompous! Supposing you give me a specimen.'

'Certainly. Can you tell me the present address of your brother Charles?'

The eyes narrowed again. Her latent energy was less apparent. It was as though she withdrew into a shell.

'I'm afraid I can't. We don't correspond much. I rather think he has left England.'

'I see.'

Poirot was silent for a minute or two.

'Was that all you wanted to know?'

'Oh, I have other questions. For one—are you satisfied with the way in which your aunt disposed of her fortune? For another—how long have you been engaged to Dr Donaldson?'

'You do jump about, don't you?'

'*Eh bien?*'

'Eh bien—since we are so foreign!—my answer to both those questions is they are none of your business! *Ça ne vous regarde pas, M. Hercule Poirot.*'

Poirot studied her for a moment or two attentively. Then, with no trace of disappointment, he got up.

'So it is like that! Ah, well, perhaps it is not surprising. Allow me, mademoiselle, to congratulate you upon your

French accent. And to wish you a very good morning. Come, Hastings.'

We had reached the door when the girl spoke. The simile of a whip-lash came again into my mind. She did not move from her position but the two words were like the flick of a whip.

'Come back!' she said.

Poirot obeyed slowly. He sat down again and looked at her inquiringly.

'Let's stop playing the fool,' she said. 'It's just possible that you might be useful to me, M. Hercule Poirot.'

'Delighted, mademoiselle—and how?'

Between two puffs of cigarette smoke she said very quietly and evenly:

'Tell me how to break that will.'

'Surely a lawyer—'

'Yes, a lawyer, perhaps—if I knew the right lawyer. But the only lawyers I know are respectable men! Their advice is that the will holds good in law and that any attempts to contest it will be useless expense.'

'But you do not believe them.'

'I believe there is always a way to do things—if you don't mind being unscrupulous and are prepared to pay. Well, *I am prepared to pay.*'

'And you take it for granted that I am prepared to be unscrupulous if I am paid?'

'I've found that to be true of most people! I don't see why you should be an exception. People always protest about their honesty and their rectitude to begin with, of course.'

'Just so, that is part of the game, eh? But what, given that I was prepared to be—unscrupulous—do you think I could do?'

'I don't know. But you're a clever man. Everyone knows that. You could think out some scheme.'

'Such as?'

Theresa Arundell shrugged her shoulders.

'That's your business. Steal the will and substitute a forgery... Kidnap the Lawson and frighten her into saying she bullied Aunt Emily into making it. Produce a later will made on old Emily's death-bed.'

'Your fertile imagination takes my breath away, mademoiselle!'

'Well, what is your answer? I've been frank enough. If it's righteous refusal, there's the door.'

'It is not righteous refusal—yet—' said Poirot.

Theresa Arundell laughed. She looked at me.

'Your friend,' she observed, 'looks shocked. Shall we send him out to chase himself round the block?'

Poirot addressed himself to me with some slight irritation.

'Control, I pray of you, your beautiful and upright nature, Hastings. I demand pardon for my friend, mademoiselle. He is, as you have perceived, honest. But he is also faithful. His loyalty to myself is absolute. In any case, let me emphasize this point'—he looked at her very hard—'whatever we are about to do will be strictly within the law.'

She raised her eyebrows slightly.

'The law,' said Poirot thoughtfully, 'has a lot of latitude.'

'I see,' she smiled faintly. 'All right, we'll let that be understood. Do you want to discuss your share of the booty—if there turns out to be any booty?'

'That, also, can be understood. Some nice little pickings—that is all I ask?'

'Done,' said Theresa.

Poirot leant forward.

'Now listen, mademoiselle, usually—in ninety-nine cases out of a hundred cases, shall we say, I am on the side of the law. The hundredth—well, the hundredth is different. For one thing, it is usually much more lucrative... But it has to be done very quietly, you understand—very, very quietly. My reputation, it must not suffer. I have to be careful.'

Theresa Arundell nodded.

'And I must have *all* the facts of the case! I must have the truth! You comprehend that once one knows the truth it is an easier matter to know just what lies to tell!'

'That seems eminently reasonable.'

'Very well then. Now, on what date was this will made?'

'On April 21st.'

'And the previous will?'

'Aunt Emily made a will five years ago.'

'Its provisions being—?'

'After a legacy to Ellen and one to a former cook, all her property was to be divided between the children of her brother Thomas and the children of her sister Arabella.'

'Was this money left in trust?'

'No, it was left to us absolutely.'

'Now, be careful. Did you all know the provisions of this will?'

'Oh, yes. Charles and I knew—and Bella knew too. Aunt Emily made no secret of it. In fact, if any of us asked for a loan she would usually say, "You'll have all my money when I'm dead and gone. Be content with that fact."'

'Would she have refused a loan if there had been a case of illness or any dire necessity?'

'No, I don't think she would,' said Theresa slowly.

'But she considered you all had enough to live on?'

'She considered so—yes.'

There was bitterness in that voice.

'But you—did not?'

Theresa waited a minute or two before speaking. Then she said:

'My father left us thirty thousand pounds each. The interest on that, safely invested, amounts to about twelve hundred a year. Income-tax takes another wedge off it. A nice little income on which one can manage very prettily. But I—' her voice changed, her slim body straightened, her head went back—all that wonderful aliveness I had sensed in her came to the fore—'but I want something better than that out of life! I want the best! The best food, the best clothes—something with line to it—beauty—not just suitable covering in the prevailing fashion. I want to live and enjoy—to go to the Mediterranean and lie in the warm summer sea—to sit round a table and play with exciting wads of money—to give parties—wild, absurd, extravagant parties—I want everything that's going in this rotten world—and I don't want it some day—I want it now!'

Her voice was wonderfully exciting, warm, exhilarating, intoxicating.

Poirot was studying her intently.

'And you have, I fancy, had it now?'

'Yes, Hercule—I've had it!'

'And how much of the thirty thousand is left?'

She laughed suddenly.

'Two hundred and twenty-one pounds, fourteen and seven-pence. That's the exact balance. So you see, little man, you've got to be paid by results. No results—no fees.'

'In that case,' said Poirot in a matter of fact manner, 'there will certainly be results.'

'You're a great little man, Hercule. I'm glad we got together.'

Poirot went on in a business-like way:

'There are a few things that are actually necessary that I should know. Do you drug?'

'No, never.'

'Drink?'

'Quite heavily—but not for the love of it. My crowd drinks and I drink with them, but I could give it up tomorrow.'

'That is very satisfactory.'

She laughed.

'I shan't give the show away in my cups, Hercule.'

Poirot proceeded:

'Love affairs?'

'Plenty in the past.'

'And the present?'

'Only Rex.'

'That is Dr Donaldson?'

'Yes.'

'He seems, somehow, very alien from the life you mention.'

'Oh, he is.'

'And yet you care for him. Why, I wonder?'

'Oh, what are reasons? Why did Juliet fall for Romeo?'

'Well for one thing, with all due deference to Shakespeare, he happened to be the first man she had seen.'

Theresa said slowly:

'Rex wasn't the first man I saw—not by a long way.' She added in a lower voice, 'But I think—I feel—he'll be the last man I'll ever see.'

'And he is a poor man, mademoiselle.'

She nodded.

'And he, too, needs money?'

'Desperately. Oh, not for the reasons I did. He doesn't want luxury—or beauty—or excitement—or any of these things. He'd wear the same suit until it went into holes—and eat a congealed chop every day for lunch quite happily, and wash in a cracked tin bath. If he had money it would all go on test-tubes and a laboratory and all the rest of it. He's ambitious. His profession means everything to him. It means more to him than—I do.'

'He knew that you would come into money when Miss Arundell died?'

'I told him so. Oh! after we were engaged. He isn't really marrying me for my money if that is what you are getting at.'

'You are still engaged?'

'Of course we are.'

Poirot did not reply. His silence seemed to disquiet her.

'Of course we are,' she repeated sharply. And then she added, 'You—have you seen him?'

'I saw him yesterday—at Market Basing.'

'Why? What did you say to him?'

'I said nothing. I only asked him for your brother's address.'

'Charles?' Her voice was sharp again. 'What did you want with Charles?'

'Charles? Who wants Charles?'

It was a new voice—a delightful, man's voice.

A bronze-faced young man with an agreeable grin strolled into the room.

'Who is talking about me?' he asked. 'I heard my name in the hall, but I didn't eavesdrop. They were very particular about eavesdropping at Borstal. Now then, Theresa my girl, what's all this? Spill the beans.'

CHAPTER 14

Charles Arundell

I must confess that from the moment I set eyes on him I entertained a sneaking liking for Charles Arundell. There was something so debonair and carefree about him. His eyes had an agreeable and humorous twinkle and his grin was one of the most disarming I have ever encountered.

He came across the room and sat down on the arm of one of the massive, upholstered chairs.

'What's it all about, old girl?' he asked.

'This is M. Hercule Poirot, Charles. He is prepared to—er—do some dirty work for us in return for a small consideration.'

'I protest,' cried Poirot. '*Not* dirty work—shall we say a little harmless deception of some kind—so that the original intention of the testator is carried out? Let us put it that way.'

'Put it any way you like,' said Charles agreeably. 'What made Theresa think of you, I wonder?'

'She did not,' said Poirot quickly. 'I came here of my own accord.'

'Offering your services?'

'Not quite that. I was asking for you. Your sister told me you had gone abroad.'

'Theresa,' said Charles, 'is a very careful sister. She hardly ever makes a mistake. In fact, she's suspicious as the devil.'

He smiled at her affectionately but she did not smile back. She looked worried and thoughtful.

'Surely,' said Charles. 'We've got things the wrong way round? Isn't M. Poirot famous for tracking down criminals? Surely not for aiding and abetting them?'

'We're not criminals,' said Theresa sharply.

'But we're willing to be,' said Charles affably. 'I'd thought of a spot of forgery myself—that's rather my line. I got sent down from Oxford because of a little misunderstanding about a cheque. That was childishly simple, though—merely a question of adding a nought. Then there was another little *fracas* with Aunt Emily and the local bank. Foolish on my part, of course. I ought to have realized the old lady was sharp as needles. However, all these incidents have been very small fry—fivers and tenners—that class. A death-bed will would be admittedly risky. One would have to get hold of the stiff and starched Ellen and—is suborn the word?—anyway, induce her to say she had witnessed it. It would take some doing, I fear. I might even marry her and then she wouldn't be able to give evidence against me afterwards.'

He grinned amiably at Poirot.

'I feel sure you've installed a secret dictaphone and Scotland Yard is listening in,' he said.

'Your problem interests me,' said Poirot with a touch of reproof in his manner. 'Naturally I could not connive at anything against the law. But there are more ways than one—' he stopped significantly.

Charles Arundell shrugged his graceful shoulders.

'I've no doubt there's an equal choice of devious ways inside the law,' he said agreeably. 'You should know.'

'By whom was the will witnessed? I mean the one made on April 21st?'

'Purvis brought down his clerk and the second witness was the gardener.'

'It was signed then in Mr Purvis's presence?'

'It was.'

'And Mr Purvis, I fancy, is a man of the highest respectability?'

'Purvis, Purvis, Charlesworth and once more Purvis are just about as respectable and impeccable as the Bank of England,' said Charles.

'He didn't like making the will,' said Theresa. 'In an ultra-correct fashion I believe he even tried to dissuade Aunt Emily from making it.'

Charles said sharply:

'Did he tell you that, Theresa?'

'Yes. I went to see him again yesterday.'

'It's no good, my sweet—you ought to realize that. Only piles up the six and eightpences.'

Theresa shrugged her shoulders.

Poirot said:

'I will ask you to give me as much information as you can about the last weeks of Miss Arundell's life. Now, to begin with, I understand that you and your brother and also Dr Tanios and his wife stayed there for Easter?'

'Yes, we did.'

'Did anything happen of significance during that weekend?'

'I don't think so.'

'Nothing? But I thought—'

Charles broke in.

'What a self-centred creature you are, Theresa. Nothing of significance happened to *you*! Wrapped in love's young dream! Let me tell you, M. Poirot, that Theresa has a blue-eyed boy in Market Basing. One of the local sawbones. She's got rather a faulty sense of proportion in consequence. As a matter of fact, my revered aunt took a header down the stairs and nearly passed out. Wish she had. It would have saved all this fuss.'

'She fell down the stairs?'

'Yes, tripped over the dog's ball. Intelligent little brute left it at the top of the stairs and she took a header over it in the night.'

'This was—when?'

'Let me see—Tuesday—the evening before we left.'

'Your aunt was seriously injured?'

'Unfortunately she didn't fall on her head. If she had we might have pleaded softening of the brain—or whatever it's called scientifically. No, she was hardly hurt at all.'

Poirot said drily:

'Very disappointing for you!'

'Eh? Oh, I see what you mean. Yes, as you say, very disappointing. Tough nuts, these old ladies.'

'And you all left on the Wednesday morning?'

'That's right.'

'That was Wednesday, the fifteenth. When did you next see your aunt?'

'Well, it wasn't the next weekend. It was the weekend after that.'

'That would be—let me see—the twenty-fifth, would it not?'

'Yes, I think that was the date.'

'And your aunt died—when?'

'The following Friday.'

'Having been taken ill on the Monday night?'

'Yes.'

'That was the Monday that you left?'

'Yes.'

'You did not return during her illness?'

'Not until the Friday. We didn't realize she was really bad.'

'You got there in time to see her alive?'

'No, she died before we arrived.'

Poirot shifted his glance to Theresa Arundell.

'You accompanied your brother on both these occasions?'

'Yes.'

'And nothing was said during the second weekend about a new will having been made?'

'Nothing,' said Theresa.

Charles, however, had answered at the same moment.

'Oh, yes,' he said. 'It was.'

He spoke airily as ever, but there was something a little constrained as though the airiness were more artificial than usual.

148

'It *was*?' said Poirot.

'Charles!' cried Theresa.

Charles seemed anxious not to meet his sister's eye. He spoke to her without looking at her.

'Surely you remember, old girl? I told you. Aunt Emily made a kind of ultimatum of it. Sat there like a judge in court. Made a kind of speech. Said she thoroughly disapproved of all her relations—that is to say, of me and Theresa. Bella, she allowed, she had nothing against, but on the other hand she disliked and distrusted her husband. Buy British was ever Aunt Emily's motto. If Bella were to inherit any considerable sum of money she said she was convinced that Tanios would somehow or other get possession of it. Trust a Greek to do that! "She's safer as she is," she went on to say. Then she said that neither I nor Theresa were fit people to be trusted with money. We would only gamble and squander it away. Therefore, she finished up, she had made a new will and had left the entire estate to Miss Lawson. "She is a fool," said Aunt Emily, "but she is a faithful soul. And I really believe she is devoted to me. She cannot help her lack of brains. I have thought it fairer to tell you this, Charles, as you may as well realize that it will not be possible for you to raise money on your expectations from me." Rather a nasty one, that. Just what I'd been trying to do.'

'Why didn't you tell me, Charles?' demanded Theresa fiercely.

Poirot asked:

'And what did you say, Mr Arundell?'

149

'I?' said Charles airily. 'Oh, I just laughed. No good cutting up rough. That's not the way. "Just as you please, Aunt Emily," I said. "Bit of a blow, perhaps, but after all, it's your own money and you can do what you like with it."'

'And your aunt's reaction to that?'

'Oh, it went down well—very well indeed. She said, "Well, I will say you're a sportsman, Charles." And I said, "Got to take the rough with the smooth. As a matter of fact, if I've no expectations what about giving me a tenner now?" And she said I was an impudent boy and actually parted with a fiver.'

'You concealed your feelings very cleverly.'

'Well, as a matter of fact, I didn't take it very seriously.'

'You didn't?'

'No. I thought it was what you might call a gesture on the old bean's part. She wanted to frighten us all. I'd a pretty shrewd suspicion that after a few weeks or perhaps months she'd tear that will up. She was pretty hot on family, Aunt Emily. And, as a matter of fact, I believe that's what she *would* have done if she hadn't died so confoundedly suddenly.'

'Ah!' said Poirot. 'It is an interesting idea that.'

He remained silent for a minute or two then went on:

'Could anyone, Miss Lawson, for instance, have over-heard your conversation?'

'Rather. We weren't speaking any too low. As a matter of fact, the Lawson bird was hovering about outside the door when I went out. Been doing a bit of snooping in my opinion.'

Poirot turned a thoughtful glance on Theresa.

'And you knew nothing of this?'

Before she could answer, Charles broke in.

'Theresa, old girl, I'm sure I told you—or hinted to you?'

There was a queer sort of pause. Charles was looking fixedly at Theresa, and there was an anxiety, a fixity, about his gaze that seemed out of all proportion to the subject matter.

Theresa said slowly:

'If you had told me—I don't think—I could have forgotten, do you, M. Poirot?'

Her long dark eyes turned to him.

Poirot said slowly:

'No, I don't think you could have forgotten, Miss Arundell.'

Then he turned sharply to Charles.

'Let me be quite clear on one point. Did Miss Arundell tell you she was about to alter her will, or did she tell you specifically that she *had* altered it?'

Charles said quickly:

'Oh, she was quite definite. As a matter of fact she showed me the will.'

Poirot leaned forward. His eyes opened wide.

'This is very important. You say that Miss Arundell actually showed you the will?'

Charles gave a sudden schoolboy wriggle—a rather disarming action. Poirot's gravity made him quite uncomfortable.

'Yes,' he said. 'She showed it to me.'

'You can swear definitely to that?'

'Of course I can.' Charles looked nervously at Poirot. 'I don't see what is so significant about that.'

There was a sudden brusque movement from Theresa. She had risen and was standing by the mantelpiece. She quickly lit another cigarette.

'And you, mademoiselle?' Poirot whirled suddenly round on her. 'Did your aunt say nothing of importance to you during that weekend?'

'I don't think so. She was—quite amiable. That is, as amiable as she usually was. Lectured me a bit about my way of life and all that. But then, she always did. She seemed perhaps a bit more jumpy than usual.'

Poirot said, smiling:

'I suppose, mademoiselle, that you were more taken up with your fiancé?'

Theresa said sharply:

'He wasn't there. He was away, he'd gone to some medical congress.'

'You had not seen him then since the Easter weekend? Was that the last time you had seen him?'

'Yes—on the evening before we left he came to dinner.'

'You had not—excuse me—had any quarrel with him then?'

'Certainly not.'

'I only thought seeing that he was away on your second visit—'

Charles broke in:

'Ah, but you see, that second weekend was rather unpremeditated. We went down on the spur of the moment.'

'Really?'

'Oh, let's have the truth,' said Theresa wearily. 'You see, Bella and her husband were down the weekend before—fussing over Aunt Emily because of her accident. We thought they might steal a march on us—'

'We thought,' said Charles with a grin, 'that we'd better show a little concern for Aunt Emily's health too. Really, though, the old lady was much too sharp to be taken in by the dutiful attention stunt. She knew very well how much it was worth. No fool, Aunt Emily.'

Theresa laughed suddenly.

'It's a pretty story, isn't it? All of us with our tongues hanging out for money.'

'Was that the case with your cousin and her husband?'

'Oh, yes, Bella's always hard up. Rather pathetic the way she tries to copy all my clothes at about an eighth of the price. Tanios speculated with her money, I believe. They're hard put to it to make both ends meet. They've got two children and want to educate them in England.'

'Can you perhaps give me their address?' said Poirot.

'They're staying at the Durham Hotel in Bloomsbury.'

'What is she like, your cousin?'

'Bella? Well, she's a dreary woman. Eh, Charles?'

'Oh, definitely a dreary woman. Rather like an earwig. She's a devoted mother. So are earwigs, I believe.'

'And her husband.'

'Tanios? Well, he looks a bit odd, but he's really a thoroughly nice fellow. Clever, amusing and a thorough good sport.'

'You agree, mademoiselle?'

'Well, I must admit I prefer him to Bella. He's a damned clever doctor, I believe. All the same, I wouldn't trust him very far.'

'Theresa,' said Charles, 'doesn't trust anybody.'

He put an arm round her.

'She doesn't trust me.'

'Anyone who trusted you, my sweet, would be mentally deficient,' said Theresa kindly.

The brother and sister moved apart and looked at Poirot.

Poirot bowed and moved to the door.

'I am—as you say—on the job! It is difficult, but mademoiselle is right. There is always a way. Ah, by the way, this Miss Lawson, is she the kind that might conceivably lose her head under cross-examination in court?'

Charles and Theresa exchanged glances.

'I should say,' said Charles, 'that a really bullying K.C. could make her say black was white!'

'That,' said Poirot, 'may be very useful.'

He skipped out of the room and I followed him. In the hall he picked up his hat, moved to the front door, opened it and shut it again quickly with a bang. Then he tiptoed to the door of the sitting-room and unblushingly applied his ear to the crack. At whatever school Poirot was educated, there were clearly no unwritten rules about eavesdropping. I was horrified but powerless. I made urgent signs to Poirot but he took no notice.

And then, clearly, in Theresa Arundell's deep, vibrant voice, there came two words:

'You fool!'

There was the noise of footsteps along the passage and Poirot quickly seized me by the arm, opened the front door and passed through, closing it noiselessly behind him.

CHAPTER 15

Miss Lawson

'Poirot,' I said. 'Have we *got* to listen at doors?'

'Calm yourself, my friend. It was only I who listened! It was not you who put your ear to the crack. On the contrary, you stood bolt upright like a soldier.'

'But I heard just the same.'

'True. Mademoiselle was hardly whispering.'

'Because she thought that we had left the flat.'

'Yes, we practised a little deception there.'

'I don't like that sort of thing.'

'Your moral attitude is irreproachable! But let us not repeat ourselves. This conversation has occurred on previous occasions. You are about to say that it is not playing the game. And my reply is that murder is not a game.'

'But there is no question of murder here.'

'Do not be sure of that.'

'The *intention*, yes, perhaps. But after all, murder, and *attempted* murder are not the same thing.'

'Morally they are exactly the same thing. But what I meant

155

was, are you so sure that it is only *attempted* murder that occupies our attention?'

I stared at him.

'But old Miss Arundell died a perfectly natural death.'

'I repeat again—*are you so sure*?'

'Everyone says so!'

'Everyone? Oh, *là, là!*'

'The doctor says so,' I pointed out. 'Dr Grainger. He ought to know.'

'Yes, he ought to know.' Poirot's voice was dissatisfied. 'But remember, Hastings, again and again a body is exhumed—and in each case a certificate has been signed in all good faith by the doctor attending the case.'

'Yes, but in this case, Miss Arundell died of a long-standing complaint.'

'It seems so—yes.'

Poirot's voice was still dissatisfied. I looked at him keenly.

'Poirot,' I said, 'I'll begin a sentence with Are you sure! Are you sure *you* are not being carried away by professional zeal? You *want* it to be murder and so you think it *must* be murder.'

The shadow on his brow deepened. He nodded his head slowly.

'It is clever what you say, there, Hastings. It is a weak spot on which you put your finger. Murder is my business. I am like a great surgeon who specializes in—say—appendicitis or some rarer operation. A patient comes to him and he regards that patient solely from the standpoint of his own specialized subject. Is there any possible reason for thinking this man suffers from so and so…? Me, I am like that, too. I say to myself always, "Can this possibly be murder?" And you see, my friend, there is nearly always a possibility.'

'I shouldn't say there was much possibility here,' I remarked.

'But she died, Hastings! You cannot get away from that fact. She *died*!'

'She was in poor health. She was past seventy. It all seems perfectly natural to me.'

'And does it also seem natural to you that Theresa Arundell should call her brother a fool with that degree of intensity?'

'What has that got to do with it?'

'Everything! Tell me, what did you think of that statement of Mr Charles Arundell's—that his aunt had shown him her new will?'

I looked at Poirot, warily.

'What do *you* make of it?' I asked.

Why should Poirot always be the one to ask the questions?

'I call it very interesting—very interesting indeed. So was Miss Theresa Arundell's reaction to it. Their passage of arms was suggestive—very suggestive.'

'H'm,' I said, in oracular fashion.

'It opens up two distinct lines of inquiry.'

'They seem a nice pair of crooks,' I remarked. 'Ready for anything. The girl's amazingly good-looking. As for young Charles, he's certainly an attractive scoundrel.'

Poirot was just hailing a taxi. It drew into the kerb and Poirot gave an address to the driver.

'17 Clanroyden Mansions, Bayswater.'

'So it's Lawson next,' I commented. 'And after that—the Tanioses?'

'Quite right, Hastings.'

'What rôle are you adopting here?' I inquired as the taxi drew up at Clanroyden Mansions. 'The biographer of General Arundell, a prospective tenant of Littlegreen House, or something more subtle still?'

'I shall present myself simply as Hercule Poirot.'

'How very disappointing,' I gibed.

Poirot merely threw me a glance and paid off the taxi.

No. 17 was on the second floor. A pert-looking maid opened the door and showed us into a room that really struck a ludicrous note after the one we had just left.

Theresa Arundell's flat had been bare to the point of emptiness. Miss Lawson's on the other hand was so crammed with furniture and odds and ends that one could hardly move about without the fear of knocking something over.

The door opened and a rather stout, middle-aged lady came in. Miss Lawson was very much as I had pictured her. She had an eager, rather foolish face, untidy greyish hair and pince-nez perched a little askew on her nose. Her style of conversation was spasmodic and consisted of gasps.

'Good morning—er—I don't think—'

'Miss Wilhelmina Lawson?'

'Yes—yes—that *is* my name...'

'My name is Poirot—Hercule Poirot. Yesterday I was looking over Littlegreen House.'

'Oh, yes?'

Miss Lawson's mouth fell a little wider open and she made some inefficient dabs at her untidy hair.

'Won't you sit down?' she went on. 'Sit here, won't you? Oh, dear, I'm afraid that table is in your way. I'm just a leetle bit crowded here. So difficult! These flats! Just a teeny bit on the small side. But *so* central! And I do like being central. Don't you?'

With a gasp she sat down on an uncomfortable-looking Victorian chair and, her pince-nez still awry, leaned forward breathlessly and looked at Poirot hopefully.

'I went to Littlegreen House in the guise of a purchaser,' went on Poirot. 'But I should like to say at once—this is in the strictest confidence—'

'Oh, yes,' breathed Miss Lawson, apparently pleasurably excited.

'The very strictest confidence,' continued Poirot, 'that I went there with another object… You may or may not be aware that shortly before she died Miss Arundell wrote to me—'

He paused and then went on:

'I am a well-known private detective.'

A variety of expressions chased themselves over Miss Lawson's slightly flushed countenance. I wondered which one Poirot would single out as relevant to his inquiry. Alarm, excitement, surprise, puzzlement…

'Oh,' she said. Then after a pause, 'Oh,' again.

And then, quite unexpectedly, she asked:

'Was it about the money?'

Poirot, even, was slightly taken aback. He said tentatively:

'You mean the money that was—'

'Yes, yes. The money that was taken from the drawer?'

Poirot said, quietly:

'Miss Arundell didn't tell you she had written to me on the subject of that money?'

'No, indeed. I had no idea—Well, really, I must say I'm very surprised—'

'You thought she would not have mentioned it to anyone?'

'I certainly didn't think so. You see, she had a very good idea—'

She stopped again. Poirot said, quickly:

'She had a very good idea who took it. That is what you would say, is it not?'

Miss Lawson nodded and continued breathlessly:

'And I shouldn't have thought she would have wanted—well, I mean she said—that is, she seemed to feel—'

Again Poirot cut in neatly into the midst of these incoherencies.

'It was a family matter?'

'Exactly.'

'But me,' said Poirot, 'I specialize in family matters. I am, you see, very very discreet.'

Miss Lawson nodded vigorously.

'Oh! of course—that makes a difference. It's not like the *police*.'

'No, no. I am not at all like the police. That would not have done at all.'

'Oh, no. Dear Miss Arundell was such a *proud* woman. Of course, there had been trouble before with Charles, but it was always hushed up. Once, I believe, he had to go to Australia!'

'Just so,' said Poirot. 'Now the facts of the case were as follows, were they not? Miss Arundell had a sum of money in a drawer—'

He paused. Miss Lawson hastened to confirm his statement.

'Yes—from the Bank. For the wages, you know, and the books.'

'And how much was missing exactly?'

'Four pound notes. No, no, I am wrong, three pound notes and two ten-shilling notes. One must be exact, I know, very exact, in such matters.' Miss Lawson looked at him earnestly and absent-mindedly knocked her pince-nez a little farther awry. Her rather prominent eyes seemed to goggle at him.

'Thank you, Miss Lawson. I see you have an excellent business sense.'

Miss Lawson bridled a little and uttered a deprecatory laugh.

'Miss Arundell suspected, no doubt with reason, that her nephew Charles was responsible for this theft,' went on Poirot.

'Yes.'

'Although there was no particular evidence to show who actually took the money?'

'Oh, but it must have been Charles! Mrs Tanios wouldn't do such a thing, and her husband was quite a stranger and wouldn't have known where the money was kept—neither of them would. And I don't think Theresa Arundell would dream of such a thing. She's got plenty of money and always so beautifully dressed.'

'It might have been one of the servants,' Poirot suggested.

Miss Lawson seemed horrified by the idea.

'Oh, no, indeed, neither Ellen nor Annie would have *dreamed* of such a thing. They are both *most* superior women and *absolutely honest* I am sure.'

Poirot waited a minute or two. Then he said:

'I wonder if you can give me any idea—I am sure you can, for if anyone possessed Miss Arundell's confidence you did—'

Miss Lawson murmured confusedly:

'Oh, I don't know about that, I'm sure—' but she was clearly flattered.

'I feel that you will be able to help me.'

'Oh, I'm sure, if I can—anything I can do—'

Poirot went on:

'This is in confidence—'

A sort of owlish expression appeared on Miss Lawson's face. The magical words 'in confidence' seemed to be a kind of Open Sesame.

'Have you any idea of the reason which caused Miss Arundell to alter her will?'

'Her will? Oh—her will?'

Miss Lawson seemed slightly taken aback.

Poirot said, watching her closely:

'It is true, is it not, that she made a new will shortly before her death, leaving all her fortune to you?'

'Yes, but I knew nothing about it. Nothing at all!' Miss Lawson was shrill in protest. 'It was the *greatest* surprise to me! A *wonderful* surprise, of course! So *good* of dear Miss Arundell. And she never even gave me a *hint*. Not the smallest hint! I was so taken aback when Mr Purvis read it out, I didn't know where to look, or whether to laugh or cry! I assure you, M. Poirot, the *shock* of it—the *shock*, you know. The *kindness*—the wonderful kindness of dear Miss Arundell. Of course, I'd hoped perhaps, for just a little something—perhaps just a teeny, teeny legacy—though of course, there was no *reason* she should have left me even that. I'd not been with her so very long. But this—it was like—it was like a fairy story! Even now I can't quite believe in it, if you know what I mean. And sometimes—well sometimes—I don't feel altogether comfortable about it. I mean—well, I mean—'

She knocked off her pince-nez, picked them up, fumbled with them and went on even more incoherently.

'Sometimes I feel that—well, flesh and blood is flesh and blood after all, and I don't feel quite comfortable at Miss Arundell's leaving all her money away from her family. I mean, it doesn't seem *right*, does it? Not *all* of it. Such a *large* fortune, too! Nobody had any *idea*! But—well—it does make one feel uncomfortable—and everyone saying things, you know—and I'm sure I've never been an *ill-natured* woman! I mean I wouldn't have dreamed of influencing Miss Arundell in any way! And it's not as though I could, either. Truth to tell, I was always just a teeny weeny bit afraid of her! She was so *sharp*, you know, so inclined to *jump* on you. And quite rude sometimes! "Don't be a downright fool," she'd snap. And really, after all, I had my feelings and sometimes I'd feel quite upset... And then to find out that all the time she'd really been fond of me—well, it was very wonderful, wasn't it? Only of course, as I say, there's been a lot of *unkindness*, and really in some ways one feels—I mean, well, it does seem a little *hard*, doesn't it, on some people?'

'You mean that you would prefer to relinquish the money?' asked Poirot.

Just for a moment I fancied a flicker of some quite different expression showed itself in Miss Lawson's dull, pale blue eyes. I imagined that, just for a moment, a shrewd, intelligent woman sat there instead of an amiable, foolish one.

She said with a little laugh.

'Well—of course, there is the other side of it too... I mean there are two sides to every question. What I say is, Miss Arundell meant me to have the money. I mean if I didn't take it I should be going against her *wishes*. And that wouldn't be right, either, would it?'

'It is a difficult question,' said Poirot, shaking his head.

'Yes, indeed, I have worried over it a great deal. Mrs Tanios—Bella—she is such a nice woman—and those dear children! I mean, I feel sure Miss Arundell wouldn't have wanted her to—I feel, you see, that dear Miss Arundell intended me to use my *discretion*. She didn't want to leave any money *outright* to Bella because she was afraid that man would get hold of it.'

'What man?'

'Her husband. You know, Mr Poirot, the poor girl is *quite* under his thumb. She does *anything* he tells her. I dare say she'd *murder* someone if he told her to! And she's afraid of him. I'm quite sure she's afraid of him. I've seen her look simply *terrified* once or twice. Now that isn't right, Mr Poirot—you can't say that's right.'

Poirot did not say so. Instead he inquired:

'What sort of man is Dr Tanios?'

'Well,' said Miss Lawson, hesitating, 'he's a very pleasant man.'

She stopped, doubtfully.

'But you don't trust him?'

'Well—no, I don't. I don't know,' went on Miss Lawson doubtfully, 'that I'd trust *any* man very much! Such *dreadful* things one hears! And all their *poor* wives go through! It's really terrible! Of course, Dr Tanios pretends to be very fond of his wife and he's quite charming to her. His manners are really *delightful*. But I don't trust foreigners. They're so *artful*! And I'm quite sure dear Miss Arundell didn't want her money to get into *his* hands!'

'It is hard on Miss Theresa Arundell and Mr Charles Arundell also to be deprived of their inheritance,' Poirot suggested.

A spot of colour came into Miss Lawson's face.

'I think Theresa has quite as much money as is good for her!' she said sharply. 'She spends hundreds of pounds on her clothes, alone. And her underclothing—it's wicked! When one thinks of so many nice, well-bred girls who have to earn their own living—'

Poirot gently completed the sentence.

'You think it would do no harm for her to earn hers for a bit?'

Miss Lawson looked at him solemnly.

'It might do her a lot of *good*,' she said. 'It might bring her to her senses. Adversity teaches us many things.'

Poirot nodded slowly. He was watching her intently.

'And Charles?'

'Charles doesn't deserve a penny,' said Miss Lawson, sharply. 'If Miss Arundell cut him out of her will, it was for a very good cause—after his wicked threats.'

'Threats?' Poirot's eyebrows rose.

'Yes, threats.'

'What threats? When did he threaten her?'

'Let me see, it was—yes, of course, it was at Easter. Actually on *Easter Sunday*—which made it even worse!'

'What did he say?'

'He asked her for money and she refused to give it him! And then he told her that it wasn't wise of her. He said if she kept up that attitude he would—now what was the phrase—a very vulgar American one—oh, yes, he said he would bump her off!'

'He threatened to bump her off?'

'Yes.'

'And what did Miss Arundell say?'

'She said: "I think you'll find, Charles, that I can look after myself."'

'You were in the room at the time?'

'Not exactly in the room,' said Miss Lawson after a momentary pause.

'Quite, quite,' said Poirot, hastily. 'And Charles, what did he say to that?'

'He said: "Don't be too sure."'

Poirot said slowly:

'Did Miss Arundell take this threat seriously?'

'Well, I don't know… She didn't say anything to me about it… But then she wouldn't do that, anyway.'

Poirot said quietly:

'You knew, of course, that Miss Arundell was making a new will?'

'No, no. I've told you, it was a complete surprise. I never dreamt—'

Poirot interrupted.

'You did not know the *contents*. But you knew the *fact*—that there *was* a will being made?'

'Well—I suspected—I mean her sending for the lawyer when she was laid up—'

'Exactly. That was after she had a fall, was it not?'

'Yes, Bob—Bob was the dog—he had left his ball at the top of the stairs—and she tripped over it and fell.'

'A nasty accident.'

'Oh, yes, why, she might easily have broken her leg or her arm. The doctor said so.'

'She might quite easily have been killed.'

'Yes, indeed.'

Her answer seemed quite natural and frank.

Poirot said, smiling:

'I think I saw Master Bob at Littlegreen House.'

'Oh, yes, I expect you did. He's a dear little doggie.'

Nothing annoys me more than to hear a sporting terrier called a dear little doggie. No wonder, I thought, that Bob despised Miss Lawson and refused to do anything she told him.

'And he is very intelligent?' went on Poirot.

'Oh, yes, very.'

'How upset he'd be if he knew he had nearly killed his mistress?'

Miss Lawson did not answer. She merely shook her head and sighed.

Poirot asked:

'Do you think it possible that that fall influenced Miss Arundell to remake her will?'

We were getting perilously near the bone here, I thought, but Miss Lawson seemed to find the question quite natural.

'You know,' she said, 'I shouldn't wonder if you weren't right. It gave her a *shock*—I'm sure of that. Old people never like to think there's any chance of their dying. But an accident like that makes one *think*. Or perhaps she might have had a *premonition* that her death wasn't far off.'

Poirot said casually:

'She was in fairly good health, was she not?'

'Oh, yes. Very well, indeed.'

'Her illness must have come on very suddenly?'

'Oh, it did. It was quite a shock. We had had some friends that evening—' Miss Lawson paused.

'Your friends, the Misses Tripp. I have met those ladies. They are quite charming.'

Miss Lawson's face flushed with pleasure.

'Yes, aren't they? Such *cultured* women! Such wide interests! And so very *spiritual*! They told you, perhaps—about our sittings? I expect you are a sceptic—but indeed, I wish I could tell you the inexpressible joy of getting into touch with those who've passed over!'

'I am sure of it. I am sure of it.'

'Do you know, Mr Poirot, my mother has spoken to me—more than once. It is such a joy to know that one's dear ones are still thinking of one and watching over one.'

'Yes, yes, I can well understand that,' said Poirot, gently. 'And was Miss Arundell also a believer?'

Miss Lawson's face clouded over a little.

'She was willing to be convinced,' she said, doubtfully. 'But I do not think she always approached the matter in the right frame of mind. She was sceptical and unbelieving—and once or twice her attitude attracted a most *undesirable* type of spirit! There were some very ribald messages—all due, I am *convinced*, to Miss Arundell's attitude.'

'I should think very likely due to Miss Arundell,' agreed Poirot.

'But on that last evening—' continued Miss Lawson, 'perhaps Isabel and Julia told you?—there were distinct phenomena. Actually the beginning of a materialization. Ectoplasm—you know what ectoplasm is perhaps?'

'Yes, yes, I am acquainted with its nature.'

'It proceeds, you know, from the medium's mouth in the form of a *ribbon* and builds itself up into a *form*. Now I am *convinced*, Mr Poirot, that *unknown to herself* Miss Arundell was a *medium*. On that evening I distinctly saw a *luminous* ribbon issuing from dear Miss Arundell's mouth! Then her head became enveloped in a luminous mist.'

169

'Most interesting!'

'And then, unfortunately, Miss Arundell was suddenly taken ill and we had to break up the *séance*.'

'You sent for the doctor—when?'

'First thing the following morning.'

'Did he think the matter grave?'

'Well, he sent in a hospital nurse the following evening, but I think he hoped she would pull through.'

'The—excuse me—the relatives were not sent for?'

Miss Lawson flushed.

'They were notified as soon as possible—that is to say, when Dr Grainger pronounced her to be in danger.'

'What was the cause of the attack? Something she had eaten?'

'No, I don't think there was anything in particular. Dr Grainger said she hadn't been quite as careful in diet as she should have been. I think he thought the attack was probably brought on by a chill. The weather had been very treacherous.'

'Theresa and Charles Arundell had been down that weekend, had they not?'

Miss Lawson pursed her lips together.

'They had.'

'The visit was not a success,' Poirot suggested, watching her.

'It was not.' She added quite spitefully. 'Miss Arundell knew what they'd come for!'

'Which was?' asked Poirot, watching her.

'Money!' snapped Miss Lawson. 'And they didn't get it.'

'No?' said Poirot.

'And I believe that's what Dr Tanios was after too,' she went on.

'Dr Tanios. He was not down that same weekend, was he?'

'Yes, he came down on the Sunday. He only stayed about an hour.'

'Everyone seems to have been after poor Miss Arundell's money,' hazarded Poirot.

'I know, it is not very nice to think of, is it?'

'No, indeed,' said Poirot. 'It must have been a shock to Charles and Theresa Arundell that weekend when they learned that Miss Arundell had definitely disinherited them!'

Miss Lawson stared at him.

Poirot said:

'Is that not so? Did she not specifically inform them of the fact?'

'As to that, I couldn't say. *I* didn't hear anything about it! There wasn't any *fuss*, or anything, as far as I know. Both Charles and his sister seemed to go away *quite* cheerful.'

'Ah! possibly I have been misinformed. Miss Arundell actually kept her will in the house, did she not?'

Miss Lawson dropped her pince-nez and stooped to pick them up.

'I really couldn't say. No, I think it was with Mr Purvis.'

'Who was the executor?'

'Mr Purvis was.'

'After the death did he come over and look through her papers?'

'Yes, he did.'

Poirot looked at her keenly and asked her an unexpected question.

'Do you like Mr Purvis?'

Miss Lawson was flustered.

'Like Mr Purvis? Well, really, that's difficult to say, isn't it? I mean, I'm sure he's a very *clever* man—that is a clever lawyer, I mean. But rather a brusque *manner*! I mean, it's not very pleasant always, to have someone speaking to you as though—well, really I can't explain what I mean—he was quite civil and yet at the same time, almost *rude* if you know what I mean.'

'A difficult situation for you,' said Poirot, sympathetically.

'Yes, indeed it was.'

Miss Lawson sighed and shook her head.

Poirot rose to his feet.

'Thank you very much, mademoiselle, for all your kindness and help.'

Miss Lawson rose too. She sounded slightly flustered.

'I'm sure there's nothing to thank *me* for—nothing at all! So glad if I've been able to do anything—if there's anything more I *can* do—'

Poirot came back from the door. He lowered his voice.

'I think, Miss Lawson, that there is something you ought to be told. Charles and Theresa Arundell are hoping to upset this will.'

A sharp flush of colour came into Miss Lawson's cheeks.

'They can't do that,' she said, sharply. 'My lawyer says so.'

'Ah,' said Poirot. 'You have consulted a lawyer, then?'

'Certainly. Why shouldn't I?'

'No reason at all. A very wise proceeding. Good day to you, mademoiselle.'

When we emerged from Clanroyden Mansions into the street Poirot drew a deep breath.

'Hastings, *mon ami*, that woman is either exactly what she seems or else she is a very good actress.'

'She doesn't believe Miss Arundell's death was anything but natural. You can see that,' I said.

Poirot did not answer. There are moments when he is conveniently deaf. He hailed a taxi.

'Durham Hotel, Bloomsbury,' he told the driver.

CHAPTER 16

Mrs Tanios

'Gentleman to see you, madam.'

The woman who was sitting writing at one of the tables in the writing-room of the Durham Hotel turned her head and then rose, coming towards us uncertainly.

Mrs Tanios might have been any age over thirty. She was a tall, thin woman with dark hair, rather prominent light 'boiled gooseberry' eyes and a worried face. A fashionable hat was perched on her head at an unfashionable angle and she wore a rather depressed-looking cotton frock.

'I don't think—' she began vaguely.

Poirot bowed.

'I have just come from your cousin, Miss Theresa Arundell.'

'Oh! from Theresa? Yes?'

'Perhaps I could have a few minutes' private conversation?'

Mrs Tanios looked about her rather vacantly. Poirot suggested a leather sofa at the far end of the room.

As we made our way there a high voice squeaked out:

'Mother, where are you going?'

'I shall be just over there. Go on with your letter, darling.'

The child, a thin, peaky-looking girl of about seven, settled down again to what was evidently a laborious task. Her tongue showed through her parted lips in the effort of composition.

The far end of the room was quite deserted. Mrs Tanios sat down, we did the same. She looked inquiringly at Poirot.

He began:

'It is in reference to the death of your aunt, the late Miss Emily Arundell.'

Was I beginning to fancy things, or did a look of alarm spring up suddenly in those pale, prominent eyes?

'Yes?'

'Miss Arundell,' said Poirot, 'altered her will a very short time before she died. By the new will everything was left to Miss Wilhelmina Lawson. What I want to know, Mrs Tanios, is whether you will join with your cousins, Miss Theresa and Mr Charles Arundell, in trying to contest that will?'

'Oh!' Mrs Tanios drew a deep breath. 'But I don't think that's possible, is it? I mean, my husband consulted a lawyer and he seemed to think that it was better not to attempt it.'

'Lawyers, madame, are cautious people. Their advice is usually to avoid litigation at all costs—and no doubt they are usually right. But there are times when it pays to take a risk. I am not a lawyer myself and therefore I look at the matter differently. Miss Arundell—Miss Theresa Arundell, I mean—is prepared to fight. What about you?'

'I—Oh! I really don't know.' She twisted her fingers nervously together: 'I should have to consult my husband.'

'Certainly, you must consult your husband before anything definite is undertaken. But what is your *own* feeling in the matter?'

'Well, really, I don't know.' Mrs Tanios looked more worried than ever. 'It depends so much on my husband.'

'But you *yourself*, what do you think, madame?'

Mrs Tanios frowned, then she said slowly:

'I don't think I like the idea very much. It seems—it seems rather indecent, doesn't it?'

'Does it, madame?'

'Yes—after all if Aunt Emily chose to leave her money away from her family, I suppose we must put up with it.'

'You do not feel aggrieved in the matter, then?'

'Oh, yes, I do.' A quick flush showed in her cheeks. 'I think it was most unfair! *Most* unfair! And so unexpected. It was so unlike Aunt Emily. And so very unfair on the children.'

'You think it is very unlike Miss Emily Arundell?'

'I think it was extraordinary of her!'

'Then isn't it possible that she was not acting of her own free will? Don't you think that perhaps she was being unduly influenced?'

Mrs Tanios frowned again. Then she said almost unwillingly:

'The difficult thing is that I can't see Aunt Emily being influenced by *anybody*! She was such a decided old lady.'

Poirot nodded approvingly.

'Yes, what you say is true. And Miss Lawson is hardly what one would describe as a strong character.'

'No, she's a nice creature really—rather foolish, perhaps—but very, very kind. That's partly why I feel—'

'Yes, madame?' said Poirot as she paused.

Mrs Tanios twisted her fingers nervously again as she answered:

'Well, that it would be mean to try and upset the will. I feel certain that it wasn't in any way Miss Lawson's doing—I'm sure she'd be quite incapable of scheming and intriguing—'

'Again, I agree with you, madame.'

'And that's why I feel that to go to law would be—well, would be undignified and spiteful, and besides it would be very expensive, wouldn't it?'

'It would be expensive, yes.'

'And probably useless, too. But you must speak to my husband about it. He's got a much better head for business than I have.'

Poirot waited a minute or two, then he said:

'What reason do you think lay behind the making of that will?'

A quick colour rose in Mrs Tanios' cheeks as she murmured:

'I haven't the least idea.'

'Madame, I have told you I am not a lawyer. But you have not asked me what my profession is.'

She looked at him inquiringly.

'I am a detective. And, a short time before she died, Miss Emily Arundell wrote me a letter.'

Mrs Tanios leaned forward, her hands pressed themselves together.

'A letter?' she asked, abruptly. 'About my husband?'

Poirot watched her for a minute or two, then he said, slowly:

'I am afraid I am not at liberty to answer that question.'

'Then it *was* about my husband.' Her voice rose slightly. 'What did she say? I can assure you, Mr—er—I don't know your name.'

'Poirot is my name. Hercule Poirot.'

'I can assure you, Mr Poirot, that if anything was said in that letter against my husband, it was entirely untrue! I know, too, who will have inspired that letter! And that is another reason why I would rather have nothing to do with *any* action undertaken by Theresa and Charles! Theresa has never liked my husband. She has said things! I know she has said things! Aunt Emily was prejudiced against my husband because he was not an Englishman, and she may therefore have believed things that Theresa said about him. But they are *not true*, Mr Poirot, you can take my word for that!'

'Mother—I've finished my letter.'

Mrs Tanios turned quickly. With an affectionate smile she took the letter the little girl held out to her.

'That's very nice, darling, very nice, indeed. And that's a beautiful drawing of Mickey Mouse.'

'What shall I do now, Mother?'

'Would you like to get a nice postcard with a picture on it? Here's the money. You go to the gentleman in the hall and choose one and then you can send it to Selim.'

The child moved away. I remembered what Charles Arundell had said. Mrs Tanios was evidently a devoted wife and mother. She was also, as he had said, a little like an earwig.

'That is your only child, madame?'

'No, I have a little boy also. He is out with his father at the moment.'

'They did not accompany you to Littlegreen House on your visits?'

'Oh yes, sometimes, but you see, my aunt was rather old and children were inclined to worry her. But she was very kind and always sent them out nice presents at Christmas.'

'Let me see, when did you last see Miss Emily Arundell?'

'I think it was about ten days before she died.'

'You and your husband and your two cousins were all down there together, were you not?'

'Oh, no, that was the weekend before—at Easter.'

'And you and your husband were down there the weekend after Easter as well?'

'Yes.'

'And Miss Arundell was in good health and spirits then?'

'Yes, she seemed much as usual.'

'She was not ill in bed?'

'She was laid up with a fall she had had, but she came downstairs again while we were there.'

'Did she say anything to you about having made a new will?'

'No, nothing at all.'

'And her manner to you was quite unchanged?'

A slightly longer pause this time before Mrs Tanios said: 'Yes.'

I feel sure that at that moment Poirot and I had the same conviction.

Mrs Tanios was lying!

Poirot paused a minute and then said:

'Perhaps I should explain that when I asked if Miss Arundell's manner to you was unchanged, I was not using the "you" plural. I referred to *you personally*.'

Mrs Tanios replied quickly.

'Oh! I see. Aunt Emily was very nice to me. She gave me a little pearl and diamond brooch and she sent ten shillings to each of the children.'

There was no constraint in her manner now. The words came freely with a rush.

'And as regards your husband—was there no change in her manner to him?'

The constraint had returned. Mrs Tanios did not meet Poirot's eye as she replied:

'No, of course not—why should there be?'

'But since you suggest that your cousin Theresa Arundell might have tried to poison your aunt's mind—'

'She did! I'm sure she did!' Mrs Tanios leant forward eagerly. 'You are quite right. There *was* a change! Aunt Emily was suddenly far more distant to him. And she behaved very oddly. There was a special digestive mixture he recommended—even went to the trouble of getting her some—going to the chemist and having it made up. She thanked him and all that—but rather stiffly, and later I actually saw her pouring the bottle down the sink!'

Her indignation was quite fierce.

Poirot's eyes flickered.

'A very odd procedure,' he said. His voice was carefully unexcited.

'I thought it *most* ungrateful,' said Dr Tanios' wife hotly.

'As you say, elderly ladies distrust foreigners sometimes,' said Poirot. 'I am sure they think that English doctors are the only doctors in the world. Insularity accounts for a lot.'

'Yes, I suppose it does.' Mrs Tanios looked slightly mollified.

'When do you return to Smyrna, madame?'

'In a few weeks' time. My husband—ah! here is my husband and Edward with him.'

CHAPTER 17

Dr Tanios

I must say that my first sight of Dr Tanios was rather a shock. I had been imbuing him in my mind with all sorts of sinister attributes. I had been picturing to myself a dark bearded foreigner with a swarthy aspect and a sinister cast of countenance.

Instead, I saw a rotund, jolly, brown-haired, brown-eyed man. And though it is true he had a beard, it was a modest brown affair that made him look more like an artist.

He spoke English perfectly. His voice had a pleasant timbre and matched the cheerful good-humour of his face.

'Here we are,' he said, smiling to his wife. 'Edward has been passionately thrilled by his first ride in the tube. He has always been in buses until today.'

Edward was not unlike his father in appearance, but both he and his little sister had a definitely foreign-looking appearance and I understood what Miss Peabody had meant when she described them as rather yellow looking children.

The presence of her husband seemed to make Mrs Tanios nervous. Stammering a little she introduced Poirot to him. Me, she ignored.

Dr Tanios took up the name sharply.

'Poirot? Monsieur Hercule Poirot? But I know that name well! And what brings you to us, M. Poirot?'

'It is the affair of a lady lately deceased. Miss Emily Arundell,' replied Poirot.

'My wife's aunt? Yes—what of her?'

Poirot said slowly:

'Certain matters have arisen in connection with her death—'

Mrs Tanios broke in suddenly.

'It's about the will, Jacob. M. Poirot has been conferring with Theresa and Charles.'

Some of the tensity went out of Dr Tanios' attitude. He dropped into a chair.

'Ah, the will! An iniquitous will—but there, it is not my business, I suppose.'

Poirot sketched an account of his interview with the two Arundells (hardly a truthful one, I may say) and cautiously hinted at a fighting chance of upsetting the will.

'You interest me, M. Poirot, very much. I may say I am of your opinion. Something could be done. I actually went as far as to consult a lawyer on the subject, but his advice was not encouraging. Therefore—' he shrugged his shoulders.

'Lawyers, as I have told your wife, are cautious people. They do not like taking chances. But me, I am different! And you?'

Dr Tanios laughed—a rich rollicking laugh.

'Oh, I'd take a chance all right! Often have, haven't I, Bella, old girl?' He smiled across at her, and she smiled back at him—but in a rather mechanical manner, I thought.

He turned his attention back to Poirot.

'I am not a lawyer,' he said. 'But in my opinion it is perfectly clear that that will was made when the old lady was not responsible for what she was doing. That Lawson woman is both clever and cunning.'

Mrs Tanios moved uneasily. Poirot looked at her quickly.

'You do not agree, madame?'

She said rather weakly:

'She has always been very kind. I shouldn't call her clever.'

'She's been kind to you,' said Dr Tanios, 'because she had nothing to fear from you, my dear Bella. You're easily taken in!'

He spoke good-humouredly, but his wife flushed.

'With me it was different,' he went on. 'She didn't like me. And she made no bones about showing it! I'll give you an instance. The old lady had a fall down the stairs when we were staying there. I insisted on coming back the following weekend to see how she was. Miss Lawson did her utmost to prevent us. She didn't succeed, but she was annoyed about it, I could see. The reason was clear. *She wanted the old lady to herself.*'

Again Poirot turned to the wife.

'You agree, madame?'

Her husband did not give her time to answer.

'Bella's too kind-hearted,' he said. 'You won't get her to impute bad motives to anybody. But I'm quite sure I was

184

right. I'll tell you another thing, M. Poirot. The secret of her ascendency over old Miss Arundell was spiritualism! That's how it was done, depend upon it!'

'You think so?'

'Sure of it, my dear fellow. I've seen a lot of that sort of thing. It gets hold of people. You'd be amazed! Especially anyone of Miss Arundell's age. I'd be prepared to bet that that's how the suggestion came. Some spirit—possibly her dead father—ordered her to alter her will and leave her money to the Lawson woman. She was in bad health—credulous—'

There was a very faint movement from Mrs Tanios. Poirot turned to her.

'You think it possible—yes?'

'Speak up, Bella,' said Dr Tanios. 'Tell us your views?'

He looked at her encouragingly. Her quick look back at him was an odd one. She hesitated, then said:

'I know so little about these things. I dare say you're right, Jacob.'

'Depend upon it I'm right, eh, M. Poirot?'

Poirot nodded his head.

'It may be—yes.' Then he said, 'You were down at Market Basing, I think, the weekend before Miss Arundell's death?'

'We were down at Easter and again the weekend after—that is right.'

'No, no, I meant the weekend after that—on the *26th*. You were there on the Sunday, I think?'

'Oh, Jacob, were you?' Mrs Tanios looked at him wide-eyed.

He turned quickly.

'Yes, you remember? I just ran down in the afternoon. I told you about it.'

Both Poirot and I were looking at her. Nervously she pushed her hat a little farther back on her head.

'Surely you remember, Bella,' her husband continued. 'What a terrible memory you've got.'

'Of course!' she apologized, a thin smile on her face. 'It's quite true, I have a shocking memory. And it's nearly two months ago now.'

'Miss Theresa Arundell and Mr Charles Arundell were there then, I believe?' said Poirot.

'They may have been,' said Tanios easily. 'I didn't see them.'

'You were not there very long then?'

'Oh, no—just half an hour or so.'

Poirot's inquiring gaze seemed to make him a little uneasy.

'Might as well confess,' he said with a twinkle. 'I hoped to get a loan—but I didn't get it. I'm afraid my wife's aunt didn't take to me as much as she might. Pity, because I liked her. She was a sporting old lady.'

'May I ask you a frank question, Dr Tanios?'

Was there or was there not a momentary apprehension in Tanios' eye?

'Certainly, M. Poirot.'

'What is your opinion of Charles and Theresa Arundell?'

The doctor looked slightly relieved.

'Charles and Theresa?' he looked at his wife with an affectionate smile. 'Bella, my dear, I don't suppose you mind my being frank about your family?'

She shook her head, smiling faintly.

'Then it's my opinion they're rotten to the core, both of them! Funnily enough I like Charles the best. He's a rogue but he's a likeable rogue. He's no moral sense but he can't help that. People are born that way.'

'And Theresa?'

He hesitated.

'I don't know. She's an amazingly attractive young woman. But she's quite ruthless, I should say. She'd murder anyone in cold blood if it suited her book. At least that's my fancy. You may have heard, perhaps, that her mother was tried for murder?'

'And acquitted,' said Poirot.

'As you say, and acquitted,' said Tanios quickly. 'But all the same, it makes one—wonder sometimes.'

'You met the young man to whom she is engaged?'

'Donaldson? Yes, he came to supper one night.'

'What do you think of him?'

'A clever fellow. I fancy he'll go far—if he gets the chance. It takes money to specialize.'

'You mean that he is clever in his profession.'

'That is what I mean, yes. A first-class brain.' He smiled. 'Not quite a shining light in society yet. A little precise and prim in manner. He and Theresa make a comic pair. The attraction of opposites. She's a social butterfly and he's a recluse.'

The two children were bombarding their mother.

'Mother, can't we go in to lunch? I'm hungry. We'll be late.'

Poirot looked at his watch and gave an exclamation.

'A thousand pardons! I delay your lunch hour.'

Glancing at her husband Mrs Tanios said, uncertainly:

'Perhaps we can offer you—'

Poirot said quickly:

'You are most amiable, madame, but I have a luncheon engagement for which I am already late.'

He shook hands with both the Tanioses and with the children. I did the same.

We delayed for a minute or two in the hall. Poirot wanted to put through a telephone call. I waited for him by the hall porter's desk. I was standing there when I saw Mrs Tanios come out into the hall and look searchingly around. She had a hunted, harried look. She saw me and came swiftly across to me.

'Your friend—M. Poirot—I suppose he has gone?'

'No, he is in the telephone box.'

'Oh.'

'You wanted to speak to him?'

She nodded. Her air of nervousness increased.

Poirot came out of the box at that moment and saw us standing together. He came quickly across to us.

'M. Poirot,' she began quickly in a low, hurried voice. 'There is something that I would like to say—that I *must* tell you—'

'Yes, madame.'

'It is important—very important. You see—'

She stopped. Dr Tanios and the two children had just emerged from the writing-room. He came across and joined us.

'Having a few last words with M. Poirot, Bella?'

His tone was good-humoured, the smile on his face pleasantness itself.

'Yes—' She hesitated, then said, "Well, that is really all, M. Poirot. I just wanted you to tell Theresa that we will back her up in anything she decides to do. I quite see that the family *must* stand together.'

She nodded brightly to us, then taking her husband's arm she moved off in the direction of the dining-room.

I caught Poirot by the shoulder.

'That wasn't what she started to say, Poirot!'

He shook his head slowly, watching the retreating couple.

'She changed her mind,' I went on.

'Yes, *mon ami*, she changed her mind.'

'Why?'

'I wish I knew,' he murmured.

'She will tell us some other time,' I said hopefully.

'I wonder. I rather fear—she may not...'

CHAPTER 18

'A Wolf in the Manger'

We had lunch at a small restaurant not far away. I was eager to learn what he made of the various members of the Arundell family.

'Well, Poirot?' I asked impatiently.

With a look of reproof Poirot turned his whole attention to the menu. When he had ordered he leaned back in his chair, broke his roll of bread in half and said with a slightly mocking intonation:

'Well, Hastings?'

'What do you think of them now you've seen them all?'

Poirot replied slowly.

'*Ma foi*, I think they are an interesting lot! Really, this case is an enchanting study! It is, how do you say, the box of surprises? Look how each time I say, "I got a letter from Miss Arundell before she died," something crops up. From Miss Lawson I learn about the missing money. Mrs Tanios says at once, "About my husband?" Why about her husband? Why should Miss Arundell write to me, Hercule Poirot, about Dr Tanios?'

'That woman has something on her mind,' I said.

'Yes, she knows something. But *what*? Miss Peabody tells us that Charles Arundell would murder his grandmother for twopence, Miss Lawson says that Mrs Tanios would murder anyone if her husband told her to do so. Dr Tanios says that Charles and Theresa are rotten to the core, and he hints that their mother was a murderess and says apparently carelessly that Theresa is capable of murdering anyone in cold blood.

'They have a pretty opinion of each other, all these people! Dr Tanios thinks, or *says* he thinks, that there was undue influence. His wife, before he came in, evidently did *not* think so. She does not want to contest the will at first. Later she veers round. See you, Hastings—it is a pot that boils and seethes and every now and then a significant fact comes to the surface and can be seen. There is *something* in the depths there—yes, there is *something*! I swear it, by my faith as Hercule Poirot, I swear it!'

I was impressed in spite of myself by his earnestness.

After a minute or two I said:

'Perhaps you are right, but it seems too vague—so nebulous.'

'But you agree with me that there is *something*?'

'Yes,' I said hesitatingly. 'I believe I do.'

Poirot leaned across the table. His eyes bored into mine.

'Yes—you have changed. You are no longer amused, superior—indulging me in my academic pleasures. But what is it that has convinced you? It is not my excellent reasoning—*non, ce n'est pas ça*! But *something*—something quite independent—has produced an effect on you. Tell me, my friend, what is it that has suddenly induced you to take this matter seriously?'

'I think,' I said slowly, 'it was Mrs Tanios. She looked—she looked—*afraid*...'

'Afraid of me?'

'No—no, not of you. It was something else. She spoke so quietly and sensibly to begin with—a natural resentment at the terms of the will, perhaps, but otherwise she seemed so resigned and willing to leave things as they are. It seemed the natural attitude of a well-bred but rather apathetic woman. And then that sudden change—the eagerness with which she came over to Dr Tanios' point of view. The way she came out into the hall after us—the—almost *furtive* way—'

Poirot nodded encouragingly.

'And another little thing which you may not have noticed—'

'I notice everything!'

'I mean the point about her husband's visit to Littlegreen House on that last Sunday. I could swear she knew nothing of it—that it was the most complete surprise to her—and yet she took her cue so quickly—agreed that he had told her about it and that she had forgotten. I—I didn't like it, Poirot.'

'You are quite right, Hastings—it was significant that.'

'It left an ugly impression of—of fear on me.'

Poirot nodded his head slowly.

'You felt the same?' I asked.

'Yes—that impression was definitely in the air.' He paused and then went on. 'And yet you liked Tanios, did you not?

You found him an agreeable man, open-hearted, good-natured, genial. Attractive in spite of your insular prejudice against the Argentines, the Portuguese and the Greeks—a thoroughly congenial personality?'

'Yes,' I admitted. 'I did.'

In the silence that ensued, I watched Poirot. Presently I said: 'What are you thinking of, Poirot?'

'I am reflecting on various people, handsome young Norman Gale, bluff, hearty Evelyn Howard, the pleasant Dr Sheppard, the quiet, reliable Knighton.'

For a moment I did not understand these references to people who had figured in past cases.

'What of them?' I asked.

'They were all delightful personalities...'

'My goodness, Poirot, do you really think that Tanios—'

'No, no. Do not jump to conclusions, Hastings. I am only pointing out that one's own personal reactions to people are singularly unsafe guides. One must go not by one's feelings but by facts.'

'H'm,' I said. 'Facts are not our strong suit. No, no, Poirot, don't go over it all again!'

'I will be brief, my friend, do not fear. To begin with, we have quite certainly a case of attempted murder. You admit that, do you not?'

'Yes,' I said slowly. 'I do.'

I had, up to now, been a little sceptical over Poirot's (as I thought) somewhat fanciful reconstruction of the events on the night of Easter Tuesday. I was forced to admit, however, that his deductions were perfectly logical.

'*Très bien*. Now one cannot have attempted murder without a murderer. One of the people present on that evening was a murderer—in intention if not in fact.'

'Granted.'

'Then that is our starting point—a murderer. We make a few inquiries—we, as you would say—stir the mud—and what do we get—several very interesting accusations uttered apparently casually in the course of conversations.'

'You think they were not casual?'

'Impossible to tell at the moment! Miss Lawson's innocent seeming way of bringing out the fact that Charles threatened his aunt may have been quite innocent or it may not. Dr Tanios' remarks about Theresa Arundell may have absolutely no malice behind them, but be merely a physician's genuine opinion. Miss Peabody, on the other hand, is probably quite genuine in her opinion of Charles Arundell's proclivities—but it is, after all, merely an opinion. So it goes on. There is a saying, is there not, a wolf in the manger. *Eh bien*, that is just what I find here. There is—not a wolf—but a murderer in our manger.'

'What I'd like to know is, what you yourself really think, Poirot?'

'Hastings—Hastings—I do not permit myself to "think"—not, that is, in the sense that you are using the word. At the moment I only make certain reflections.'

'Such as?'

'I consider the question of motive. What are the likely *motives* for Miss Arundell's death? Clearly the most obvious one is *gain*. Who would have gained by Miss Arundell's death—if she had died on Easter Tuesday?'

'Everyone—with the exception of Miss Lawson.'

'Precisely.'

'Well, at any rate, one person is automatically cleared.'

'Yes,' said Poirot thoughtfully. 'It would seem so. But the interesting thing is that the person who would have gained nothing if death had occurred on Easter Tuesday, gains everything when death occurs two weeks later.'

'What are you getting at, Poirot?' I said, slightly puzzled.

''Cause and effect, my friend, cause and effect.'

I looked at him doubtfully.

He went on:

'Proceed logically! What exactly happened—after the accident?'

I hate Poirot in this mood. Whatever one says is bound to be wrong! I proceeded with intense caution.

'Miss Arundell was laid up in bed.'

'Exactly. With plenty of time to think. What next?'

'She wrote to you.' Poirot nodded.

'Yes, she wrote to me. And the letter was not posted. A thousand pities, that.'

'Do you suspect that there was something fishy about that letter not being posted?'

Poirot frowned.

'There, Hastings, I have to confess that I do not know. I think—in view of everything I am almost sure—that the letter was genuinely mislaid. I believe—but I cannot be sure—that the fact that such a letter was written was unsuspected by anybody. Continue—what happened next?'

I reflected.

'The lawyer's visit,' I suggested.

'Yes—she sent for her lawyer and in due course he arrived.'

'And she made a new will,' I continued.

'Precisely. She made a new and very unexpected will. Now, in view of that will we have to consider very carefully a statement made to us by Ellen. Ellen said, if you remember, that Miss Lawson was particularly anxious that the news that Bob had been out all night should not get to Miss Arundell's ears.'

'But—oh, I see—no, I don't. Or do I begin to see what you are hinting at...?'

'I doubt it!' said Poirot. 'But if you do, you realize, I hope, the *supreme importance* of that statement.'

He fixed me with a fierce eye.

'Of course. Of course,' I said hurriedly.

'And then,' continued Poirot, 'various other things happen. Charles and Theresa come for the weekend, and Miss Arundell shows the new will to Charles—or so he *says*.'

'Don't you believe him?'

'I only believe statements that are *checked*. Miss Arundell does not show it to Theresa.'

'Because she thought Charles would tell her.'

'But he doesn't. *Why* doesn't he?'

'According to Charles himself he *did* tell her.'

'Theresa said quite positively that he *didn't*—a very interesting and suggestive little clash. And when we depart she calls him a fool.'

'I'm getting fogged, Poirot,' I said plaintively.

'Let us return to the sequence of events. Dr Tanios comes down on Sunday—possibly without the knowledge of his wife.'

'I should say certainly without her knowledge.'

'Let us say *probably*. To proceed! Charles and Theresa leave on the Monday. Miss Arundell is in good health and spirits. She eats a good dinner and sits in the dark with the Tripps and the Lawson. Towards the end of the *séance* she is taken ill. She retires to bed and dies four days later and Miss Lawson inherits all her money, and Captain Hastings says she died a natural death!'

'Whereas Hercule Poirot says she was given poison in her dinner on no evidence at all!'

'I have *some* evidence, Hastings. Think over our conversation with the Misses Tripp. And also one statement that stood out from Miss Lawson's somewhat rambling conversation.'

'Do you mean the fact that she had curry for dinner? Curry would mask the taste of a drug. Is that what you meant?'

Poirot said slowly:

'Yes, the curry has a certain significance, perhaps.'

'But,' I said, 'if what you advance (in defiance of all the medical evidence) is true, only Miss Lawson or one of the maids could have killed her.'

'I wonder.'

'Or the Tripp women? Nonsense. I can't believe that! All these people are palpably innocent.'

Poirot shrugged his shoulders.

'Remember this, Hastings, stupidity—or even silliness, for that matter—can go hand in hand with intense cunning. And do not forget the original attempt at murder. That was not the handiwork of a particularly clever or complex brain. It was a very *simple* little murder, suggested by Bob and his habit of leaving the ball at the top of the stairs. The thought of putting a thread across the stairs was quite simple and easy—a child could have thought of it!'

I frowned.

'You mean—'

'I mean that what we are seeking to find here is just one thing—the wish to kill. Nothing more than that.'

'But the poison must have been a very skilful one to leave no trace,' I argued. 'Something that the ordinary person would have difficulty in getting hold of. Oh, damn it all, Poirot. I simply can't believe it now. You can't *know*! It's all pure hypothesis.'

'You are wrong, my friend. As the result of our various conversations this morning. I have now something definite to go upon. Certain faint but unmistakable indications. The only thing is—I am afraid.'

'Afraid? Of what?'

He said gravely:

'Of disturbing the dogs that sleep. That is one of your proverbs, is it not? To let the sleeping dogs lie! That is what our murderer does at present—sleeps happily in the sun... Do we not know, you and I, Hastings, how often a murderer, his confidence disturbed, turns and kills a second—or even a *third* time!'

'You are afraid of that happening?'

He nodded.

'Yes. *If* there is a murderer in the woodpile—and I think there is, Hastings. Yes, I think there is...'

CHAPTER 19

Visit to Mr Purvis

Poirot called for his bill and paid it.

'What do we do next?' I asked.

'We are going to do what you suggested earlier in the morning. We are going to Harchester to interview Mr Purvis. That is why I telephoned from the Durham Hotel.'

'You telephoned to Purvis?'

'No, to Theresa Arundell. I asked her to write me a letter of introduction to him. To approach him with any chance of success we must be accredited by the family. She promised to send it round to my flat by hand. It should be awaiting us there now.'

We found not only the letter but Charles Arundell who had brought it round in person.

'Nice place you have here, M. Poirot,' he remarked, glancing round the sitting-room of the flat.

At that moment my eye was caught by an imperfectly shut drawer in the desk. A small slip of paper was preventing it from shutting.

Now if there was one thing absolutely incredible it was that Poirot should shut a drawer in such a fashion! I looked thoughtfully at Charles. He had been alone in this room awaiting our arrival. I had no doubt that he had been passing the time by snooping among Poirot's papers. What a young crook the fellow was! I felt myself burning with indignation.

Charles himself was in a most cheerful mood.

'Here we are,' he remarked, presenting a letter. 'All present and correct—and I hope you'll have more luck with old Purvis than we did.'

'He held out very little hope, I suppose?'

'Definitely discouraging… In his opinion the Lawson bird had clearly got away with the doings.'

'You and your sister have never considered an appeal to the lady's feelings?'

Charles grinned.

'I considered it—yes. But there seemed to be nothing doing. My eloquence was in vain. The pathetic picture of the disinherited black sheep—and a sheep not so black as he was painted—(or so I endeavoured to suggest)—failed to move the woman! You know, she definitely seems to dislike me! I don't know why.' He laughed. 'Most old women fall for me quite easily. They think I've never been properly understood and that I've never had a fair chance!'

'A useful point of view.'

'Oh, it's been extremely useful before now. But, as I say, with the Lawson, nothing doing. I think she's rather anti-man. Probably used to chain herself to railings and wave a suffragette flag in good old pre-war days.'

'Ah, well,' said Poirot, shaking his head. 'If simpler methods fail—'

'We must take to crime,' said Charles cheerfully.

'Aha,' said Poirot. 'Now, speaking of crime, young man, is it true that you threatened your aunt—that you said that you would "bump her off," or words to that effect?'

Charles sat down in a chair, stretched his legs out in front of him and stared hard at Poirot.

'Now who told you that?' he said.

'No matter. Is it true?'

'Well, there are elements of truth about it.'

'Come, come, let me hear the story—the *true* story, mind.'

'Oh, you can have it, sir. There was nothing melodramatic about it. I'd been attempting a touch—if you gather what I mean.'

'I comprehend.'

'Well, that didn't go according to plan. Aunt Emily intimated that any efforts to separate her and her money would be quite unavailing! Well, I didn't lose my temper, but I put it to her plainly. "Now look here, Aunt Emily," I said, "you know, you're going about things in such a way that you'll end by getting bumped off!" She said, rather sniffily, what did I mean. "Just that," I said. "Here are your friends and relations all hanging around with their mouths open, all as poor as church mice—whatever church mice may be—all hoping. And what do you do? Sit down on the dibs and refuse to part. That's the way people get themselves murdered. Take it from me, if you're bumped off, you'll only have yourself to blame."

'She looked at me then, over the top of her spectacles in a way she had. Looked at me rather nastily. "Oh," she said drily enough, "so that's your opinion, is it?" "It is," I said. "You loosen up a bit, that's my advice to you." "Thank you, Charles," she said, "for your well-meant advice. But I think you'll find I'm well able to take care of myself." "Please yourself, Aunt Emily," I said. I was grinning all over my face—and I fancy she wasn't as grim as she tried to look. "Don't say I didn't warn you." "I'll remember it," she said.'

He paused.

'That's all there was to it.'

'And so,' said Poirot, 'you contented yourself with a few pound notes you found in a drawer.'

Charles stared at him, then burst out laughing.

'I take off my hat to you,' he said. 'You're some sleuth! How did you get hold of *that*?'

'It is true, then?'

'Oh, it's true enough! I was damned hard up. Had to get money somewhere. Found a nice little wad of notes in a drawer and helped myself to a few. I was very modest—didn't think my little subtraction would be noticed. Even then, they'd probably think it was the servants.'

Poirot said drily:

'It would be very serious for the servants if such an idea had been entertained.'

Charles shrugged his shoulders.

'Every one for himself,' he murmured.

'And *le diable* takes the hindermost,' said Poirot. 'That is your creed, is it?'

Charles was looking at him curiously.

'I didn't know the old lady had ever spotted it. How did you come to know about it—and about the bumping-off conversation?'

'Miss Lawson told me.'

'The sly old pussy cat!' He looked, I thought, just a shade disturbed. 'She doesn't like me and she doesn't like Theresa,' he said presently. 'You don't think—she's got anything more up her sleeve?'

'What could she have?'

'Oh, I don't know. It's just that she strikes me as a malicious old devil.' He paused. 'She hates Theresa...' he added.

'Did you know, Mr Arundell, that Dr Tanios came down to see your aunt on the Sunday before she died?'

'What—on the Sunday that we were there?'

'Yes. You did not see him?'

'No. We were out for a walk in the afternoon. I suppose he must have come then. Funny that Aunt Emily didn't mention his visit. Who told you?'

'Miss Lawson.'

'Lawson again? She seems to be a mine of information.'

He paused and then said:

'You know, Tanios is a nice fellow. I like him. Such a jolly, smiling chap.'

'He has an attractive personality, yes,' said Poirot.

Charles rose to his feet.

'If I'd been him I'd have murdered the dreary Bella years ago! Doesn't she strike you as the type of woman who is marked out by fate to be a victim? You know, I should never be surprised if bits of her turned up in a trunk at Margate or somewhere!'

'It is not a pretty action that you attribute there to her husband the good doctor,' said Poirot severely.

'No,' said Charles meditatively. 'And I don't think really that Tanios would hurt a fly. He's much too kind-hearted.'

'And what about you? Would you do murder if it were made worth your while?'

Charles laughed—a ringing, genuine laugh.

'Thinking about a spot of blackmail, M. Poirot? Nothing doing. I can assure you that I didn't put—' he stopped suddenly and then went on—'strychnine in Aunt Emily's soup.'

With a careless wave of his hand he departed.

'Were you trying to frighten him, Poirot?' I asked. 'If so, I don't think you succeeded. He showed no guilty reactions whatsoever.'

'No?'

'No. He seemed quite unruffled.'

'Curious that pause he made,' said Poirot. 'A pause?'

'Yes. A pause before the word strychnine. Almost as though he had been about to say something else and thought better of it.'

I shrugged my shoulders.

'He was probably thinking of a good, venomous-sounding poison.'

'It is possible. It is possible. But let us set off. We will, I think, stay the night at the George in Market Basing.'

Ten minutes later saw us speeding through London, bound once more for the country.

We arrived in Harchester about four o'clock and made our way straight to the offices of Purvis, Purvis, Charlesworth and Purvis.

Mr Purvis was a big solidly-built man with white hair and a rosy complexion. He had a little the look of a country squire. His manner was courteous but reserved.

He read the letter we had brought and then looked at us across the top of his desk. It was a shrewd look and a somewhat searching one.

'I know you by name, of course, M. Poirot,' he said politely. 'Miss Arundell and her brother have, I gather, engaged your services in this matter, but exactly in what capacity you propose to be of use to them I am at a loss to imagine.'

'Shall we say, Mr Purvis, a fuller investigation of all the circumstances?'

The lawyer said drily:

'Miss Arundell and her brother have already had my opinion as to the legal position. The circumstances were perfectly clear and admit of no misrepresentation.'

'Perfectly, perfectly,' said Poirot quickly. 'But you will not, I am sure, object to just repeating them so that I can envisage the situation clearly.'

The lawyer bowed his head.

'I am at your service.'

Poirot began:

'Miss Arundell wrote to you giving you instructions on the seventeenth of April, I believe?'

Mr Purvis consulted some papers on the table before him.

'Yes, that is correct.'

'Can you tell me what she said?'

'She asked me to draw up a will. There were to be legacies to two servants and to three or four charities. The rest of her estate was to pass to Wilhelmina Lawson absolutely.'

'You will pardon me, Mr Purvis, but you were surprised?'

'I will admit that—yes, I was surprised.'

'Miss Arundell had made a will previously?'

'Yes, she had made a will five years ago.'

'That will, after certain small legacies, left her property to her nephew and nieces?'

'The bulk of her estate was to be divided equally between the children of her brother Thomas and the daughter of Arabella Biggs, her sister.'

'What has happened to that will?'

'At Miss Arundell's request I brought it with me when I visited her at Littlegreen House on April 21st.'

'I should be much obliged to you, Mr Purvis, if you would give me a full description of everything that occurred on that occasion.'

The lawyer paused for a minute or two. Then he said, very precisely:

'I arrived at Littlegreen House at three o'clock in the afternoon. One of my clerks accompanied me. Miss Arundell received me in the drawing-room.'

'How did she look to you?'

'She seemed to me in good health in spite of the fact that she was walking with a stick. That, I understand, was on account of a fall she had had recently. Her general health, as I say, seemed good. She struck me as slightly nervous and over-excited in manner.'

'Was Miss Lawson with her?'

'She was with her when I arrived. But she left us immediately.'

'And then?'

'Miss Arundell asked me if I had done what she had asked me to do, and if I had brought the new will with me for her to sign.

'I said I had done so. I—er—' he hesitated for a minute or two, then went on stiffly. 'I may as well say that, as far as it was proper for me to do so, I remonstrated with Miss Arundell. I pointed out to her that this new will might be regarded as grossly unfair to her family who were, after all, her own flesh and blood.'

'And her answer?'

'She asked me if the money was or was not her own to do with as she liked. I replied that certainly that was the case. "Very well then," she said. I reminded her that she had known this Miss Lawson a very short time, and I asked her if she was quite sure that the injustice she was doing her own family was legitimate. Her reply was, "My dear friend, I know perfectly what I am doing."'

'Her manner was excited, you say.'

'I think I can definitely say that it was, but understand me, M. Poirot, she was in full possession of her faculties. She was in every sense of the word fully competent to manage her own affairs. Though my sympathies are entirely with Miss Arundell's family, I should be obliged to maintain that in any court of law.'

'That is quite understood. Proceed, I pray you.'

'Miss Arundell read through her existing will. Then she stretched out her hand for the one I had had drawn up. I may say that I would have preferred to submit a draft first but she had impressed upon me that the will must be brought her ready to sign. That presented no difficulties as its provisions were so simple. She read it through, nodded her head and said she would sign it straightaway. I felt it my duty to enter one last protest. She heard me out patiently, but said that her mind was quite made up. I called in my clerk and he and the gardener acted as witnesses to her signature. The servants, of course, were ineligible owing to the fact that they were beneficiaries under the will.'

'And afterwards, did she entrust the will to you for safe keeping?'

'No, she placed it in a drawer of her desk, which drawer she locked.'

'What was done with the original will? Did she destroy it?'

'No, she locked it away with the other.'

'After her death, where was the will found?'

'In that same drawer. As executor I had her keys and went through her papers and business documents.'

'Were both wills in the drawer?'

'Yes, exactly as she had placed them there.'

'Did you question her at all as to the motive for this rather surprising action?'

'I did. But I got no satisfactory answer. She merely assured me that "she knew what she was doing."'

'Nevertheless you were surprised at the proceeding?'

'Very surprised. Miss Arundell, I should say, had always shown herself to have a strong sense of family feeling.'

Poirot was silent a minute, then he asked:

'You did not, I suppose, have any conversation with Miss Lawson on the subject?'

'Certainly not. Such a proceeding would have been highly improper.'

Mr Purvis looked scandalized at the mere suggestion.

'Did Miss Arundell say anything to indicate that Miss Lawson knew that a will was being drawn in her favour?'

'On the contrary. I asked her if Miss Lawson was aware of what was being done, and Miss Arundell snapped out that she knew nothing about it.

'It was advisable, I thought, that Miss Lawson should not be aware of what had happened. I endeavoured to hint as much and Miss Arundell seemed quite of my opinion.'

'Just why did you stress that point, Mr Purvis?'

The old gentleman returned his glance with dignity.

'Such things, in my opinion, are better undiscussed. Also it might have led to future disappointment.'

'Ah,' Poirot drew a long breath. 'I take it that *you thought it probable that Miss Arundell might change her mind in the near future*?'

The lawyer bowed his head.

'That is so. I fancied that Miss Arundell had had some violent altercation with her family. I thought it probable that when she cooled down, she would repent of her rash decision.'

'In which case she would have done—what?'

'She would have given me instructions to prepare a new will.'

'She might have taken the simpler course of merely destroying the will lately made, in which case the older will would have been good?'

'That is a somewhat debatable point. All earlier wills, you understand, had been definitely revoked by the testator.'

'But Miss Arundell would not have had the legal knowledge to appreciate that point. She may have thought that by destroying the latter will, the earlier one would stand.'

'It is quite possible.'

'Actually, if she died intestate, her money would pass to her family?'

'Yes. One half to Mrs Tanios, one half divisible between Charles and Theresa Arundell. But the fact remains, however, that she did *not* change her mind! She died with her decision unchanged.'

'But that,' said Poirot, 'is where I come in.'

The lawyer looked at him inquiringly.

Poirot leaned forward.

'Supposing,' he said, 'that Miss Arundell, on her deathbed, *wished to destroy that will*. Supposing that she believed that she *had* destroyed it—but that, in reality, she only destroyed the *first* will.'

Mr Purvis shook his head.

'No, *both* wills were intact.'

'Then supposing she destroyed a *dummy* will—*under the impression that she was destroying the genuine document.* She was very ill, remember, it would be easy to deceive her.'

'You would have to bring evidence to that effect,' said the lawyer sharply.

'Oh! undoubtedly—undoubtedly...'

'Is there—may I ask—is there any reason to believe something of that kind happened?'

Poirot drew back a little.

'I should not like to commit myself at this stage—'

'Naturally, naturally,' said Mr Purvis, agreeing with a phrase that was familiar to him.

'But may I say, strictly in confidence, that there are some curious features about this business!'

'Really? You don't say so?'

Mr Purvis rubbed his hands together with a kind of pleasurable anticipation.

'What I wanted from you and what I have got,' continued Poirot, 'is your opinion that Miss Arundell would, sooner or later, have changed her mind and relented towards her family.'

'That is only my personal opinion, of course,' the lawyer pointed out.

'My dear sir, I quite understand. You do not, I believe, act for Miss Lawson?'

'I advised Miss Lawson to consult an independent solicitor,' said Mr Purvis.

His tone was wooden.

Poirot shook hands with him, thanking him for his kindness and the information he had given us.

CHAPTER 20

Second Visit to Littlegreen House

On our way from Harchester to Market Basing, a matter of some ten miles, we discussed the situation.

'Have you any grounds at all, Poirot, for that suggestion you threw out?'

'You mean that Miss Arundell may have believed that that particular will was destroyed? No, *mon ami*—frankly, no. But it was incumbent upon me—you must perceive that—to make *some* sort of suggestion! Mr Purvis is a shrewd man. Unless I threw out some hint of the kind I did, he would ask himself what I could be doing in this affair.'

'Do you know what you remind me of, Poirot?' I said.

'No, *mon ami*.'

'Of a juggler juggling with a lot of different coloured balls! They are all in the air at once.'

'The different coloured balls are the different lies I tell—eh?'

'That's about the size of it.'

'And some day, you think, there will come the grand crash?'

'You can't keep it up for ever,' I pointed out.

'That is true. There will come the grand moment when I catch the balls one by one, make my bow, and walk off the stage.'

'To the sound of thunderous applause from the audience.'

Poirot looked at me rather suspiciously.

'That well may be, yes.'

'We didn't learn very much from Mr Purvis,' I remarked, edging away from the danger-point.

'No, except that it confirmed our general ideas.'

'And it confirmed Miss Lawson's statement that she knew nothing about the will until after the old lady's death.'

'Me, I do not see that it confirmed anything of the sort.'

'Purvis advised Miss Arundell not to tell her, and Miss Arundell replied that she had no intention of doing so.'

'Yes, that is all very nice and clear. But there are keyholes, my friend, and keys that unlock locked drawers.'

'Do you really think that Miss Lawson would eavesdrop and poke and pry around?' I asked rather shocked.

Poirot smiled.

'Miss Lawson—she is not an old school tie, *mon cher*. We know that she overheard *one* conversation which she was not supposed to have heard—I refer to the one in which Charles and his aunt discussed the question of bumping-off miserly relatives.'

I admitted the truth of that.

'So you see, Hastings, she may easily have overheard some of the conversation between Mr Purvis and Miss Arundell. He has a good resonant voice.'

'As for poking and prying,' went on Poirot. 'More people do it than you would suppose. Timid and easily frightened people such as Miss Lawson often acquire a number of mildly dishonourable habits which are a great solace and recreation to them.'

'Really, Poirot!' I protested.

He nodded his head a good many times.

'But yes, it is so, it is so.'

We arrived at the George and took a couple of rooms. Then we strolled off in the direction of Littlegreen House.

When we rang the bell, Bob immediately answered the challenge. Dashing across the hall, barking furiously, he flung himself against the front door.

'I'll have your liver and your lights!' he snarled. 'I'll tear you limb from limb! I'll teach you to try and get into *this* house! Just wait until I get my teeth into you.'

A soothing murmur added itself to the clamour.

'Now then, boy. Now then, there's a good doggie. Come in here.'

Bob, dragged by the collar, was immured in the morning-room much against his will.

'Always spoiling a fellow's sport,' he grumbled. 'First chance I've had of giving anyone a really good fright for ever so long. Just aching to get my teeth into a trouser leg. You be careful of yourself without me to protect you.'

The door of the morning-room was shut on him, and Ellen drew back bolts and bars and opened the front door.

'Oh, it's you, sir,' she exclaimed.

She drew the door right back. A look of highly pleasurable excitement spread over her face.

'Come in, sir, if you please, sir.'

We entered the hall. From beneath the door on the left, loud snuffling sounds proceeded, interspersed with growls. Bob was endeavouring to 'place' us correctly.

'You can let him out,' I suggested.

'I will, sir. He's quite all right, really, but he makes such a noise and rushes at people so it frightens them. He's a splendid watchdog though.'

She opened the morning-room door, and Bob shot through like a suddenly projected cannon-ball.

'Who is it? Where are they? Oh, there you are. Dear me, don't I seem to remember—' sniff—sniff—sniff—prolonged snort. 'Of course! We *have* met!'

'Hullo, old man,' I said. 'How goes it?'

Bob wagged his tail perfunctorily.

'Nicely, thank you. Let me just see—' he resumed his researches. 'Been talking to a spaniel lately, I smell. Foolish dogs, I think. What's this? A cat? That is interesting. Wish we had her here. We'd have rare sport. H'm—not a bad bull-terrier.'

Having correctly diagnosed a visit I had lately paid to some doggy friends, he transferred his attention to Poirot, inhaled a noseful of benzine and walked away reproachfully.

'Bob,' I called.

He threw me a look over his shoulder.

'It's all right. I know what I'm doing. I'll be back in a jiffy.'

'The house is all shut up. I hope you'll excuse—' Ellen hurried into the morning-room and began to unfasten the shutters.

'Excellent, this is excellent,' said Poirot, following her in and sitting down. As I was about to join him, Bob reappeared from some mysterious region, ball in mouth. He dashed up the stairs and sprawled himself on the top step, his ball between his paws. His tail wagged slowly.

'Come on,' he said. 'Come on. Let's have a game.'

My interest in detection momentarily eclipsed, we played for some minutes, then with a feeling of guilt I hurried into the morning-room.

Poirot and Ellen seemed to be well away on the subject of illness and medicines.

'Some little white pills, sir, that's all she used to take. Two or three after every meal. That was Dr Grainger's orders. Oh, yes, she was very good about it. Tiny little things they were. And then there was some stuff Miss Lawson swore by. Capsules, they were, Dr Loughbarrow's Liver Capsules. You can see advertisements of them on all the hoardings.'

'She took those too?'

'Yes. Miss Lawson got her them to begin with, and she thought they did her good.'

'Did Dr Grainger know?'

'Oh, sir, he didn't mind. "You take 'em if you think they do you good," he'd say to her. And she said, "Well, you may laugh, but they *do* do me good. A lot better than any of *your* physic." And Dr Grainger, he laughed, and said faith was worth all the drugs ever invented.'

'She didn't take anything else?'

'No. Miss Bella's husband, the foreign doctor, he went out and got her a bottle of something, but although she thanked him very politely she poured it away and that I know for a fact! And I think she was right. You don't know where you are with these foreign things.'

'Mrs Tanios saw her pouring it away, didn't she?'

'Yes, and I'm afraid she was rather hurt about it, poor lady. I'm sorry, too, for no doubt it was kindly meant on the doctor's part.'

'No doubt. No doubt. I suppose any medicines that were left in the house were thrown away when Miss Arundell died?'

Ellen looked a little surprised at the question.

'Oh, yes, sir. The nurse threw away some and Miss Lawson got rid of all the old lot in the medicine-cupboard in the bathroom.'

'Is that where the—er—Dr Loughbarrow's Liver Capsules were kept?'

'No, they were kept in the corner-cupboard in the dining-room so as to be handy for taking after meals as directed.'

'What nurse attended Miss Arundell? Can you give me her name and address?'

Ellen could supply that at once and did.

Poirot continued to ask questions about Miss Arundell's last illness.

Ellen gave details with relish, describing the sickness, the pain, the onset of jaundice, and the final delirium. I don't know whether Poirot got any satisfaction out of the catalogue. He listened patiently enough and occasionally interpolated some pertinent little question, usually about Miss Lawson and the amount of time she spent in the sickroom. He was also exceedingly interested in the diet administered to the ill woman, comparing it with that administered to some dead relative (non-existent) of his own.

Seeing that they were enjoying themselves so much, I stole out in the hall again. Bob had gone to sleep on the landing, his ball lying under his chin.

I whistled to him and he sprang up, alert at once. This time, however, doubtless out of offended dignity, he made a protracted business of despatching the ball down to me, several times catching it back at the last minute.

'Disappointed, aren't you? Well, perhaps I *will* let you have it this time.'

When I next went back to the morning-room, Poirot was talking about Dr Tanios' surprise visit on the Sunday before the old lady's death.

'Yes, sir, Mr Charles and Miss Theresa were out for a walk. Dr Tanios wasn't expected, I know. The mistress was lying down and she was very surprised when I told her who it was. "Dr Tanios?" she said. "Is Mrs Tanios with him?" I told her no, the gentleman had come alone. So she said to tell him she'd be down in a minute.'

'Did he stay long?'

'Not above an hour, sir. He didn't look too pleased when he went away.'

'Have you any idea of the—er—purpose of his visit?'

'I couldn't say, I'm sure, sir.'

'You did not happen to hear anything?'

Ellen's face flushed suddenly.

'No, I did *not*, sir! I've never been one to listen at doors, no matter what *some* people will do—and people who ought to know better!'

'Oh, but you misunderstand me.' Poirot was eager, apologetic.

'It just occurred to me that perhaps you might have brought in tea while the gentleman was there and if so, you could hardly have helped hearing what he and your mistress were talking about.'

Ellen was mollified.

'I'm sorry, sir, I misunderstood you. No, Dr Tanios didn't stay for tea.'

Poirot looked up at her and twinkled a little.

'And if I want to know what he came down for—well, it is possible that Miss Lawson might be in a position to know? Is that it?'

'Well, if she doesn't know, sir, nobody does,' said Ellen with a sniff.

'Let me see,' Poirot frowned as though trying to remember. 'Miss Lawson's bedroom—was it next to Miss Arundell's?'

'No, sir. Miss Lawson's room is right at the top of the staircase. I can show you, sir.'

Poirot accepted the offer. As he went up the stairs he kept close to the wall side, and just as he reached the top uttered an exclamation and stooped to his trouser-leg.

'Ah—I have just caught a thread—ah, yes, there is a nail here in the skirting-board.'

'Yes, there is, sir. I think it must have worked loose or something. I've caught my dress on it once or twice.'

'Has it been like that long?'

'Well, some time, I'm afraid, sir. I noticed it first when the mistress was laid up—after her accident, that was, sir—I tried to pull it out but I couldn't.'

'It had a thread round it some time, I think.'

'That's right, sir, there was a little loop of thread, I remember. I can't think what for, I'm sure.'

But there was no suspicion in Ellen's voice. To her it was just one of the things that occur in houses and which one does not bother to explain!

Poirot had stepped into the room at the top of the stairs. It was of moderate size. There were two windows directly facing us. There was a dressing-table across one corner and between the windows was a wardrobe with a long mirror. The bed was to the right behind the door facing the windows. On the left-hand wall of the room was a big mahogany chest of drawers and a marble-topped wash-stand.

Poirot looked round the room thoughtfully and then came out again on the landing. He went along the passage, passing two other bedrooms and then came to the large bedchamber which had belonged to Emily Arundell.

'The nurse had the little room next door,' Ellen explained.

Poirot nodded thoughtfully.

As we descended the stairs, he asked if he might walk round the garden.

'Oh, yes, sir, certainly. It looks lovely just now.'

'The gardener is still employed?'

'Angus? Oh, yes, Angus is still here. Miss Lawson wants everything kept nice because she thinks it will sell better that way.'

'I think she is wise. To let a place run to seed is not the good policy.'

The garden was very peaceful and beautiful. The wide borders were full of lupins and delphiniums and great scarlet poppies. The peonies were in bud. Wandering along we came presently to a potting-shed where a big, rugged old man was busy. He saluted us respectfully and Poirot engaged him in conversation.

A mention that we had seen Mr Charles that day thawed the old man and he became quite garrulous.

'Always a one, he was! I've known him come out here with half a gooseberry pie and the cook hunting high and low for it! And he'd go back with such an innocent face that durned if they wouldn't say it must have been the cat, though I've never known a cat eat a gooseberry pie! Oh, he's a one, Mr Charles is!'

'He was down here in April, wasn't he?'

'Yes, down here two weekends. Just before the missus died, it was.'

'Did you see much of him?'

'A good bit, I did. There wasn't much for a young gentleman to do down here, and that's a fact. Used to stroll up to the George and have one. And then he'd potter round here, asking me questions about one thing and another.'

'About flowers?'

'Yes—flowers—and weeds too.' The old man chuckled.

'Weeds?'

Poirot's voice held a sudden, tentative note. He turned his head and looked searchingly along the shelves. His eye stopped at a tin.

'Perhaps he wanted to know how you got rid of them?'

'He did that!'

'I suppose this is the stuff you use.'

Poirot turned the tin gently round and read the label.

'That's it,' said Angus. 'Very handy stuff it is.'

'Dangerous stuff?'

'Not if you use it right. It's arsenic, of course. Had a bit of a joke about that, Mr Charles and I did. Said as how when he had a wife and didn't like her, he'd come to me and get a little of that stuff to put her away with! Maybe, I sez, *she'll* be the one that wants to do away with *you*! Ah, that made him laugh proper, that did! It was a good one, that!'

We laughed as in duty bound. Poirot prised up the lid of the tin.

'Nearly empty,' he murmured.

The old man had a look.

'Aye, there's more gone than I thought. No idea I'd used that much. I'll be having to order some more.'

'Yes,' said Poirot smiling. 'I'm afraid there's hardly enough for you to spare me some for *my* wife!'

We all had another good laugh over this witticism.

'You're not married, I take it, mister?'

'No.'

'Ah! it's always them as isn't that can afford to joke about it. Those that isn't don't know what trouble is!'

'I gather that your wife—?' Poirot paused delicately.

'She's alive all right—very much so.'

Angus seemed a little depressed about it.

Complimenting him on his garden, we bade him farewell.

CHAPTER 21

The Chemist; The Nurse; The Doctor

The tin of weed-killer had started a new train of thought in my mind. It was the first definite suspicious circumstance that I had encountered. Charles' interest in it, the old gardener's obvious surprise at finding the tin almost empty—it all seemed to point in the right direction.

Poirot was, as usual when I am excited, very non-committal.

'Even if some of the weed-killer *has* been taken, there is as yet no evidence that Charles was the person to take it, Hastings.'

'But he talked so much to the gardener about it!'

'Not a very wise procedure if he was going to help himself to some.'

Then he went on:

'What is the first and simplest poison to come into your mind if you were asked to name one quickly?'

'Arsenic, I suppose.'

'Yes. You understand then, that very marked pause before the word strychnine when Charles was talking to us today.'

'You mean—?'

'That he was about to say "arsenic in the soup," and stopped himself.'

'Ah!' I said, 'and why did he stop himself?'

'Exactly. *Why?* I may say, Hastings, that it was to find the answer to that particular "why?" which made me go out into the garden in search of any likely source of weed-killer.'

'And you found it!'

'And I found it.'

I shook my head.

'It begins to look rather bad for young Charles. You had a good talk with Ellen over the old lady's illness. Did her symptoms resemble those of arsenic poisoning?'

Poirot rubbed his nose.

'It is difficult to say. There was abdominal pain—sickness.'

'Of course—that's it!'

'H'm, I am not so sure.'

'What poison did it resemble?'

'*Eh bien*, my friend, it resembled not so much poison as disease of the liver and death from that cause!'

'Oh, Poirot,' I cried. 'It *can't* be natural death! It's got to be murder!'

'Oh, *là, là*, we seem to have changed places, you and I.'

He turned abruptly into a chemist's shop. After a long discussion of Poirot's particular internal troubles, he purchased a small box of indigestion lozenges. Then, when his purchase was wrapped up and he was about to leave the shop, his attention was taken by an attractively-wrapped package of Dr Loughbarrow's Liver Capsules.

'Yes, sir, a very good preparation.' The chemist was a middle-aged man of a chatty disposition. 'You'll find them very efficacious.'

'Miss Arundell used to take them, I remember. Miss Emily Arundell.'

'Indeed she did, sir. Miss Arundell of Littlegreen House. A fine old lady, one of the old school. I used to serve her.'

'Did she take many patent medicines?'

'Not really, sir. Not so many as some elderly ladies I could name. Miss Lawson, now, her companion, the one that's come into all the money—'

Poirot nodded.

'She was a one for this, that, and the other. Pills, lozenges, dyspepsia tablets, digestive mixtures, blood mixtures. Really enjoyed herself among the bottles.' He smiled ruefully. 'I wish there were more like her. People nowadays don't take to medicines as they used. Still, we sell a lot of toilet preparations to make up for it.'

'Did Miss Arundell take these Liver Capsules regularly?'

'Yes, she'd been taking them for three months, I think, before she died.'

'A relative of hers, a Dr Tanios, came in to have a mixture made up one day, didn't he?'

'Yes, of course, the Greek gentleman that married Miss Arundell's niece. Yes, a very interesting mixture it was. One I've not previously become acquainted with.'

The man spoke as of a rare botanical trophy.

'It makes a change sir, when you get something new. Very interesting combination of drugs, I remember. Of course, the gentleman is a doctor. Very nice he was—a pleasant way with him.'

'Did his wife do any shopping here?'

'Did she now? I don't recall. Oh, yes, came in for a sleeping-draught—chloral it was, I remember. A double quantity the prescription was for. It's always a little difficult for us with hypnotic drugs. You see, most doctors don't prescribe much at a time.'

'Whose prescription was it?'

'Her husband's I think. Oh, of course, it was quite all *right*—but, you know, we have to be careful nowadays. Perhaps you don't know the fact, but if a doctor makes a mistake in a prescription and we make it up in all good faith and anything goes wrong it's we who have to take the blame—not the doctor.'

'That seems very unfair!'

'It's worrying, I'll admit. Ah, well, I can't complain. No trouble has come *my* way—touching wood.'

He rapped the counter sharply with his knuckles.

Poirot decided to buy a package of Dr Loughbarrow's Liver Capsules.

'Thank you, sir. Which size? 25, 50, 100?'

'I suppose the larger ones are better value—but still—'

'Have the 50, sir. That's the size Miss Arundell had. Eight and six.'

Poirot agreed, paid over eight and six and received the parcel.

Then we left the shop.

'So Mrs Tanios bought a sleeping-draught,' I exclaimed as we got out into the street. 'An overdose of that would kill anyone, wouldn't it?'

'With the greatest of ease.'

'Do you think old Miss Arundell—'

I was remembering Miss Lawson's words, '*I dare say she'd murder someone if he told her to!*'

Poirot shook his head.

'Chloral is a narcotic, and a hypnotic. Used to alleviate pain and as a sleeping-draught. It can also become a habit.'

'Do you think Mrs Tanios had acquired the habit?'

Poirot shook his head perplexedly.

'No, I hardly think so. But it is curious. I can think of one explanation. But that would mean—'

He broke off and looked at his watch.

'Come, let us see if we can find this Nurse Carruthers who was with Miss Arundell in her last illness.'

Nurse Carruthers proved to be a sensible-looking, middle-aged woman.

Poirot now appeared in yet another rôle and with one more fictitious relative. This time he had an aged mother for whom he was anxious to find a sympathetic hospital nurse.

'You comprehend—I am going to speak to you quite frankly. My mother, she is difficult. We have had some excellent nurses, young women, fully competent, but the very fact that they are young has been against them. My mother dislikes young women, she insults them, she is rude and fractious, she fights against open windows and modern hygiene. It is very difficult.'

He sighed mournfully.

'I know,' said Nurse Carruthers sympathetically. 'It's very trying sometimes. One has to use a lot of tact. It's no use upsetting a patient. Better to give in to them as far as you can. And once they feel you're not trying to force things on them, they very often relax and give in like lambs.'

'Ah, I see that you would be ideal in the part. You understand old ladies.'

'I've had to do with a few in my time,' said Nurse Carruthers with a laugh. 'You can do a lot with patience and good-humour.'

'That is so wise. You nursed Miss Arundell, I believe. Now, she could not have been an easy old lady.'

'Oh, I don't know. She was strong willed, but I didn't find her difficult at all. Of course, I wasn't there any length of time. She died on the fourth day.'

'I was talking to her niece, Miss Theresa Arundell, only yesterday.'

'Really. Fancy that now! What I always say is—the world's a small place!'

'You know her, I expect?'

'Well, of course, she came down after her aunt's death and she was here for the funeral. And, of course, I've seen her about before when she's been staying down here. A very handsome girl.'

'Yes, indeed—but too thin—definitely too thin.'

Nurse Carruthers, conscious of her own comfortable plumpness, preened herself slightly.

'Of course,' she said, 'one shouldn't be *too* thin.'

'Poor girl,' continued Poirot. 'I am sorry for her. *Entre nous*,' he leaned forward confidentially, 'her aunt's will was a great blow.'

'I suppose it must have been,' said Nurse Carruthers. 'I know it caused a good deal of *talk*.'

'I cannot imagine what induced Miss Arundell to disinherit all her family. It seems an extraordinary procedure.'

'Most extraordinary. I agree with you. And, of course, people say there must have been something behind it all.'

'Did you ever get any idea of the *reason*? Did old Miss Arundell say anything?'

'No. Not to me, that is.'

'But to somebody else?'

'Well, I rather fancy she mentioned *something* to Miss Lawson because I heard Miss Lawson say, "Yes, dear, but you see it's at the lawyer's." And Miss Arundell said, "I'm sure it's in the drawer downstairs." And Miss Lawson said, "No, you sent it to Mr Purvis. Don't you remember?" And then my patient had an attack of nausea again and Miss Lawson went away while I saw to her, but I've often wondered if it was the will they were talking about.'

'It certainly seems probable.'

Nurse Carruthers went on:

'If so, I expect Miss Arundell was worried and perhaps wanted to alter it—but there, she was so ill, poor dear, after that—that she was past thinking of anything.'

'Did Miss Lawson take part in the nursing at all?' asked Poirot.

'Oh, dear no, she was no manner of good! Too fussy, you know. She only irritated my patient.'

'Did you, then, do all the nursing yourself? *C'est formidable ça*.'

229

'The maid—what was her name—Ellen, helped me. Ellen was very good. She was used to illness and used to looking after the old lady. We managed pretty well between us. As a matter of fact, Dr Grainger was sending in a night nurse on the Friday, but Miss Arundell died before the night nurse arrived.'

'Perhaps Miss Lawson helped to prepare some of the invalid's food?'

'No, she didn't do anything at all. There wasn't really anything to prepare. I had the Valentine and the brandy—and the Brand's and glucose and all that. All Miss Lawson did was to go about the house crying and getting in everyone's way.'

The nurse's tone held distinct acrimony.

'I can see,' said Poirot smiling, 'that you have not a very high opinion of Miss Lawson's usefulness.'

'Companions are usually a poor lot, in my opinion. They're not *trained*, you see, in any way. Just *amateurs*. And usually they're women who wouldn't be any good at anything else.'

'Do you think Miss Lawson was very attached to Miss Arundell?'

'She seemed to be. Very upset and took on terribly when the old lady died. More than the relatives did, in *my* opinion,' Nurse Carruthers finished with a sniff.

'Perhaps, then,' said Poirot nodding his head sagely, 'Miss Arundell knew what she was doing when she left her money as she did.'

'She was a very shrewd old lady,' said the nurse. 'There wasn't much *she* didn't take in and know about, I must say!'

'Did she mention the dog, Bob, at all?'

'It's funny you should say that! She talked about him a lot—when she was delirious. Something about his ball and a fall she'd had. A nice dog, Bob was—I'm very fond of dogs. Poor fellow, he was very miserable when she died. Wonderful, aren't they? Quite human.'

And on the note of the humanity of dogs, we parted.

'There is one who had clearly no suspicions,' remarked Poirot after we had left.

He sounded slightly discouraged.

We had a bad dinner at the George—Poirot groaning a good deal, especially over the soup.

'And it is so easy, Hastings, to make good soup. *Le pot au feu*—'

I avoided a disquisition on cookery with some difficulty.

After dinner we had a surprise.

We were sitting in the 'lounge' which we had to ourselves. There had been one other man at dinner—a commercial traveller by his appearance—but he had gone out. I was just idly turning over the pages of an antiquated *Stock Breeder's Gazette* or some such periodical when I suddenly heard Poirot's name being mentioned.

The voice in question was somewhere outside.

'Where is he? In here? Right—I can find him.'

The door was flung violently open, and Dr Grainger, his face rather red, his eyebrows working irritably, strode into the room. He paused to close the door and then advanced upon us in no uncertain fashion.

'Oh, here you are! Now then, M. Hercule Poirot, what

the devil do you mean by coming round to see me and telling me a pack of lies?'

'One of the juggler's balls?' I murmured maliciously.

Poirot said in his oiliest voice:

'My dear doctor, you must allow me to explain—'

'Allow you? Allow you? Damn it, I'll *force* you to explain! You're a detective, that's what you are! A nosing, prying detective! Coming round to me and feeding me up with a pack of lies about writing old General Arundell's biography! More fool me to be taken in by such a damn' fool story.'

'Who told you of my identity?' asked Poirot.

'Who told me? Miss Peabody told me. *She* saw through you all right!'

'Miss Peabody—yes.' Poirot sounded reflective. 'I rather thought—'

Dr Grainger cut in angrily.

'Now then, sir, I'm waiting for your explanation!'

'Certainly. My explanation is very simple. *Attempted murder.*'

'What? What's that?'

Poirot said quietly:

'Miss Arundell had a fall, did she not? A fall down the stairs shortly before her death?'

'Yes, what of it? She slipped on that damned dog's ball.'

Poirot shook his head.

'No, Doctor, *she did not. A thread* was fastened across the top of the stairs so as to trip her up.'

Dr Grainger stared.

'Then why didn't she tell me so?' he demanded. 'Never said a word to me about it.'

'That is perhaps understandable—if it were a *member of her own family* who placed that thread there!'

'H'm—I see.' Grainger cast a sharp glance at Poirot, then threw himself into a chair. 'Well?' he said. 'How did you come to be mixed up in this affair?'

'Miss Arundell wrote to me, stressing the utmost secrecy. Unfortunately the letter was delayed.'

Poirot proceeded to give certain carefully-edited details and explained the finding of the nail driven into the skirting-board.

The doctor listened with a grave face. His anger had abated.

'You can comprehend my position was a difficult one,' Poirot finished. 'I was employed, you see, by a dead woman. But I counted the obligation none the less strong for that.'

Dr Grainger's brows were drawn together in thought.

'And you've no idea who it was stretched that thread across the head of the stairs?' he asked.

'I have no *evidence* as to who it was. I will not say I have no *idea*.'

'It's a nasty story,' said Grainger, his face grim.

'Yes. You can understand, can you not, that to begin with I was uncertain whether there had or had not been a sequel?'

'Eh? What's that?'

'To all intents and purposes Miss Arundell died a natural death, but could one be sure of that? There had been *one* attempt on her life. How could I be sure that there had not been a second? And this time a successful one!'

Grainger nodded thoughtfully.

'I suppose you are *sure*, Dr Grainger—please do not get angry—that Miss Arundell's death *was* a natural one? I have come across certain evidence today—'

He detailed the conversation he had had with old Angus, Charles Arundell's interest in the weed-killer, and finally the old man's surprise at the emptiness of the tin.

Grainger listened with keen attention. When Poirot had finished he said, quietly:

'I see your point. Many a case of arsenical poisoning has been diagnosed as acute gastroenteritis and a certificate given—especially when there are no suspicious contributing circumstances. In any case, arsenical poisoning presents certain difficulties—it has so many different forms. It may be acute, subacute, nervous or chronic. There may be vomiting and abdominal pain—these symptoms may be entirely absent—the person may fall suddenly to the ground and expire shortly afterwards—there may be narcotism and paralysis. The symptoms vary widely.'

Poirot said:

'*Eh bien*, taking the facts into account, what is your opinion?'

Dr Grainger was silent for a minute or two. Then he said slowly:

'Taking everything into account, and without any bias whatever, I am of the opinion that no form of arsenical poisoning could account for the symptoms in Miss Arundell's case. She died, I am quite convinced, of yellow atrophy of the liver. I have, as you know, attended her for many years, and she has suffered previously from attacks similar to that which caused her death. That is my considered opinion, M. Poirot.'

And there, perforce, the matter had to rest.

It seemed rather an anti-climax when, somewhat apologetically, Poirot produced the package of Liver Capsules he had bought at the chemists.

'Miss Arundell took these, I believe?' he said. 'I suppose they could not be injurious in any way?'

'That stuff? No harm at all. *Aloes*—podophyllin—all quite mild and harmless,' said Grainger. 'She liked trying the stuff. I didn't mind.'

He got up.

'You dispensed certain medicines for her yourself?' asked Poirot.

'Yes—a mild liver pill to be taken after food.' His eyes twinkled. 'She could have taken a boxful without hurting herself. I'm not given to poisoning my patients, M. Poirot.'

Then, with a smile, he shook hands with us both and departed.

Poirot undid the package he had purchased at the chemists. The medicament consisted of transparent capsules, three-quarters full of dark brown powder.

'They look like a seasick remedy I once took,' I remarked.

Poirot opened a capsule, examined its contents and tasted it gingerly with his tongue. He made a grimace.

'Well,' I said, throwing myself back in my chair and yawning, 'everything seems harmless enough. Dr Loughbarrow's specialities, and Dr Grainger's pills! And Dr Grainger seems definitely to negative the arsenic theory. Are you convinced at last, my stubborn Poirot?'

'It is true that I am pig-headed—that is your expression, I think?—Yes, definitely I have the head of the pig,' said my friend, meditatively.

'Then, in spite of having the chemist, the nurse and the doctor, against you, you still think that Miss Arundell was murdered?'

Poirot said, quietly:

'That is what I believe. No—more than believe. I am *sure* of it, Hastings.'

'There's one way of proving it, I suppose,' I said slowly. 'Exhumation.'

Poirot nodded.

'Is that the next step?'

'My friend, I have to go carefully.'

'Why?'

'Because,' his voice dropped, 'I am afraid of a second tragedy.'

'You mean—?'

'I am afraid, Hastings, I am afraid. Let us leave it at that.'

CHAPTER 22

The Woman on the Stairs

On the following morning a note arrived by hand. It was in a rather weak, uncertain handwriting slanting very much uphill.

Dear M. Poirot,

I hear from Ellen that you were at Littlegreen House yesterday. I shall be much obliged if you would call and see me some time today.

Yours truly,

Wilhelmina Lawson.

'So *she's* down here,' I remarked.

'Yes.'

'Why has she come, I wonder?'

Poirot smiled.

'I do not suppose there is any sinister reason. After all, the house belongs to her.'

'Yes, that's true, of course. You know, Poirot, that's the

worst of this game of ours. Every single little thing that anyone does is open to the most sinister constructions.'

'It is true that I myself have enjoined upon you the motto, "suspect everyone."'

'Are you still in that state yourself?'

'No—for me it has boiled down to this. I suspect one particular person.'

'Which one?'

'Since, at the moment, it is only suspicion and there is no definite proof, I think I must leave you to draw your own deductions, Hastings. And do not neglect the psychology— that is important. The character of the murder—implying as it does a certain temperament in the murderer—that is an essential clue to the crime.'

'I can't consider the character of the murderer if I don't know who the murderer is!'

'No, no, you have not paid attention to what I have just said. If you reflect sufficiently on the character—the necessary character of the *murder*—then you will realize *who* the murderer is!'

'Do you really know, Poirot?' I asked, curiously.

'I cannot say I *know* because I have no proofs. That is why I cannot say more at the present. But I am quite sure—yes, my friend, in my own mind I am very sure.'

'Well,' I said, laughing, 'mind he doesn't get *you*! That *would* be a tragedy!'

Poirot started a little. He did not take the matter as a joke. Instead he murmured: 'You are right. I must be careful—extremely careful.'

'You ought to wear a coat of chain mail,' I said, chaffingly. 'And employ a taster in case of poison! In fact, you ought to have a regular band of gunmen to protect you!'

'*Merci*, Hastings, I shall rely on my wits.'

He then wrote a note to Miss Lawson saying that he would call at Littlegreen House at eleven o'clock.

After that we breakfasted and then strolled out into the Square. It was about a quarter past ten and a hot sleepy morning.

I was looking into the window of the antique shop at a very nice set of Hepplewhite chairs when I received a highly painful lunge in the ribs, and a sharp, penetrating voice said: 'Hi!'

I spun round indignantly to find myself face to face with Miss Peabody. In her hand (the instrument of her assault upon me) was a large and powerful umbrella with a spiked point.

Apparently completely callous to the severe pain she had inflicted, she observed in a satisfied voice:

'Ha! Thought it was you. Don't often make a mistake.'

I said rather coldly:

'Er—Good morning. Can I do anything for you?'

'You can tell me how that friend of yours is getting on with his book—Life of General Arundell?'

'He hasn't actually started to write it yet,' I said.

Miss Peabody indulged in a little silent but apparently satisfying laughter. She shook like a jelly. Recovering from that attack, she remarked:

'No, I don't suppose he will be starting to write it.'

I said, smiling:

'So you saw through our little fiction?'

'What d'you take me for—a fool?' asked Miss Peabody. 'I saw soon enough what your downy friend was after! Wanted me to talk! Well, *I* didn't mind. I like talking. Hard to get anyone to listen nowadays. Quite enjoyed myself that afternoon.'

She cocked a shrewd eye at me.

'What's it all about, eh? What's it all about?'

I was hesitating what exactly to reply when Poirot joined us. He bowed with *empressement* to Miss Peabody.

'Good morning, mademoiselle. Enchanted to encounter you.'

'Good mornin',' said Miss Peabody. 'What are you this morning, Parotti or Poirot—eh?'

'It was very clever of you to pierce my disguise so rapidly,' said Poirot, smiling.

'Wasn't much disguise to pierce! Not many like you about, are there? Don't know if that's a good thing or a bad one. Difficult to say.'

'I prefer, mademoiselle, to be unique.'

'You've got your wish, I should say,' said Miss Peabody, drily. 'Now then, Mr Poirot, I gave you all the gossip you wanted the other day. Now it's my turn to ask questions. What's it all about? Eh? What's it all about?'

'Are you not asking a question to which you already know the answer?'

'I wonder.' She shot a glance at him. 'Something fishy about that will? Or is it something else? Going to dig Emily up? Is that it?'

Poirot did not answer.

Miss Peabody nodded her head slowly and thoughtfully as though she had received a reply.

'Often wondered,' she said inconsequently, 'what it would feel like... Readin' the papers, you know—wondered if anyone would ever be dug up in Market Basing... Didn't think it would be Emily Arundell...'

She gave him a sudden, piercing look.

'She wouldn't have liked it, you know. I suppose you've thought of that—hey?'

'Yes, I have thought of it.'

'I suppose you would do—you're not a fool! Don't think you're particularly officious either.'

Poirot bowed.

'Thank you, mademoiselle.'

'And that's more than most people would say—looking at your moustache. Why d'you have a moustache like that? D'you like it?'

I turned away convulsed with laughter.

'In England the cult of the moustache is lamentably neglected,' said Poirot. His hand surreptitiously caressed the hirsute adornment.

'Oh, I see! Funny,' said Miss Peabody. 'Knew a woman who once had a goitre and was proud of it! Wouldn't believe that, but it's true! Well, what I say is, it's lucky when you're pleased with what the Lord has given you. It's usually the other way about.' She shook her head and sighed.

'Never thought there would be a murder in this out of the world spot.' Again she shot a sudden, piercing look at Poirot. 'Which of 'em did it?'

'Am I to shout that to you here in the street?'

'Probably means you don't know. or do you? Oh, well—bad blood—bad blood. I'd like to know whether that Varley woman poisoned her husband or not. Makes a difference.'

'You believe in heredity?'

Miss Peabody said, suddenly:

'I'd rather it was Tanios. An outsider! But wishes ain't horses, worse luck. Well, I'll be getting along. I can see you're not goin' to tell me anything… Who are you actin' for, by the way?'

Poirot said, gravely:

'I am acting for the dead, mademoiselle.'

I am sorry to say that Miss Peabody received this remark with a sudden shriek of laughter. Quickly subduing her mirth she said:

'Excuse me. It sounded like Isabel Tripp—that's all! What an awful woman! Julia's worse, I think. So painfully girlish. Never did like mutton dressed lamb fashion. Well, goodbye. Seen Dr Grainger at all?'

'Mademoiselle, I have the bone to pick with you. You betrayed my secret.'

Miss Peabody indulged in her peculiar throaty chuckle.

'Men are simple! He'd swallowed that preposterous tissue of lies you told him. Wasn't he mad when I told him? Went away snorting with rage! He's looking for you.'

'He found me last night.'

'Oh! I wish I'd been there.'

'I wish you had, mademoiselle,' said Poirot gallantly.

Miss Peabody laughed and prepared to waddle away. She addressed me over her shoulder.

'Goodbye, young man. Don't you go buying those chairs. They're a fake.'

She moved off, chuckling.

'That,' said Poirot, 'is a very clever old woman.'

'Even although she did not admire your moustaches?'

'Taste is one thing,' said Poirot coldly. 'Brains are another.'

We passed into the shop and spent a pleasant twenty minutes looking round. We emerged unscathed in pocket and proceeded in the direction of Littlegreen House.

Ellen, rather redder in the face than usual, admitted us and showed us into the drawing-room. Presently footsteps were heard descending the stairs and Miss Lawson came in. She seemed somewhat out of breath and flustered. Her hair was pinned up in a silk handkerchief.

'I hope you'll excuse my coming in like this, M. Poirot. I've been going through some locked-up cupboards—so many things—old people are inclined to *hoard* a little, I'm afraid—dear Miss Arundell was no exception—and one gets so much dust in one's *hair*—astonishing, you know, the things people collect—if you can believe me, two dozen needlebooks—actually, two dozen.'

'You mean that Miss Arundell had bought two dozen needlebooks?'

'Yes, and put them away and forgot about them—and, of course, now the needles are all rusty—such a pity. She used to give them to the maids as Christmas presents.'

'She was very forgetful—yes?'

'Oh, *very*. Especially in the way of putting things away. Like a dog with a bone, you know. That's what we used to call it between us. "Now don't go and dog and bone it," I used to say to her.'

She laughed and then producing a small handkerchief from her pocket suddenly began to sniff.

'Oh, dear,' she said tearfully. 'It seems so dreadful of me to be laughing here.'

'You have too much sensibility,' said Poirot. 'You feel things too much.'

'That's what my mother always used to say to me, M. Poirot. "You take things to heart too much, Minnie," she used to say. It's a great drawback, M. Poirot, to be so sensitive. Especially when one has one's living to get.'

'Ah, yes, indeed, but that is all a thing of the past. You are now your own mistress. You can enjoy yourself—travel—you have absolutely no worries or anxieties.'

'I suppose that's true,' said Miss Lawson, rather doubtfully.

'Assuredly it is true. Now talking of Miss Arundell's forgetfulness I see how it was that her letter to me never reached me for so long a time.'

He explained the circumstances of the finding of the letter. A red spot showed in Miss Lawson's cheek. She said sharply:

'Ellen should have told *me*! To send that letter off to you without a word was great impertinence! She should have consulted me first. *Great* impertinence, I call it! Not one word did I hear about the whole thing. Disgraceful!'

'Oh, my dear lady, I am sure it was done in all good faith.'

'Well, I think it was very *peculiar* myself! *Very* peculiar! Servants really do the oddest things. Ellen should have remembered that I am the mistress of the house now.'

She drew herself up, importantly.

'Ellen was very devoted to her mistress, was she not?' said Poirot.

'Yes, I dare say, but that makes no difference. I should have been *told*!'

'The important thing is—that I received the letter,' said Poirot.

'Oh, I agree that it's no good making a fuss after things have happened, but all the same I think Ellen ought to be told that she mustn't take it upon herself to do things without asking first!'

She stopped, a red spot on each cheekbone.

Poirot was silent for a minute, then he said:

'You wanted to see me today? In what way can I be of service to you?'

Miss Lawson's annoyance subsided as promptly as it had arisen. She began to be flustered and incoherent again.

'Well, really—you see, I just *wondered*... Well, to tell the truth, M. Poirot, I arrived down here yesterday and, of course, Ellen told me you had been here, and I just wondered—well, as you hadn't *mentioned* to me that you were coming—Well, it seemed rather *odd*—that I couldn't see—'

'You couldn't see what I was doing down here?' Poirot finished for her.

'I—well—no, that's exactly it. I couldn't.'

She looked at him, flushed but inquiring.

'I must make a little confession to you,' said Poirot. 'I have permitted you to remain under a misapprehension, I am afraid. You assumed that the letter I received from Miss Arundell concerned itself with the question of a small sum of money, abstracted by—in all possibility—Mr Charles Arundell.'

Miss Lawson nodded.

'But that, you see, was not the case... In fact, the first I heard of the stolen money was from you... Miss Arundell wrote to me on the subject of her accident.'

'Her accident?'

'Yes, she had a fall down the stairs, I understand.'

'Oh, quite—quite—' Miss Lawson looked bewildered. She stared vacantly at Poirot. She went on. 'But—I'm sorry—I'm sure it's very stupid of me—but why should she write to *you*? I understand—in fact, I think you said so—that you are a detective. You're not a—a doctor, too? Or a faith healer, perhaps?'

'No, I am not a doctor—nor a faith healer. But, like the doctor, I concern myself sometimes with so-called accidental deaths.'

'With accidental deaths?'

'With *so-called* accidental deaths, I said. It is true that Miss Arundell did not *die*—but she might have died!'

'Oh, dear me, yes, the doctor said so, but I don't understand—'

Miss Lawson sounded still bewildered.

'The cause of the accident was supposed to be the ball of the little Bob, was it not?'

'Yes, yes, that was it. It was Bob's ball.'

'Oh, no, it was not Bob's ball.'

'But, excuse me, M. Poirot, I saw it there myself—as we all ran down.'

'You saw it—yes, perhaps. But *it was not the cause of the accident. The cause of the accident, Miss Lawson, was a dark-coloured thread stretched about a foot above the top of the stairs!'*

'But—but a dog couldn't—'

'Exactly,' said Poirot quickly. 'A dog could not do that—he is not sufficiently intelligent—or, if you like, he is not sufficiently *evil*... A *human being* put that thread in position...'

Miss Lawson's face had gone deadly white. She raised a shaking hand to her face.

'Oh, M. Poirot—I can't believe it—you don't mean—but that is awful—really awful. You mean it was done on *purpose*?'

'Yes, it was done on purpose.'

'But that's dreadful. It's almost like—like killing a person.'

'If it had succeeded it *would* have been killing a person! In other words—it would have been murder!'

Miss Lawson gave a little shrill cry.

Poirot went on in the same grave tone.

'A nail was driven into the skirting board so that the thread could be attached. That nail was varnished so as not to show. Tell me, do you ever remember a smell of varnish that you could not account for?'

Miss Lawson gave a cry.

'Oh, how extraordinary! To think of that! Why, of course! And to think I never thought—never dreamed—but then, how could I? And yet it did seem odd to me at the time.'

Poirot leant forward.

'So—you can help us, mademoiselle. Once again you can help us. *C'est épatant!*'

'To think that was it! Oh, well, it all fits in.'

'Tell me, I pray of you. You smelt varnish—yes?'

247

'Yes. Of course, I didn't know what it was. I thought—dear me—is it paint—no, it's more like floor stain, and then, of course, I thought I must have *imagined* it.'

'When was this?'

'Now let me see—when was it?'

'Was it during that Easter weekend when the house was full of guests?'

'Yes, that was the time—but I'm trying to recall just which day it was… Now, let me see, it wasn't Sunday. No, and it wasn't on Tuesday—that was the night Dr Donaldson came to dinner. And on the Wednesday they had all left. No, of course, it was the *Monday*—Bank Holiday. I'd been lying awake—rather worried, you know. I always think Bank Holiday is such a worrying day! There had been only just enough cold beef to go round at supper and I was afraid Miss Arundell might be annoyed about it. You see *I'd* ordered the joint on the Saturday, and of course I ought to have said seven pounds but I thought five pounds would do nicely, but Miss Arundell was always so vexed if there was any shortage—she was so hospitable—'

Miss Lawson paused to draw a deep breath and then rushed on.

'And so I was lying awake and wondering whether she'd say anything about it tomorrow, and what with one thing and another I was a long time dropping off—and then just as I was going off something seemed to wake me up—a sort of rap or tap—and I sat up in bed, and then I sniffed. Of course, I'm always terrified of fire—sometimes I think I smell fire two or three times a night—(so awful wouldn't it be if one were *trapped*?) Anyway there was a smell, and I sniffed hard but it wasn't smoke or anything like that. And I said to myself it's more like paint or floor stain—but of course, one wouldn't smell that in the middle of the night. But it was quite strong and I sat up sniffing and sniffing, and then I saw her in the glass—'

'Saw *her*? Saw whom?'

'In my looking-glass, you know, it's really most convenient. I left my door open a little always, so as to hear Miss Arundell if she were to call, and if she went up and down stairs I could see her. The one light was always left switched on in the passage. That's how I came to see her kneeling on the stair—Theresa, I mean. She was kneeling on about the third step with her head bent down over something and I was just thinking, "How odd, I wonder if she's *ill*?" when she got up and went away, so I supposed she'd just slipped or something. Or perhaps was stooping to pick something up. But, of course, I never thought about it again one way or another.'

'The tap that aroused you would be the tap of the hammer on the nail,' mused Poirot.

'Yes, I suppose it would. But oh, M. Poirot, how *dreadful*—how truly dreadful. I've always felt Theresa was, perhaps a little *wild*, but to do a thing like that.'

'You are sure it was Theresa?'

'Oh, dear me, yes.'

'It couldn't have been Mrs Tanios or one of the maids, for instance?'

'Oh, no, it was Theresa.'

Miss Lawson shook her head and murmured to herself: 'Oh, dear. Oh, dear,' several times.

Poirot was staring at her in a way I found it hard to understand.

'Permit me,' he said suddenly, 'to make an experiment. Let us go upstairs and endeavour to reconstruct this little scene.'

'Reconstruction? Oh, really—I don't know—I mean I don't quite see—'

'I will show you,' said Poirot, cutting in upon these doubts in an authoritative manner.

Somewhat flustered, Miss Lawson led the way upstairs.

'I hope the room's tidy—so much to do—what with one thing and another—' she tailed off incoherently.

The room was indeed somewhat heavily littered with miscellaneous articles, obviously the result of Miss Lawson's turning out of cupboards. With her usual incoherence Miss Lawson managed to indicate her own position and Poirot was able to verify for himself the fact that a portion of the staircase was reflected in the wall-mirror.

'And now, mademoiselle,' he suggested, 'if you will be so good as to go out and reproduce the actions that you saw.'

Miss Lawson, still murmuring, 'Oh, dear—' bustled out to fulfil her part. Poirot acted the part of the observer.

The performance concluded, he went out on the landing and asked which electric light had been left switched on.

'This one—this one along here. Just outside Miss Arundell's door.'

Poirot reached up, detached the bulb and examined it.

'A forty watt lamp, I see. Not very powerful.'

'No, it was just so that the passage shouldn't be quite dark.'

Poirot retraced his steps to the top of the stairs.

'You will pardon me, mademoiselle, but with the light being fairly dim and the way that shadow falls it is hardly possible that you can have seen very clearly. Can you be positive it was Miss Theresa Arundell and not just an indeterminate female figure in a dressing-gown?'

Miss Lawson was indignant.

'No, indeed, M. Poirot! I'm *perfectly* sure! I know Theresa well enough, I should hope! Oh, it was her all right. Her dark dressing-gown and that big shining brooch she wears with the initials—I saw that plainly.'

'So that there is no possible doubt. You saw the initials?'

'Yes, T.A. I know the brooch. Theresa often wore it. Oh, yes, I could swear to its being Theresa—and I will swear to it if necessary!'

There was a firmness and decision in those last two sentences that was quite at variance with her usual manner.

Poirot looked at her. Again there was something curious in his glance. It was aloof, appraising—and had also a queer appearance of finality about it.

'You would swear to that, yes?' he said.

'If—if—it's necessary. But I suppose it—will it be necessary?'

Again Poirot turned that appraising glance upon her.

'That will depend on the result of the exhumation,' he said.

'Ex—exhumation?'

Poirot put out a restraining hand. In her excitement Miss Lawson very nearly went headlong down the stairs.

'It may possibly be a question of exhumation,' he said.

'Oh, but surely—how *very* unpleasant! But I mean, I'm sure the family would oppose the idea very strongly—very strongly indeed.'

'Probably they will.'

'I'm quite sure they won't hear of such a thing!'

'Ah, but if it is as an order from the Home Office.'

'But M. Poirot—*why*? I mean it's not as though—not as though—'

'Not as though what?'

'Not as though there were anything—*wrong*.'

'You think not?'

'No, of course not. Why, there *couldn't* be! I mean the doctor and the nurse and everything—'

'Do not upset yourself,' said Poirot calmly and soothingly.

'Oh, but I can't help it! Poor dear Miss Arundell! It's not even as though Theresa had been here in the house when she died.'

'No, she left on the Monday before she was taken ill, did she not?'

'Quite early in the morning. So you see, *she* can't have had anything to do with it!'

'Let us hope not,' said Poirot.

'Oh, dear.' Miss Lawson clasped her hands together. 'I've never known *anything* so dreadful as all this! Really, I don't know whether I'm on my head or my heels.'

Poirot glanced at his watch.

'We must depart. We are returning to London. And you, mademoiselle, you are remaining down here some little time?'

'No—no... I have really no settled plans. Actually I'm going back myself today... I only came down just for a night to—to settle things a little.'

'I see. Well, goodbye, mademoiselle, and forgive me if I have upset you at all.'

'Oh, M. Poirot. *Upset* me? I feel quite *ill*! Oh dear—Oh, dear, it's such a *wicked* world! Such a dreadfully wicked world!'

Poirot cut short her lamentations by taking her hand firmly in his.

'Quite so. And you are still ready to swear *that you saw Theresa Arundell kneeling on the stairs on the night of Easter Bank Holiday?*'

'Oh, yes, I can swear to that.'

'And you can also swear that you saw a halo of light round Miss Arundell's head during the *séance*?'

Miss Lawson's mouth fell open.

'Oh, M. Poirot, don't—don't joke about these things.'

'I am not joking. I am perfectly serious.'

Miss Lawson said with dignity:

'It wasn't exactly a halo. It was more like the beginning of a manifestation. A ribbon of some luminous material. I think it was beginning to form into a face.'

'Extremely interesting. *Au revoir*, mademoiselle, and please keep all this to yourself.'

'Oh, of course—of course. I shouldn't dream of doing anything else...'

The last we saw of Miss Lawson was her rather sheep-like face gazing after us from the front door step.

CHAPTER 23

Dr Tanios Calls on Us

No sooner had we left the house than Poirot's manner changed. His face was grim and set.

'*Dépêchons nous*, Hastings,' he said. 'We must get back to London as soon as possible.'

'I'm willing.' I quickened my pace to suit his. I stole a look at his grave face.

'Who do you suspect, Poirot?' I asked. 'I wish you'd tell me. Do you believe it was Theresa Arundell on the stairs or not?'

Poirot did not reply to my questions. Instead he asked a question of his own.

'Did it strike you—reflect before you answer—did it strike you that there was something *wrong* with that statement of Miss Lawson's?'

'How do you mean—wrong with it?'

'If I knew that I should not be asking you!'

'Yes, but wrong in what way?'

'That is just it. I cannot be precise. But as she was talking I had, somehow, a feeling of unreality...as though there was something—some small point that was wrong—that was, yes, that was the feeling—something that was *impossible*...'

'She seemed quite positive it was Theresa!'

'Yes, yes.'

'But after all, the light couldn't have been very good. I don't see how she can be quite so sure.'

'No, no, Hastings, you are not helping me. It was some small point—something connected with—yes, I am sure of it—with the bedroom.'

'With the bedroom?' I repeated, trying to recall the details of the room. 'No,' I said at last. 'I can't help you.'

Poirot shook his head, vexedly.

'Why did you bring up that spiritualistic business again?' I asked.

'Because it is important.'

'What is important? Miss Lawson's luminous "ribbon development"?'

'You remember the Misses Tripp's description of the *séance*?'

'I know they saw a halo round the old lady's head.' I laughed in spite of myself. '*I* shouldn't think she was a saint by all accounts! Miss Lawson seems to have been terrified by her. I felt quite sorry for the poor woman when she described how she lay awake, worried to death because she might get into trouble over ordering too small a sirloin of beef.'

'Yes, it was an interesting touch that.'

'What are we going to do when we get to London?' I asked as we turned into the George and Poirot asked for the bill.

'We must go and see Theresa Arundell immediately.'

'And find out the truth? But won't she deny the whole thing anyway?'

'*Mon cher*, it is not a criminal offence to kneel upon a flight of stairs! She may have been picking up a pin to bring her luck—something of that sort!'

'And the smell of varnish?'

We could say no more just then, as the waiter arrived with the bill.

On the way to London we talked very little. I am not fond of talking and driving, and Poirot was so busy protecting his moustaches with his muffler from the disastrous effects of wind and dust that speech was quite beyond him.

We arrived at the flat at about twenty to two.

George, Poirot's immaculate and extremely English manservant, opened the door.

'A Dr Tanios is waiting to see you, sir. He has been here for half an hour.'

'Dr Tanios? Where is he?'

'In the sitting-room, sir. A lady also called to see you, sir. She seemed very distressed to find you were absent from home. It was before I received your telephone message, sir, so I could not tell her when you would be returning to London.'

'Describe this lady.'

'She was about five foot seven, sir, with dark hair and light blue eyes. She was wearing a grey coat and skirt and a hat worn very much to the back of the head instead of over the right eye.'

'Mrs Tanios,' I ejaculated in a low voice.

'She seemed in a condition of great nervous excitement, sir. Said it was of the utmost importance she should find you quickly.'

'What time was this?'

'About half-past ten, sir.'

Poirot shook his head as he passed on towards the sitting-room.

'That is the second time I have missed hearing what Mrs Tanios has to say. What would you say, Hastings? Is there a fate in it?'

'Third time lucky,' I said consolingly.

Poirot shook his head doubtfully.

'Will there be a third time? I wonder. Come, let us hear what the husband has to say.'

Dr Tanios was sitting in an arm-chair reading one of Poirot's books on psychology. He sprang up and greeted us.

'You must forgive this intrusion. I hope you don't mind my forcing my way in and waiting for you like this.'

'*Du tout, du tout.* Pray sit down. Permit me to offer you a glass of sherry.'

'Thank you. As a matter of fact I have an excuse. M. Poirot, I am worried, terribly worried, about my wife.'

'About your wife? I'm very sorry. What's the matter?'

Tanios said:

'You have seen her perhaps lately?'

It seemed quite a natural question, but the quick look that accompanied it was not so natural.

Poirot replied in the most matter of fact manner.

'No, not since I saw her at the hotel with you yesterday.'

'Ah—I thought perhaps she might have called upon you.'

Poirot was busy pouring out three glasses of sherry.

He said in a slightly abstracted voice:

'No. Was there any—reason for her calling on me?'

'No, no.' Dr Tanios accepted his sherry. 'Thank you. Thank you very much. No, there was no exact *reason*, but to be frank I am very much concerned about my wife's state of health.'

'Ah, she is not strong?'

'Her bodily health,' said Tanios slowly, 'is good. I wish I could say the same for her mind.'

'Ah?'

'I fear, M. Poirot, that she is on the verge of a complete nervous breakdown.'

'My dear Dr Tanios, I am extremely sorry to hear this.'

'This condition has been growing for some time. During the last two months her manner towards me has completely changed. She is nervous, easily startled, and she has the oddest fancies—actually they are more than fancies—they are *delusions*!'

'Really?'

'Yes. She is suffering from what is commonly known as persecution mania—a fairly well-known condition.'

Poirot made a sympathetic noise with his tongue.

'You can understand my anxiety!'

'Naturally. Naturally. But what I do not quite understand is why you have come to me. How can I help you?'

Dr Tanios seemed a little embarrassed.

'It occurred to me that my wife might have—or may yet—come to you with some extraordinary tale. She may conceivably say that she is in danger from me—something of the kind.'

'But why should she come to *me*?'

Dr Tanios smiled—it was a charming smile—genial yet wistful.

'You are a celebrated detective, M. Poirot. I saw—I could see at once—that my wife was very impressed at meeting you yesterday. The mere fact of meeting a detective would make a powerful impression on her in her present state. It seems to me highly probable that she might seek you out and—and—well, confide in you. That is the way these nervous affections go! There is a tendency to turn against those nearest and dearest to you.'

'Very distressing.'

'Yes, indeed. I am very fond of my wife.' There was a rich tenderness in his voice. 'I always feel it was so brave of her to marry me—a man of another race—to come out to a far country—to leave all her own friends and surroundings. For the last few days I have been really distraught... I can see only one thing for it...'

'Yes?'

'Perfect rest and quiet—and suitable psychological treatment. There is a splendid home I know of run by a first-class man. I want to take her there—it is in Norfolk—straightaway. Perfect rest and isolation from outside influence—that is what is needed. I feel convinced that once she has been there a month or two under skilled treatment there will be a change for the better.'

'I see,' said Poirot.

He uttered the words in a matter of fact manner without any clue to the feelings that prompted him.

Tanios again shot a quick glance at him.

'That is why, if she should come to you, I should be obliged if you will let me know at once.'

'But certainly. I will telephone you. You are at the Durham Hotel still?'

'Yes. I am going back there now.'

'And your wife is not there?'

'She went out directly after breakfast.'

'Without telling you where she was going?'

'Without saying a word. That is most unlike her.'

'And the children?'

'She took them with her.'

'I see.'

Tanios got up.

'I thank you so much, M. Poirot. I need hardly say that if she does tell you any high-flown stories of intimidation and persecution pay no attention to them. It is, unfortunately, a part of her malady.'

'Most distressing,' said Poirot with sympathy.

'It is indeed. Although one knows, medically speaking, that it is part of a recognized mental disease, yet one cannot help being hurt when a person very near and dear to you turns against you and all their affection changes to dislike.'

'You have my deepest sympathy,' said Poirot as he shook hands with his guest.

'By the way—' Poirot's voice recalled Tanios just as he was at the door.

'Yes?'

'Do you ever prescribe chloral for your wife?'

Tanios gave a startled movement.

'I—no—at least I may have done. But not lately. She seems to have taken an aversion to any form of sleeping draught.'

'Ah! I suppose because she does not trust you?'

'M. Poirot!'

Tanios came striding forward angrily.

'That would be part of the disease,' said Poirot smoothly.

'Yes, yes, of course.'

'She is probably highly suspicious of anything you give her to eat or drink. Probably suspects you of wanting to poison her?'

'Dear me, M. Poirot, you are quite right. You know something of such cases, then?'

'One comes across them now and then in my profession, naturally. But do not let me detain you. You may find her waiting for you at the hotel.'

'True. I hope I shall. I feel terribly anxious.'

He hurried out of the room.

Poirot went swiftly to the telephone. He flicked over the pages of the telephone directory and asked for a number.

'Allo—Allo—is that the Durham Hotel. Can you tell me if Mrs Tanios is in? What? T A N I O S. Yes, that is right. Yes? Yes? Oh, I see.'

He replaced the receiver.

'Mrs Tanios left the hotel this morning early. She returned at eleven, waited in the taxi whilst her luggage was brought down and drove away with it.'

'Does Tanios know she took away her luggage?'

'I think not as yet.'

'Where has she gone?'

'Impossible to tell.'

'Do you think she will come back here?'

'Possibly. I cannot tell.'

'Perhaps she will write.'

'Perhaps.'

'What can we do?'

Poirot shook his head. He looked worried and distressed.

'Nothing at the moment. A hasty lunch and then we will go and see Theresa Arundell.'

'Do you believe it *was* her on the stairs?'

'Impossible to tell. One thing I made sure of—Miss Lawson could not have seen her face. She saw a tall figure in a dark dressing-gown, that is all.'

'And the brooch.'

'My dear friend, a brooch is not part of a person's anatomy! It can be detached from that person. It can be lost—or borrowed—or even stolen.'

'In other words you don't want to believe Theresa Arundell guilty.'

'I want to hear what she has to say on the matter.'

'And if Mrs Tanios comes back?'

'I will arrange for that.'

George brought in an omelette.

'Listen, George,' said Poirot. 'If that lady comes back, you will ask her to wait. If Dr Tanios comes while she is here on no account let him in. If he asks if his wife is here, you will tell him she is not. You understand?'

'Perfectly, sir.'

Poirot attacked the omelette.

'This business complicates itself,' he said. 'We must step very carefully. If not—the murderer will strike again.'

'If he did you might get him.'

'Quite possibly, but I prefer the life of the innocent to the conviction of the guilty. We must go very, very carefully.'

CHAPTER 24

Theresa's Denial

We found Theresa Arundell just preparing to go out.

She was looking extraordinarily attractive. A small hat of the most outrageous fashion descended rakishly over one eye. I recognized with momentary amusement that Bella Tanios had worn a cheap imitation of such a hat yesterday and had worn it—as George had put it—on the back of the head instead of over the right eye. I remembered well how she had pushed it farther and farther back on her untidy hair.

Poirot said, politely:

'Can I have just a minute or two, mademoiselle, or will it delay you too much?'

Theresa laughed.

'Oh, it doesn't matter. I'm always three-quarters of an hour late for everything. I might just as well make it an hour.'

She led him into the sitting-room. To my surprise Dr Donaldson rose from a chair by the window.

'You've met M. Poirot already, Rex, haven't you?'

'We met at Market Basing,' said Donaldson, stiffly.

'You were pretending to write the life of my drunken grandfather, I understand,' said Theresa. 'Rex, my angel, will you leave us?'

'Thank you, Theresa, but I think that from every point of view it would be advisable for me to be present at this interview.'

There was a brief duel of eyes. Theresa's were commanding. Donaldson's were impervious. She showed a quick flash of anger.

'All right, stay then, damn you!'

Dr Donaldson seemed unperturbed.

He seated himself again in the chair by the window, laying down his book on the arm of it. It was a book on the pituitary gland, I noticed.

Theresa sat down on her favourite low stool and looked impatiently at Poirot.

'Well, you've seen Purvis? What about it?'

Poirot said in a non-committal voice:

'There are—possibilities, mademoiselle.'

She looked at him thoughtfully. Then she sent a very faint glance in the direction of the doctor. It was, I think, intended as a warning to Poirot.

'But it would be well, I think,' went on Poirot, 'for me to report later when my plans are more advanced.'

A faint smile showed for a minute on Theresa's face.

Poirot continued:

'I have today come from Market Basing and while there I have talked to Miss Lawson. Tell me, mademoiselle, did you on the night of April 13th (that was the night of the

Easter Bank Holiday) kneel upon the stairs after everyone had gone to bed?'

'My dear Hercule Poirot, what an extraordinary question. Why should I?'

'The question, mademoiselle, is not why you *should*, but whether you *did*.'

'I'm sure I don't know. I should think it most unlikely.'

'You comprehend, mademoiselle, Miss Lawson *says you did*.'

Theresa shrugged her attractive shoulders.

'Does it matter?'

'It matters very much.'

She stared at him. In a perfectly amiable fashion, Poirot stared back.

'Loopy!' said Theresa.

'*Pardon?*'

'Definitely loopy!' said Theresa. 'Don't you think so, Rex?'

Dr Donaldson coughed.

'Excuse me, M. Poirot, but what is the point of the question?'

My friend spread out his hands.

'It is most simple! Someone drove in a nail in a convenient position at the head of the stairs. The nail was just touched with brown varnish to match the skirting board.'

'Is this a new kind of witchcraft?' asked Theresa.

'No, mademoiselle, it is much more homely and simple than that. On the following evening, the Tuesday, *someone* attached a string or thread from the nail to the balusters with the result that when Miss Arundell came out of her room she caught her foot in it and went headlong down the stairs.'

Theresa drew in her breath sharply.

'That was Bob's ball!'

'*Pardon*, it was not.'

There was a pause. It was broken by Donaldson who said in his quiet, precise voice:

'Excuse me, but what evidence have you in support of this statement?'

Poirot said quietly:

'The evidence of the nail, the evidence of Miss Arundell's own written words, and finally the evidence of Miss Lawson's eyes.'

Theresa found her voice.

'She says *I* did it, does she?'

Poirot did not answer except by bending his head a little.

'Well, it's a lie! I had nothing to do with it!'

'You were kneeling on the stairs for quite another reason?'

'I wasn't kneeling on the stairs at all!'

'Be careful, mademoiselle.'

'I wasn't there! I never came out of my room after I went to bed on any evening I was there.'

'Miss Lawson recognized you.'

'It was probably Bella Tanios or one of the maids she saw.'

'She says it was you.'

'She's a damned liar!'

'She recognized your dressing-gown and a brooch you wear.'

'A brooch—what brooch?'

'A brooch with your initials.'

'Oh, I know the one! What a circumstantial liar she is!'

'You still deny that it was you she saw?'

'If it's my word against hers—'

'You are a better liar than she is—eh?'

Theresa said, calmly:

'That's probably quite true. But in this case I'm speaking the truth. I wasn't preparing a booby trap, or saying my prayers, or picking up gold or silver, or doing anything at all on the stairs.'

'Have you this brooch that was mentioned?'

'Probably. Do you want to see it?'

'If you please, mademoiselle.'

Theresa got up and left the room. There was an awkward silence. Dr Donaldson looked at Poirot much as I imagined he might have looked at an anatomical specimen.

Theresa returned.

'Here it is.'

She almost flung the ornament at Poirot. It was a large rather showy chromium or stainless steel brooch with T.A. enclosed in a circle. I had to admit that it was large enough and showy enough to be easily seen in Miss Lawson's mirror.

'I never wear it now. I'm tired of it,' said Theresa. 'London's been flooded with them. Every little skivvy wears one.'

'But it was expensive when you bought it?'

'Oh, yes. They were quite exclusive to begin with.'

'When was that?'

'Last Christmas, I think it was. Yes, about then.'

'Have you ever lent it to anyone?'

'No.'

'You had it with you at Littlegreen House?'

'I suppose I did. Yes, I did. I remember.'

'Did you leave it about at all? Was it out of your possession while you were there?'

'No, it wasn't. I wore it on a green jumper. I remember. And I wore the same jumper every day.'

'And at night?'

'It was still in the jumper.'

'And the jumper.'

'Oh, hell, the jumper was sitting on a chair.'

'You are sure no one removed the brooch and put it back again the next day?'

'We'll say so in court if you like—if you think that's the best lie to tell! Actually I'm *quite sure* that nothing like that happened! It's a pretty idea that somebody framed me—but I don't think it's true.'

Poirot frowned. Then he got up, attached the brooch carefully to his coat lapel and approached a mirror on a table at the other end of the room. He stood in front of it and then moved slowly backward, getting an effect of distance.

Then he uttered a grunt.

'Imbecile that I am! Of course!'

He came back and handed the brooch to Theresa with a bow.

'You are quite right, mademoiselle. The brooch did *not* leave your possession! I have been regrettably dense.'

'I do like modesty,' said Theresa, pinning the brooch on carelessly.

She looked up at him.

'Anything more? I ought to be going.'

'Nothing that cannot be discussed later.'

Theresa moved towards the door. Poirot went on in a quiet voice:

'There is a question of exhumation, it is true—'

Theresa stopped dead. The brooch fell to the ground.

'What's that?'

Poirot said clearly:

'It is possible that the body of Miss Emily Arundell may be exhumed.'

Theresa stood still, her hands clenched. She said in a low, angry voice:

'Is this *your* doing? It can't be done without an application from the family!'

'You are wrong, mademoiselle. It can be done on an order from the Home Office.'

'My God!' said Theresa.

She turned and walked swiftly up and down.

Donaldson said quietly:

'I really don't see that there is any need to be upset, Tessa. I dare say that to an outsider the idea is not very pleasant, but—'

She interrupted him.

'Don't be a fool, Rex!'

Poirot asked:

'The idea disturbs you, mademoiselle?'

'Of course it does! It isn't decent. Poor old Aunt Emily. Why the devil *should* she be exhumed?'

'I presume,' said Donaldson, 'that there is some doubt as to the cause of death?' He looked inquiringly at Poirot. He went on. 'I confess that I am surprised. I think that there is no doubt that Miss Arundell died a natural death from a disease of long standing.'

'You told me something about a rabbit and liver trouble once,' said Theresa. 'I've forgotten it now, but you infect a rabbit with blood from a person with yellow atrophy of the liver, and then you inject that rabbit's blood into another rabbit, and then that second rabbit's blood into a person and the person gets a diseased liver. Something like that.'

'That was merely an illustration of serum therapeutics,' said Donaldson patiently.

'Pity there are so many rabbits in the story!' said Theresa with a reckless laugh. 'None of us keep rabbits.' She turned on Poirot and her voice altered.

'M. Poirot, is this *true*?' she asked.

'It is true enough, but—there are ways of avoiding such a contingency, mademoiselle.'

'Then avoid it!' her voice sank almost to a whisper. It was urgent, compelling. 'Avoid it *at all costs*!'

Poirot rose to his feet.

'Those are your instructions?' His voice was formal.

'Those are my instructions.'

'But Tessa—' Donaldson interrupted.

She whirled round on her fiancé.

'Be quiet! She was *my* aunt, wasn't she? Why should *my* aunt be dug up? Don't you know there will be paragraphs in the papers and gossip and general unpleasantness?' She swung round again on Poirot.

'You must stop it! I give you *carte blanche*. Do anything you like, but *stop it*!'

Poirot bowed formally.

'I will do what I can. *Au revoir, mademoiselle, au revoir,* doctor.'

'Oh, go away!' cried Theresa. 'And take St Leonards with you. I wish I'd never set eyes on either of you.'

We left the room. Poirot did not this time deliberately place his ear to the crack but he dallied—yes, he dallied.

And not in vain. Theresa's voice rose clear and defiant: 'Don't look at me like that, Rex.'

And then suddenly, with a break in her voice—'Darling.'

Dr Donaldson's precise voice answered her.

He said very clearly:

'That man means mischief.'

Poirot grinned suddenly. He drew me through the front door.

'Come, St Leonards,' he said. '*C'est drôle, ça!*'

Personally I thought the joke a particularly stupid one.

CHAPTER 25

I Lie Back and Reflect

No, I thought, as I hurried after Poirot, there was no doubt about it now. Miss Arundell had been murdered and Theresa knew it. But was she herself the criminal or was there another explanation?

She was afraid—yes. But was she afraid for herself or for someone else? Could that someone be the quiet, precise young doctor with the calm, aloof manner?

Had the old lady died of genuine disease *artificially induced*?

Up to a point it all fitted in—Donaldson's ambitions, his belief that Theresa would inherit money at her aunt's death. Even the fact that he had been at dinner there on the evening of the accident. How easy to leave a convenient window open and return in the dead of night to tie the murderous thread across the staircase. But then, what about the placing of the nail in position?

No, Theresa must have done that. Theresa, his fiancée and accomplice. With the two of them working in together, the whole thing seemed clear enough. In that case it was probably Theresa who had actually placed the thread in position. The *first* crime, the crime that failed, had been *her* work. The second crime, the crime that had succeeded, was Donaldson's more scientific masterpiece.

Yes—it all fitted in.

Yet even now there were loose strands. Why had Theresa blurted out those facts about inducing liver disease in human beings? It was almost as though she did not realize the truth... But in that case—and I felt my mind growing bewildered, and I interrupted my speculations to ask:

'Where are we going, Poirot?'

'Back to my flat. It is possible that we may find Mrs Tanios there.'

My thoughts switched off on a different track.

Mrs Tanios! That was another mystery! If Donaldson and Theresa were guilty, where did Mrs Tanios and her smiling husband come in? What did the woman want to tell Poirot and what was Tanios' anxiety to prevent her doing so?

'Poirot,' I said humbly. 'I'm getting rather muddled. They're not *all* in it, are they?'

'Murder by a syndicate? A family syndicate? No, not this time. There is the mark of one brain and one brain only in this. The psychology is very clear.'

'You mean that either Theresa or Donaldson did it—but not *both* of them? Did he get her to hammer that nail in on some entirely innocent pretext, then?'

'My dear friend, from the moment I heard Miss Lawson's story I realized that there were three possibilities. (1) That Miss Lawson was telling the exact truth. (2) That Miss

Lawson had invented the story for reasons of her own. (3) That Miss Lawson actually believed her own story, but that her identification rested upon the brooch—and as I have already pointed out to you—a brooch is easily detachable from its owner.'

'Yes, but Theresa insists that the brooch did not leave her possession.'

'And she is perfectly right. I had overlooked a small but intensely significant fact.'

'Very unlike you, Poirot,' I said solemnly.

'*N'est ce pas?* But one has one's lapses.'

'Age will tell!'

'Age has nothing to do with it,' said Poirot coldly.

'Well, what is the significant fact?' I asked as we turned in at the entrance of the Mansions.

'I will show you.'

We had just reached the flat.

George opened the door to us. In reply to Poirot's anxious question he shook his head.

'No, sir. Mrs Tanios has not called. Neither has she telephoned.' Poirot went into the sitting-room. He paced up and down for a few minutes. Then he picked up the telephone. He got first on to the Durham Hotel.

'Yes—yes, please. Ah, Dr Tanios, this is Hercule Poirot speaking. Your wife has returned? Oh, not returned. Dear me... Taken her luggage, you say... And the children... You have no idea where she has gone... Yes, quite... Oh, perfectly... If my professional services are of any use to you? I have certain experience in these matters... Such things can be done quite discreetly... No, of course not... Yes, of course that is true... Certainly—certainly. I shall respect your wishes in the matter.'

He hung up the receiver thoughtfully.

'He does not know where she is,' he said thoughtfully. 'I think that is quite genuine. The anxiety in his voice is unmistakable. He does not want to go to the police, that is understandable. Yes, I understand that. He does not want my assistance either. That is, perhaps, not quite so understandable... He wants her found—but he does not want *me* to find her... No, definitely he does not want me to find her... He seems confident that he can manage the matter himself. He does not think she can remain long hidden, for she has very little money with her. Also she has the children. Yes, I fancy he will be able to hunt her down before long. But, I think, Hastings, that we shall be a little quicker than he is. It is important, I think, that we should be.'

'Do you think it's true that she is slightly batty?' I asked.

'I think that she is in a highly nervous, overwrought condition.'

'But not to such a point that she ought to be in a mental home?'

'That, very definitely, no.'

'You know, Poirot, I don't quite understand all this.'

'If you will pardon my saying so, Hastings, you do not understand at all!'

'There seem so many—well—side issues.'

'Naturally there are side issues. To separate the main issue from the side issues is the first task of the orderly mind.'

'Tell me, Poirot, have you realized all along that there were *eight* possible suspects and not seven?'

Poirot replied drily:

'I have taken that fact into consideration from the moment that Theresa Arundell mentioned that the last time she saw Dr Donaldson was when he dined at Littlegreen House on April 14th.'

'I can't quite see—' I broke off.

'What is it you cannot quite see?'

'Well, if Donaldson had planned to do away with Miss Arundell by scientific means—by inoculation, that is to say—I can't see why he resorted to such a clumsy device as a string across the stairs.'

'*En vérité*, Hastings, there are moments when I lose patience with you! One method is a highly scientific one needing fully-specialized knowledge. That is so, is it not?'

'Yes.'

'And the other is a homely simple method—"the kind that mother makes"—as the advertisements say. Is that not right?'

'Yes, exactly.'

'Then think, Hastings—*think*. Lie back in your chair, close the eyes, employ the little grey cells.'

I obeyed. That is to say, I leant back in the chair and closed my eyes and endeavoured to carry out the third part of Poirot's instructions. The result, however, did not seem to clarify matters much.

I opened my eyes to find Poirot regarding me with the kindly attention a nurse might display towards a childish charge.

'*Eh bien?*'

I made a desperate attempt to emulate Poirot's manner.

'Well,' I said, 'it seems to me that the kind of person who laid the original booby-trap is not the kind of person to plan out a scientific murder.'

'Exactly.'

'And I doubt if a mind trained to scientific complexities would think of anything so childish as the accident plan—it would be altogether too haphazard.'

'Very clearly reasoned.'

Emboldened, I went on:

'Therefore, the only logical solution seems to be this—the two attempts were planned by two different people. We have here to deal with murder attempted by two entirely different people.'

'You do not think that is too much of a coincidence?'

'You said yourself once that one coincidence is nearly always found in a murder case.'

'Yes, that is true. I have to admit it.'

'Well, then.'

'And who do you suggest for your villains?'

'Donaldson and Theresa Arundell. A doctor is clearly indicated for the final successful murder. On the other hand we know that Theresa Arundell is concerned in the first attempt. I think it's possible that they acted quite independently of each other.'

'You are so fond of saying, "we know," Hastings. I can assure you that no matter what *you* know, I do not know that Theresa was implicated.'

'But Miss Lawson's story.'

'Miss Lawson's story is Miss Lawson's story. Just that.'

'But she says—'

'She says—she says... Always you are so ready to take what people say for a proved and accepted fact. Now listen, *mon cher*, I told you at the time, did I not, that something struck me as wrong about Miss Lawson's story?'

'Yes, I remember your saying so. But you couldn't get hold of what it was.'

'Well, I have done so now. A little moment and I will show you what I, imbecile that I am, ought to have seen at once.' He went over to the desk and opening a drawer took out a sheet of cardboard. He cut into this with a pair of scissors, motioning to me not to overlook what he was doing.

'Patience, Hastings, in a little moment we will proceed to our experiment.'

I averted my eyes obligingly.

In a minute or two Poirot uttered an exclamation of satisfaction. He put away the scissors, dropped the fragments of cardboard into the waste-paper basket and came across the room to me.

'Now, do not look. Continue to avert the eyes while I pin something to the lapel of your coat.'

I humoured him. Poirot completed the proceeding to his satisfaction, then, propelling me gently to my feet he drew me across the room, and into the adjoining bedroom.

'Now, Hastings, regard yourself in the glass. You are wearing, are you not, a fashionable brooch with your initials on it—only, *bien entendu*, the brooch is made not of chromium nor stainless steel, nor gold, nor platinum—but of humble cardboard!'

I looked at myself and smiled. Poirot is uncommonly neat with his fingers. I was wearing a very fair representation of Theresa Arundell's brooch—a circle cut out of cardboard and enclosing my initials. A.H.

'*Eh bien*,' said Poirot. 'You are satisfied? You have there, have you not, a very smart brooch with your initials?'

'A most handsome affair,' I agreed.

'It is true that it does not gleam and reflect the light, but all the same you are prepared to admit that that brooch could be seen plainly from some distance away?'

'I've never doubted it.'

'Quite so. Doubt is not your strong point. Simple faith is more characteristic of you. And now, Hastings, be so good as to remove your coat.'

Wondering a little, I did so. Poirot divested himself of his own coat and slipped on mine, turning away a little as he did so.

'And now,' he said. 'Regard how the brooch—the brooch with *your* initials—becomes me?'

He whisked round. I stared at him—for the moment uncomprehendingly. Then I saw the point.

'What a blithering fool I am! Of course. It's H.A. in the brooch, not A.H. at all.'

Poirot beamed on me, as he reassumed his own clothes and handed me mine.

'Exactly—and now you see what struck me as wrong with Miss Lawson's story. She stated that she had seen Theresa's initials clearly on the brooch she was wearing. But she saw Theresa in the *glass*. *So, if she saw the initials at all*, she must have seen them *reversed*.'

'Well,' I argued, 'perhaps she did, and realized that they were reversed.'

'*Mon cher*, did that occur to you just now? Did you exclaim, "Ha! Poirot, you've got it wrong. That's H.A. really—not A.H." No, you did not. And yet you are a good deal more intelligent, I should say, than Miss Lawson. Do not tell me that a muddle-headed woman like that woke up suddenly, and still half-asleep, realized that A.T. was really T.A. No, that is not at all consistent with the mentality of Miss Lawson.'

'She was determined it should be Theresa,' I said slowly.

'You are getting nearer, my friend. You remember, I hint to her that she could not really see the face of anyone on the stairs, and immediately—what does she do?'

'Remembers Theresa's brooch and lugs that in—forgetting that the mere fact of having seen it in the glass gave her own story the lie.'

The telephone bell rang sharply. Poirot crossed to it.

He only spoke a few non-committal words.

'Yes? Yes... certainly. Yes, quite convenient. The afternoon, I think. Yes, two o'clock will do admirably.' He replaced the receiver and turned to me with a smile.

'Dr Donaldson is anxious to have a talk with me. He is coming here tomorrow afternoon at two o'clock. We progress, *mon ami*, we progress.'

CHAPTER 26

Mrs Tanios Refuses to Speak

When I came round after breakfast the following morning I found Poirot busy at the writing-table.

He raised a hand in salutation, then proceeded with his task. Presently he gathered up the sheets, enclosed them in an envelope and sealed them up carefully.

'Well, old boy, what are you doing?' I asked facetiously. 'Writing an account of the case to be placed in safe keeping in case someone bumps you off during the course of the day?'

'You know, Hastings, you are not so far wrong as you think.'

His manner was serious.

'Is our murderer really about to get dangerous?'

'A murderer is always dangerous,' said Poirot gravely. 'Astonishing how often that fact is overlooked.'

'Any news?'

'Dr Tanios rang up.'

'Still no trace of his wife?'

'No.'

'Then that's all right.'

'I wonder.'

'Dash it all, Poirot, you don't think she's been bumped off, do you?'

Poirot shook his head doubtfully.

'I confess,' he murmured, 'that I should like to know where she is.'

'Oh, well,' I said. 'She'll turn up.'

'Your cheerful optimism never fails to delight me, Hastings!'

'My goodness, Poirot, you don't think she'll turn up in parcels or dismembered in a trunk?'

Poirot said slowly:

'I find the anxiety of Dr Tanios somewhat excessive—but no more of that. The first thing to do is to interview Miss Lawson.'

'Are you going to point out that little error over the brooch?'

'Certainly not. That little fact remains up my sleeve until the right moment comes.'

'Then what are you going to say to her?'

'That, *mon ami*, you will hear in due course.'

'More lies, I suppose?'

'You are really offensive sometimes, Hastings. Anybody would think I enjoyed telling lies.'

'I rather think you do. In fact, I'm sure of it.'

'It is true that I sometimes compliment myself upon my ingenuity,' Poirot confessed naively.

I could not help giving a shout of laughter. Poirot looked at me reproachfully and we set off for Clanroyden Mansions.

We were shown into the same crowded sitting-room and Miss Lawson came bustling in, her manner even more incoherent than usual.

'Oh, dear, M. Poirot, good-morning. Such a to do—rather untidy, I'm afraid. But then, everything is at sixes and sevens this morning. Ever since Bella arrived—'

'What is that you say? Bella?'

'Yes, Bella Tanios. She turned up half an hour ago—*and* the children—completely exhausted, poor soul! Really, I don't know what to do about it. You see, she's left her husband.'

'Left him?'

'So she says. Of course, I've no doubt she's fully *justified*, poor thing.'

'She has confided in you?'

'Well—not exactly *that*. In fact, she won't say anything at all. Just repeats that she's left him and that nothing will induce her to go back to him!'

'That is a very serious step to take?'

'Of course it is! In fact, if he'd been an Englishman, I would have advised her—but there, he isn't an Englishman... And she looks so peculiar, poor thing, so—well, so *scared*. What can he have been doing to her? I believe Turks are frightfully cruel sometimes.'

'Dr Tanios is a Greek.'

'Yes, of course, that's the other way about—I mean, they're usually the ones who get massacred by the Turks—or am I thinking of Armenians? But all the same, I don't like to think of it. I don't think she *ought* to go back to him, do you, M. Poirot? Anyway, I mean, she says she won't...

She doesn't even want him to know where she is.'

'As bad as that?'

'Yes, you see it's the *children*. She's so afraid he could take them back to Smyrna. Poor soul, she really is in a terrible way. You see, she's got no money—no money at all. She doesn't know where to go or what to do. She wants to try and earn her living but really, you know, M. Poirot, that's not so easy as it sounds. I know that. It's not as though she were *trained* for anything.'

'When did she leave her husband?'

'Yesterday. She spent last night in a little hotel near Paddington. She came to me because she couldn't think of anyone else to go to, poor thing.'

'And are you going to help her? That is very good of you.'

'Well, you see, M. Poirot, I really feel it's my *duty*. But of course, it's all very difficult. This is a very small flat and there's no room—and what with one thing and another.'

'You could send her to Littlegreen House?'

'I suppose I could—but you see, her husband might think of that. Just for the moment I've got her rooms at the Wellington Hotel in Queen's Road. She's staying there under the name of Mrs Peters.'

'I see,' said Poirot.

He paused for a minute, then said:

'I would like to see Mrs Tanios. You see, she called at my flat yesterday but I was out.'

'Oh, did she? She didn't tell me that. I'll tell her, shall I?'

'If you would be so good.'

Miss Lawson hurried out of the room. We could hear her voice.

'Bella—Bella—my dear, will you come and see M. Poirot?'

We did not hear Mrs Tanios' reply, but a minute or two later she came into the room.

I was really shocked at her appearance. There were dark circles under her eyes and her cheeks were completely destitute of colour, but what struck me far more than this was her obvious air of terror. She started at the least provocation, and she seemed to be continually listening.

Poirot greeted her in his most soothing manner. He came forward, shook hands, arranged a chair for her and handed her a cushion. He treated the pale, frightened woman as though she had been a queen.

'And now, madame, let us have a little chat. You came to see me yesterday, I believe?'

She nodded.

'I regret very much that I was away from home.'

'Yes—yes, I wish you had been there.'

'You came because you wanted to tell me something?'

'Yes, I—I meant to—'

'*Eh bien*, I am here, at your service.'

Mrs Tanios did not respond. She sat quite still, twisting a ring round and round on her finger.

'Well, madame?'

Slowly, almost reluctantly, she shook her head.

'No,' she said. 'I daren't.'

'You *daren't*, madame?'

'No. I—if he knew—he'd—Oh, something would happen to me!'

'Come, come, madame—that is absurd.'

'Oh, but it isn't absurd—it isn't absurd at all. You don't know him...'

'By *him*, you mean your husband, madame?'

'Yes, of course.'

Poirot was silent a minute or two, then he said:

'Your husband came to see me yesterday, madame.'

A quick look of alarm sprang up in her face.

'Oh, no! You didn't tell him—but of course you didn't! You couldn't. You didn't know where I was. Did he—did he say I was *mad*?'

Poirot answered cautiously.

'He said that you were—highly nervous.'

But she shook her head, undeceived.

'No, he said that I was mad—or that I was going mad! He wants to shut me up so that I shan't be able to tell anyone ever.'

'Tell anyone—what?'

But she shook her head. Twisting her fingers nervously round and round, she muttered:

'I'm afraid...'

'But madame, once you have *told* me—you are *safe*! The secret is out! That fact will protect you automatically.'

But she did not reply. She went on twisting—twisting at her ring.

'You must see that yourself,' said Poirot gently.

She gave a sort of gasp.

'How am I to know... Oh, dear, it's terrible. He's so *plausible*! And he's a doctor! People will believe him and not me. I know they will. I should myself. Nobody will believe me. How could they?'

'You will not even give me the chance?'

She shot a troubled glance at him.

'How do I know? You may be on his side.'

'I am on no-one's side, madame. I am—always—on the side of the truth.'

'I don't know,' said Mrs Tanios hopelessly. 'Oh, I don't know.' She went on, her words gathering volume, tumbling over each other.

'It's been so awful—for years now. I've seen things happening again and again. And I couldn't say anything or do anything. There have been the children. It's been like a long nightmare. And now this... But I won't go back to him. I won't let him have the children! I'll go somewhere where he can't find me. Minnie Lawson will help me. She's been so kind—so wonderfully kind. Nobody could have been kinder.' She stopped, then shot a quick look at Poirot and asked:

'What did he say about me? Did he say I had delusions?'

'He said, madame, that you had—changed towards him.'

She nodded.

'And he said I had delusions. He *did* say that, didn't he?'

'Yes, madame, to be frank, he did.'

'That's it, you see. That's what it will sound like. And I've no proof—no real proof.'

Poirot leaned back in his chair. When he next spoke it was with an entire change of manner.

He spoke in a matter of fact, business-like voice with as little emotion as if he had been discussing some dry matter of business.

'Do you suspect your husband of doing away with Miss Emily Arundell?'

Her answer came quickly—a spontaneous flash.

'I don't suspect—I know.'

'Then, madame, it is your duty to speak.'

'Ah, but it isn't so easy—no, it isn't so easy.'

'How did he kill her?'

'I don't know exactly—but he did kill her.'

'But you don't know the method he employed?'

'No—it was something—something he did that last Sunday.'

'The Sunday he went down to see her?'

'Yes.'

'But you don't know what it was?'

'No.'

'Then how, forgive me, madame, can you be so sure?'

'Because he—' she stopped and said slowly, 'I *am* sure!'

'*Pardon*, madame, but there is something you are keeping back. Something you have not yet told me?'

'Yes.'

'Come, then.'

Bella Tanios got up suddenly.

'No. No. I can't do that. The children. Their father. I can't. I simply can't...'

'But madame—'

'I can't, I tell you.'

Her voice rose almost to a scream. The door opened and Miss Lawson came in, her head cocked on one side with a sort of pleasurable excitement.

'May I come in? Have you had your little talk? Bella, my dear, don't you think you ought to have a cup of tea, or some soup, or perhaps a little brandy even?'

Mrs Tanios shook her head.

'I'm quite all right.' She gave a weak smile. 'I must be getting back to the children. I have left them to unpack.'

'Dear little things,' said Miss Lawson. 'I'm so fond of children.'

Mrs Tanios turned to her suddenly.

'I don't know what I should do without you,' she said. 'You—you've been wonderfully kind.'

'There, there, my dear, don't cry. Everything's going to be all right. You shall come round and see my lawyer—such a nice man, so sympathetic, and he'll advise you the best way to get a divorce. Divorce is so simple nowadays, isn't it, everybody says so? Oh, dear, there's the bell. I wonder who that is.'

She left the room hurriedly. There was a murmur of voices in the hall. Miss Lawson reappeared. She tiptoed in and shut the door carefully behind her. She spoke in an excited whisper, mouthing the words exaggeratedly.

'Oh, dear, Bella, it's your husband. I'm sure I don't know—'

Mrs Tanios gave one bound towards a door at the other end of the room. Miss Lawson nodded her head violently.

'That's right, dear, go in there, and then you can slip out when I've brought him in here.'

Mrs Tanios whispered:

'Don't say I've been here. Don't say you've seen me.'

'No, no, of course I won't.'

Mrs Tanios slipped through the door. Poirot and I followed hastily. We found ourselves in a small dining-room.

Poirot crossed to the door into the hall, opened it a crack and listened. Then he beckoned.

'All is clear. Miss Lawson has taken him into the other room.'

We crept through the hall and out by the front door. Poirot drew it to as noiselessly as possible after him.

Mrs Tanios began to run down the steps, stumbling and clutching at the banisters. Poirot steadied her with a hand under her arm.

'*Du calme—du calme*. All is well.'

We reached the entrance-hall.

'Come with me,' said Mrs Tanios piteously. She looked as though she might be going to faint.

'Certainly I will come,' said Poirot reassuringly.

We crossed the road, turned a corner, and found ourselves in Queen's Road. The Wellington was a small, inconspicuous hotel of the boarding-house variety.

When we were inside Mrs Tanios sank down on a plush sofa. Her hand was on her beating heart.

Poirot patted her reassuringly on the shoulder.

'It was the narrow squeak—yes. Now, madame, you are to listen to me very carefully.'

'I can't tell you anything more, M. Poirot. It wouldn't be *right*. You—you know what I think—what I believe. You—you must be satisfied with that.'

'I asked you to listen, madame. Supposing—this is a supposition only—*that I already know the facts of the case*. Supposing that what you could tell me *I have already guessed*—that would make a difference, would it not?'

She looked at him doubtfully. Her eyes were painful in their intensity.

'Oh, believe me, madame, I am not trying to trap you into saying what you do not wish to. But it *would* make a difference—yes?'

'I—I suppose it would.'

'Good. Then let me say this. *I, Hercule Poirot, know the truth.* I am not going to ask you to accept my word for it. Take this.' He thrust upon her the bulky envelope I had seen him seal up that morning. 'The facts are there. After you have read them, if they satisfy you, ring me up. My number is on the notepaper.'

Almost reluctantly she accepted the envelope.

Poirot went on briskly:

'And now, one more point, you must leave this hotel at once.'

'But why?'

'You will go to the Coniston Hotel near Euston. Tell no one where you are going.'

'But surely—here—Minnie Lawson won't tell my husband where I am.'

'You think not?'

'Oh, no—she's entirely on my side.'

'Yes, but your husband, madame, is a very clever man. He will not find it difficult to turn a middle-aged lady inside out. It is essential—*essential*, you understand, that your husband should not know where you are.'

She nodded dumbly.

Poirot held out a sheet of paper.

'Here is the address. Pack up and drive there with the children as soon as possible. You understand?'

She nodded.

'I understand.'

'It is the children you must think of, madame, not yourself. You love your children.'

He had touched the right note.

A little colour crept into her cheeks, her head went back. She looked, not a frightened drudge, but an arrogant, almost handsome woman.

'It is arranged, then,' said Poirot.

He shook hands and he and I departed. But not far. From the shelter of a convenient café, we sipped coffee and watched the entrance of the hotel. In about five minutes we saw Dr Tanios walking down the street. He did not even glance up at the Wellington. He passed it, his head bowed in thought, then he turned into the Underground station.

About ten minutes later we saw Mrs Tanios and the children get into the taxi with their luggage and drive away.

'*Bien*,' said Poirot, rising with the check in his hand. 'We have done our part. Now it is on the knees of the gods.'

CHAPTER 27

Visit of Dr Donaldson

Donaldson arrived punctually at two o'clock. He was as calm and precise as ever.

The personality of Donaldson had begun to intrigue me. I had started by regarding him as a rather nondescript young man. I had wondered what a vivid, compelling creature like Theresa could see in him. But I now began to realize that Donaldson was anything but negligible. Behind that pedantic manner there was force.

After our preliminary greetings were over, Donaldson said:

'The reason for my visit is this. I am at a loss to understand exactly what your position is in this matter, M. Poirot?'

Poirot replied guardedly:

'You know my profession, I think?'

'Certainly. I may say that I have taken the trouble to make inquiries about you.'

'You are a careful man, doctor.'

Donaldson said drily:

'I like to be sure of my facts.'

'You have the scientific mind!'

'I may say that all reports on you are the same. You are obviously a very clever man in your profession. You have also the reputation of being a scrupulous and honest one.'

'You are too flattering,' murmured Poirot.

'That is why I am at a loss to explain your connection with this affair.'

'And yet it is so simple!'

'Hardly that,' said Donaldson. 'You first present yourself as a writer of biographies.'

'A pardonable deception, do you not think? One cannot go everywhere announcing the fact that one is a detective—though that, too, has its uses sometimes.'

'So I should imagine.' Again Donaldson's tone was dry. 'Your next proceeding,' he went on, 'was to call on Miss Theresa Arundell and represent to her that her aunt's will might conceivably be set aside.'

Poirot merely bowed his head in assent.

'That, of course, was ridiculous.' Donaldson's voice was sharp. 'You knew perfectly well that that will was valid in law and that nothing could be done about it.'

'You think that is the case?'

'I am not a fool, M. Poirot—'

'No, Dr Donaldson, you are certainly not a fool.'

'I know something—not very much, but enough—of the law. That will can certainly not be upset. Why did you pretend it could? Clearly for reasons of your own—reasons which Miss Theresa Arundell did not for a moment grasp.'

'You seem very certain of her reactions.'

Agatha Christie

A very faint smile passed across the young man's face. He said unexpectedly:

'I know a good deal more about Theresa than she suspects. I have no doubt that she and Charles think they have enlisted your aid in some questionable business. Charles is almost completely amoral. Theresa has a bad heredity and her upbringing has been unfortunate.'

'It is thus you speak of your fiancée—as though she was a guinea-pig?'

Donaldson peered at him through his pince-nez.

'I see no occasion to blink the truth. I love Theresa Arundell and I love her for what she is and not for any imagined qualities.'

'Do you realize that Theresa Arundell is devoted to you and that her wish for money is mainly in order that your ambitions should be gratified?'

'Of course I realize it. I've already told you I'm not a fool. But I have no intention of allowing Theresa to embroil herself in any questionable situation on my account. In many ways Theresa is a child still. I am quite capable of furthering my career by my own efforts. I do not say that a substantial legacy would not have been acceptable. It would have been most acceptable. But it would merely have provided a short cut.'

'You have, in fact, full confidence in your own abilities?'

'It probably sounds conceited, but I have,' said Donaldson composedly.

'Let us proceed, then. I admit that I gained Miss Theresa's confidence by a trick. I let her think that I would be—shall we say, reasonably dishonest—for money. She believed that without the least difficulty.'

'Theresa believes that anyone would do anything for money,' said the young doctor in the matter-of-fact tone one uses when stating a self-evident truth.

'True. That seems to be her attitude—her brother's also.'

'Charles probably *would* do anything for money!'

'You have no illusions, I see, about your future brother-in-law.'

'No. I find him quite an interesting study. There is, I think, some deep-seated neurosis—but that is talking shop. To return to what we are discussing. I have asked myself *why* you should act in the way you have done, and I have found only one answer. It is clear that you suspect either Theresa or Charles of having a hand in Miss Arundell's death. No, please don't bother to contradict me! Your mention of exhumation was, I think, a mere device to see what reaction you would get. Have you, in actual fact, taken any steps towards getting a Home Office order for exhumation?'

'I will be frank with you. As yet, I have not.'

Donaldson nodded.

'So I thought. I suppose you have considered the possibility that Miss Arundell's death may turn out to be from natural causes?'

'I have considered the fact that it may appear to be so—yes.'

'But your own mind is made up?'

'Very definitely. If you have a case of—say—tuberculosis that looks like tuberculosis, behaves like tuberculosis, and in which the blood gives a positive reaction—*eh bien*, you consider it *is* tuberculosis, do you not?'

'You look at it that way? Then what exactly are you waiting for?'

'I am waiting for a final piece of evidence.'

The telephone bell rang. At a gesture from Poirot I got up and answered it. I recognized the voice.

'Captain Hastings? This is Mrs Tanios speaking. Will you tell M. Poirot that he is perfectly right. If he will come here tomorrow morning at ten o'clock, I will give him what he wants.'

'At ten o'clock tomorrow?'

'Yes.'

'Right, I'll tell him.'

Poirot's eyes asked a question. I nodded.

He turned to Donaldson. His manner had changed. It was brisk—assured.

'Let me make myself clear,' he said. 'I have diagnosed this case of mine as a case of murder. It looked like murder, it gave all the characteristic reactions of murder—in fact, it *was* murder! Of that there is not the least doubt.'

'Where then, does the doubt—for I perceive there *is* a doubt—lie?'

'The doubt lay in the *identity of the murderer*—but that is a doubt no longer!'

'Really? You know?'

'Let us say that I shall have definite proof in my hands tomorrow.'

Dr Donaldson's eyebrows rose in a slightly ironical fashion.

'Ah,' he said. 'Tomorrow! Sometimes, M. Poirot, tomorrow is a long way off.'

'On the contrary,' said Poirot, 'I always find that it succeeds today with monotonous regularity.'

Donaldson smiled. He rose.

'I fear I have wasted your time, M. Poirot.'

'Not at all. It is always as well to understand each other.'

With a slight bow Dr Donaldson left the room.

CHAPTER 28

Another Victim

'That is a clever man,' said Poirot thoughtfully.

'It's rather difficult to know what he is driving at.'

'Yes. He is a little inhuman. But extremely perceptive.'

'That telephone call was from Mrs Tanios.'

'So I gathered.'

I repeated the message. Poirot nodded approval.

'Good. All marches well. Twenty-four hours, Hastings, and I think we shall know exactly where we stand.'

'I'm still a little fogged. Who exactly do we suspect?'

'I really could not say who *you* suspect, Hastings! Everybody in turn, I should imagine!'

'Sometimes I think you *like* to get me into that state!'

'No, no, I would not amuse myself in such a way.'

'I wouldn't put it past you.'

Poirot shook his head, but somewhat absently. I studied him.

'Is anything the matter?' I asked.

'My friend, I am always nervous towards the end of a case. If anything should go wrong—'

'Is anything likely to go wrong?'

'I do not think so.' He paused—frowning. 'I have, I think, provided against every contingency.'

'Then, supposing we forget crime and go to a show?'

'*Ma foi, Hastings*, that is a good idea!'

We passed a very pleasant evening, though I made the slight mistake of taking Poirot to a crook play. There is one piece of advice I offer all my readers. Never take a soldier to a military play, a sailor to a naval play, a Scotsman to a Scottish play, a detective to a thriller—and an actor to any play whatsoever! The shower of destructive criticism in each case is somewhat devastating. Poirot never ceased to complain of faulty psychology, and the hero detective's lack of order and method nearly drove him demented. We parted that night with Poirot still explaining how the whole business might have been laid bare in the first half of the first act.

'But in that case, Poirot, there would have been no play,' I pointed out.

Poirot was forced to admit that perhaps that was so.

It was a few minutes past nine when I entered the sitting-room the next morning. Poirot was at the breakfast table—as usual neatly slitting open his letters.

The telephone rang and I answered it.

A heavy-breathing female voice spoke:

'Is that M. Poirot? Oh, it's you, Captain Hastings.'

There was a sort of gasp and a sob.

'Is that Miss Lawson?' I asked.

'Yes, yes, such a terrible thing has happened!'

I grasped the receiver tightly.

'What is it?'

'She left the Wellington, you know—Bella, I mean. I went there late in the afternoon yesterday and they said she'd left. Without a word to me, either! *Most* extraordinary! It makes me feel that perhaps after all, Dr Tanios was *right*. He spoke so *nicely* about her and seemed so *distressed*, and now it really looks as though he were right after all.'

'But what's happened, Miss Lawson? Is is just that Mrs Tanios left the hotel without telling you?'

'Oh, no, it's not *that*! Oh, dear me, no. If that were all it would be *quite* all right. Though I do think it was *odd*, you know. Dr Tanios did say that he was afraid she wasn't quite—not *quite*—if you know what I mean. Persecution mania, he called it.'

'Yes.' (Damn the woman!) 'But what's *happened*?'

'Oh, dear—it is terrible. Died in her sleep. An overdose of some sleeping stuff. And those *poor* children! It all seems so dreadfully *sad*! I've done nothing but cry since I heard.'

'How did you hear? Tell me all about it.'

Out of the tail of my eye I noticed that Poirot had stopped opening his letters. He was listening to my side of the conversation. I did not like to cede my place to him. If I did it seemed highly probable that Miss Lawson would start with lamentations all over again.

'They rang me up. From the hotel. The Coniston it's called. It seems they found my name and address in her bag. Oh, dear, M. Poirot—Captain Hastings, I mean, *isn't it terrible?* Those poor children left motherless.'

'Look here,' I said. 'Are you sure it's an accident? They didn't think it could be suicide?'

'Oh, what a *dreadful* idea, Captain Hastings! Oh, dear, I don't know, I'm sure. Do you think it could be? That would be *dreadful*. Of course she *did* seem very depressed. But she needn't have. I mean there wouldn't have been any difficulty about *money*. I was going to *share* with her—indeed I was. Dear Miss Arundell would have wished it. I'm sure of that! It seems so awful to think of her taking her own life—but perhaps she didn't... The hotel people seemed to think it was an accident?'

'What did she take?'

'One of those sleeping things. Veronal, I think. No, chloral. Yes, that was it. Chloral. Oh, dear, Captain Hastings, do you think—'

Unceremoniously I banged down the receiver. I turned to Poirot.

'Mrs Tanios—'

He raised a hand.

'Yes, yes, I know what you are going to say. She is dead, is she not?'

'Yes. Overdose of sleeping draught. Chloral.'

Poirot got up.

'Come, Hastings, we must go there at once.'

'Is this what you feared—last night? When you said you were always nervous towards the end of a case?'

'I feared another death—yes.'

Poirot's face was set and stern. We said very little as we drove towards Euston. Once or twice Poirot shook his head.

I said timidly:

'You don't think—? Could it be an accident?'

'No, Hastings—no. It was not an accident.'

'How on earth did he find out where she had gone?'

Poirot only shook his head without replying.

The Coniston was an unsavoury-looking place quite near Euston station. Poirot, with his card, and a suddenly bullying manner, soon fought his way into the manager's office.

The facts were quite simple.

Mrs Peters as she had called herself and her two children had arrived about half-past twelve. They had had lunch at one o'clock.

At four o'clock a man had arrived with a note for Mrs Peters. The note had been sent up to her. A few minutes later she had come down with the two children and a suitcase. The children had then left with the visitor. Mrs Peters had gone to the office and explained that she should only want the one room after all.

She had not appeared exceptionally distressed or upset, indeed she had seemed quite calm and collected. She had had dinner about seven-thirty and had gone to her room soon afterwards.

On calling her in the morning the chambermaid had found her dead.

A doctor had been sent for and had pronounced her to have been dead for some hours. An empty glass was found on the table by the bed. It seemed fairly obvious that she had taken a sleeping-draught, and by mistake, taken an overdose. Chloral hydrate, the doctor said, was a somewhat uncertain drug. There were no indications of suicide. No letter had been left. Searching for means of notifying her relations, Miss Lawson's name and address had been found and she had been communicated with by telephone.

Poirot asked if anything had been found in the way of letters or papers. The letter, for instance, brought by the man who had called for the children.

No papers of any kind had been found, the man said, but there was a pile of charred paper on the hearth.

Poirot nodded thoughtfully.

As far as anyone could say, Mrs Peters had had no visitors and no-one had come to her room—with the solitary exception of the man who had called for the two children.

I questioned the porter myself as to his appearance, but the man was very vague. A man of medium height—he thought fair-haired—rather military build—of somewhat nondescript appearance. No, he was positive the man had no beard.

'It wasn't Tanios,' I murmured to Poirot.

'My dear Hastings! Do you really believe that Mrs Tanios, after all the trouble she was taking to get the children away from their father, would quite meekly hand them over to him without the least fuss or protest? Ah, that, no!'

'Then who was the man?'

'Clearly it was someone in whom Mrs Tanios had confidence or rather it was someone sent by a third person in whom Mrs Tanios had confidence.'

'A man of medium height,' I mused.

'You need hardly trouble yourself about his appearance, Hastings. I am quite sure that the man who actually called for the children was some quite unimportant personage. The real agent kept himself in the background!'

'And the note was from this third person?'

'Yes.'

'Someone in whom Mrs Tanios had confidence?'

'Obviously.'

'And the note is now burnt?'

'Yes, she was instructed to burn it.'

'What about that résumé of the case that you gave her?'

Poirot's face looked unusually grim.

'That, too, is burned. But that does not matter!'

'No?'

'No. For you see—it is all in the head of Hercule Poirot.'

He took me by the arm.

'Come, Hastings, let us leave here. Our concern is not with the dead but with the living. It is with them I have to deal.'

CHAPTER 29

Inquest at Littlegreen House

It was eleven o'clock the following morning.

Seven people were assembled at Littlegreen House.

Hercule Poirot stood by the mantelpiece. Charles and Theresa were on the sofa, Charles on the arm of it with his hand on Theresa's shoulder. Dr Tanios sat in a grandfather chair. His eyes were red-rimmed and he wore a black band round his arm.

On an upright chair by a round table sat the owner of the house, Miss Lawson. She, too, had red eyes. Her hair was even untidier than usual. Dr Donaldson sat directly facing Poirot. His face was quite expressionless.

My interest quickened as I looked at each face in turn.

In the course of my association with Poirot I had assisted at many such a scene. A little company of people, all outwardly composed with well-bred masks for faces. And I had seen Poirot strip the mask from one face and show it for what it was—*the face of a killer*!

Yes, there was no doubt of it. *One of these people was*

a murderer! But which? Even now I was not *sure*.

Poirot cleared his throat—a little pompously as was his habit—and began to speak.

'We are assembled here, ladies and gentlemen, to inquire into the death of Emily Arundell on the first of May last. There are four possibilities—that she died naturally—that she died as the result of an accident—that she took her own life—or lastly that she met her death at the hands of some person known or unknown.

'No inquest was held at the time of her death, since it was assumed that she died from natural causes and a medical certificate to that effect was given by Dr Grainger.

'In a case where suspicion arises after burial has taken place it is usual to exhume the body of the person in question. There are reasons why I have not advocated that course. The chief of them is that my client would not have liked it.'

It was Dr Donaldson who interrupted. He said:

'Your client?'

Poirot turned to him.

'My client is Miss Emily Arundell. I am acting for her. Her greatest desire was that there should be no scandal.'

I will pass over the next ten minutes since it would involve much needless repetition. Poirot told of the letter he had received, and producing it he read it aloud. He went on to explain the steps he had taken on coming to Market Basing, and of his discovery of the means taken to bring about the accident.

Then he paused, cleared his throat once more, and went on:

'I am now going to take you over the ground I travelled to get at the truth. I am going to show you what I believe to be a true reconstruction of the facts of the case.

'To begin with it is necessary to picture exactly what passed in Miss Arundell's mind. That, I think, is fairly easy. She has a fall, her fall is supposed to be occasioned by a dog's ball, but *she herself knows better*. Lying there on her bed her active and shrewd mind goes over the circumstances of her fall and she comes to a very definite conclusion about it. Someone has deliberately tried to injure—perhaps to kill her.

'From that conclusion she passes to a consideration of who that person can be. There were *seven* people in the house—four guests, her companion and two servants. Of these seven people only one can be entirely exonerated—since to that one person no advantage could accrue. She does not seriously suspect the two servants, both of whom have been with her for many years and whom she knows to be devoted to her. There remain then, *four* persons, three of them members of her family, and one of them a connection by marriage. *Each of those four persons benefit, three directly, one indirectly, by her death.*

'She is in a difficult position since she is a woman with a strong sense of family feeling. Essentially she is not one who wishes to wash the dirty linen in public, as the saying goes. On the other hand, she is not one to submit tamely to attempted murder!

'She takes her decision and writes to me. She also takes a further step. That further step was, I believe, actuated by two motives. One, I think, was a distinct feeling of *spite* against her entire family! She suspected them all impartially, and she determined at all costs to score off them! The second and more reasoned motive was a wish to protect herself and a realization of how this could be accomplished. As you know, she wrote to her lawyer, Mr Purvis, and directed him to draw up a will in favour of the one person in the house whom, she felt convinced, could have had no hand in her accident.

'Now I may say that, from the terms of her letter to me and from her subsequent actions, I am quite sure that Miss Arundell passed from *indefinite* suspicion of four people to *definite* suspicion of *one* of those four. The whole tenor of her letter to me is an insistence that this business must be kept strictly private since the honour of the family is involved.

'I think that, from a Victorian point of view, this means that a person of *her own name* was indicated—and preferably a *man*.

'If she had suspected Mrs Tanios she would have been quite as anxious to secure her own safety, but not quite as concerned for the family honour. She might have felt much the same about Theresa Arundell, but not nearly as intensely as she would feel about Charles.

'Charles was an *Arundell*. He bore the family *name*! Her reasons for suspecting him seem quite clear. To begin with, she had no illusions about Charles. He had come near to disgracing the family once before. That is, she knew him to be not only a *potential* but an *actual* criminal! He had already forged her name to a cheque. After forgery—a step further—murder!

'Also she had had a somewhat suggestive conversation with him only two days before her accident. He had asked her for money and she had refused and he had thereupon remarked—oh, lightly enough—that she was going the right way to get herself bumped off. To this she had responded that she could take care of herself! To this, we are told, her nephew responded, "Don't be too sure." *And two days later this sinister accident takes place.*

'It is hardly to be wondered at that lying there and brooding over the occurrence, Miss Arundell came definitely to the conclusion that it was *Charles Arundell* who had made an attempt upon her life.

'The sequence of events is perfectly clear. The conversation with Charles. The accident. The letter written to me in great distress of mind. The letter to the lawyer. On the following Tuesday, the 21st, Mr Purvis brings the will and she signs it.

'Charles and Theresa Arundell come down the following weekend and Miss Arundell at once takes the necessary steps to safeguard herself. *She tells Charles about the will.* She not only *tells* him but she actually *shows* it to him! That, to my mind, *is absolutely conclusive. She is making it quite clear to a would-be murderer that murder would bring him nothing whatever!*

'She probably thought that Charles would pass on that information to his sister. But he did not do so. Why? I fancy that he had a very good reason—he felt guilty! He believed that it was *his* doing that the will had been made. But *why* did he feel guilty? Because he had really attempted murder?

Agatha Christie

Or merely because he had helped himself to a small sum of ready cash? Either the serious crime or the petty one might account for his reluctance. He said nothing, hoping that his aunt would relent and change her mind.

'As far as Miss Arundell's state of mind was concerned I felt that I had reconstructed events with a fair amount of correctness. I had next to make up my mind if her suspicions were, in actual fact, justified.

'Just as she had done, I realized that my suspicions were limited to a narrow circle—seven people to be exact. Charles and Theresa Arundell, Dr Tanios and Mrs Tanios. The two servants, Miss Lawson. There was an eighth person who had to be taken into account—namely, Dr Donaldson, who dined there that night, but I did not learn of his presence until later.

'These seven persons that I was considering fell easily into two categories. Six of them stood to benefit in a greater or lesser degree by Miss Arundell's death. If any one of those six had committed the crime the reason was probably a plain matter of *gain*. The second category contained one person only—Miss Lawson. Miss Lawson did *not* stand to gain by Miss Arundell's death, but *as a result of the accident*, she did benefit considerably *later*!

'That meant that if Miss Lawson staged the so-called accident—'

'I never did anything of the kind!' Miss Lawson interrupted. 'It's disgraceful! Standing up there and saying such things!'

'A little patience, mademoiselle. And be kind enough not to interrupt,' said Poirot.

Miss Lawson tossed her head angrily.

'I insist on making my protest! Disgraceful, that's what it is! Disgraceful!'

Poirot went on unheeding.

'I was saying that *if* Miss Lawson staged that accident she did so for an entirely *different* reason—that is, she engineered it so that Miss Arundell *would naturally suspect her own family and become alienated from them.* That *was* a possibility! I searched to see if there were any confirmation or otherwise and I unearthed one very definite fact. If Miss Lawson wanted Miss Arundell to suspect her own family, she would have stressed the fact of the dog, Bob, being *out* that night. But on the contrary Miss Lawson took the utmost pains to *prevent* Miss Arundell hearing of that. Therefore, I argued, Miss Lawson *must* be innocent.'

Miss Lawson said sharply:

'I should hope so!'

'I next considered the problem of Miss Arundell's death. If one attempt to murder a person is made, a second attempt usually follows. It seemed to me significant that within a fortnight of the first attempt Miss Arundell should have died. I began to make inquiries.

'Dr Grainger did not seem to think there was anything unusual about his patient's death. That was a little damping to my theory. But, inquiring into the happenings of the last evening before she was taken ill, I came across a significant fact. Miss Isabel Tripp mentioned a halo of light that had appeared round Miss Arundell's head. Her sister confirmed her statement. They might, of course, be inventing—in a romantic spirit—but I did not think that the incident was quite a likely one to occur to them unprompted. When questioning Miss Lawson she also gave me an interesting piece of information. She referred to a luminous ribbon issuing from Miss Arundell's mouth and forming a luminous haze round her head.

'Obviously, though described somewhat differently by two different observers, the actual *fact* was the same. What it amounted to, shorn of spiritualistic significance, was this: *On the night in question Miss Arundell's breath was phosphorescent!*'

Dr Donaldson moved a little in his chair.

Poirot nodded to him.

'Yes, you begin to see. There are not very many phospho-rescent substances. The first and most common one gave me exactly what I was looking for. I will read you a short extract from an article on phosphorus poisoning.

'*The person's breath may be phosphorescent before he feels in any way affected.* That is what Miss Lawson and the Misses Tripp saw in the dark—Miss Arundell's phosphores-cent breath—"a luminous haze". And here I will read you again. *The jaundice having thoroughly pronounced itself, the system may be considered as not only under the influ-ence of the toxic action of phosphorus, but as suffering in addition from all the accidents incidental to the retention of the biliary secretion in the blood, nor is there from this point any special difference between phosphorus poisoning and certain affections of the liver—such for example as yellow atrophy.*

'You see the cleverness of that? Miss Arundell has suffered for years from liver trouble. The symptoms of phosphorus poisoning would only look like *another attack of the same complaint*. There will be nothing new, nothing startling about it.

'Oh! It was well-planned! Foreign matches—vermin paste? It is not difficult to get hold of phosphorus and a very small dose will kill. The medicinal dose is from 1/100 to 1/30 grain.

'*Voilà*. How clear—how marvellously clear the whole business becomes! Naturally, the doctor is deceived—especially as I find his sense of smell is affected—the garlic odour of the breath is a distinct symptom of phosphorus poisoning. He had no suspicions—why should he have? There were no suspicious circumstances and the one thing that might have given him a hint was the one thing he would never hear—or if he did hear it he would only class it as spiritualistic nonsense.

'I was now sure (from the evidence of Miss Lawson and the Misses Tripp) that murder had been committed. The question still was by *whom*? I eliminated the servants—their mentality was obviously not adapted to such a crime. I eliminated Miss Lawson since she would hardly have prattled on about luminous ectoplasm if she had been connected with the crime. I eliminated Charles Arundell *since he knew, having seen the will, that he would gain nothing by his aunt's death*.

'There remained his sister Theresa, Dr Tanios, Mrs Tanios and Dr Donaldson whom I discovered to have been dining in the house on the evening of the dog's ball incident.

'At this point I had very little to help me. I had to fall back upon the psychology of the crime and the *personality* of the murderer! Both crimes had roughly *the same outline*. They were both *simple*. They were cunning, and carried out with efficiency. They required a certain amount of knowledge but not a great deal. The facts about phosphorus poisoning are easily learned, and the stuff itself, as I say, is quite easily obtained, especially abroad.

'I considered first the two men. Both of them were doctors, and both were clever men. Either of them might have thought of phosphorus and its suitability in this particular case, but the incident of the dog's ball did not seem to fit a masculine mind. The incident of the ball seemed to me essentially a *woman's* idea.

'I considered first of all Theresa Arundell. She had certain potentialities. She was bold, ruthless, and not over scrupulous. She had led a selfish and greedy life. She had always had everything she wanted and she had reached a point where she was desperate for money—both for herself and for the man she loved. Her manner, also, showed plainly that she knew her aunt had been murdered.

'There was an interesting little passage between her and her brother. I conceived the idea that *each suspected the other of the crime*. Charles endeavoured to make her say that *she knew of the existence of the new will*. Why? Clearly because if she knew of it she could not be suspected of the murder. She, on the other hand, clearly did not believe Charles' statement that Miss Arundell had shown it to him! She regarded it as a singularly clumsy attempt on his part to divert suspicion from himself.

'There was another significant point. Charles displayed a reluctance to use the word arsenic. Later I found that he had questioned the old gardener at length upon the strength of some weed-killer. It was clear what had been in his mind.'

Charles Arundell shifted his position a little.

'I thought of it,' he said. 'But—well, I suppose I hadn't got the nerve.'

Poirot nodded at him.

'Precisely, *it is not in your psychology*. Your crimes will always be the crimes of weakness. To steal, to forge—yes, it is the easiest way—but to kill—*no*! To kill one needs the type of mind that can be obsessed by an idea.'

He resumed his lecturing manner.

'Theresa Arundell, I decided, had quite sufficient strength of mind to carry such a design through, but there were other facts to take into consideration. She had never been thwarted, she had lived fully and selfishly—but that type of person is *not the type that kills*—except perhaps in sudden anger. And yet—I felt sure—*it was Theresa Arundell who had taken the weed-killer from the tin.*'

Theresa spoke suddenly:

'I'll tell you the truth. I thought of it. I actually took some weed-killer from a tin down at Littlegreen House. But I couldn't do it! I'm too fond of living—of being alive—I couldn't do that to anyone—take life from them... I may be bad and selfish but there are things I can't do! I couldn't kill a living, breathing human creature!'

Poirot nodded.

'No, that is true. And you are not as bad as you paint yourself, mademoiselle. You are only young—and reckless.'

He went on:

'There remained Mrs Tanios. As soon as I saw her I realized that she was afraid. She saw that I realized that and she very quickly made capital out of that momentary betrayal. She gave a very convincing portrait of a woman *who is afraid for her husband*. A little later she changed her tactics. It was very cleverly done—but the change did not deceive me. A woman can be afraid *for* her husband or she can be afraid *of* her husband—but she can hardly be *both*. Mrs Tanios decided on the latter rôle—and she played her part cleverly—even to coming out after me into the hall of the hotel and pretending that there was something she wanted to tell me. When her husband followed her as she knew he would, she pretended that she could not speak before him.

'I realized at once, not that she feared her husband, but that she disliked him. And at once, summing the matter up, I felt convinced that here was the exact character I had been looking for. Here was—not a self-indulgent woman—but a thwarted one. A plain girl, leading a dull existence, unable to attract the men she would like to attract, finally accepting a man she did not care for rather than be left an old maid. I could trace her growing dissatisfaction with life, her life in Smyrna exiled from all she cared for in life. Then the birth of her children and her passionate attachment to them.

'Her husband was devoted to her but she came secretly to dislike him more and more. He had speculated with her money and lost it—another grudge against him.

'There was only one thing that illuminated her drab life, the expectation of her Aunt Emily's death. Then she would have money, independence, the means to educate her children as she wished—and remember education meant a lot to her—she was a Professor's daughter!

'She may have already planned the crime, or had the idea of it in her mind, before she came to England. She had a certain knowledge of chemistry, having assisted her father in the laboratory. She knew the nature of Miss Arundell's complaint and she was well aware that phosphorus would be an ideal substance for her purpose.

'Then, when she came to Littlegreen House, a simpler method presented itself to her. The dog's ball—a thread or string across the top of the stairs. A simple, ingenious woman's idea.

'She made her attempt—and failed. I do not think that she had any idea that Miss Arundell was aware of the true facts of the matter. Miss Arundell's suspicions were directed entirely against Charles. I doubt if her manner to Bella showed any alteration. And so, quietly and determinedly, this self-contained, unhappy, ambitious woman put her original plan into execution. She found an excellent vehicle for the poison, some patent capsules that Miss Arundell was in the habit of taking after meals. To open a capsule, place the phosphorus inside and close it again, was child's play.

'The capsule was replaced among the others. Sooner or later Miss Arundell would swallow it. Poison was not likely to be suspected. Even if, by some unlikely chance it was, she herself would be nowhere near Market Basing at the time.

'Yet she took one precaution. She obtained a double supply of chloral hydrate at the chemist's, forging her husband's name to the prescription. I have no doubt of what that was for—to keep by her in case anything went wrong.

'As I say, I was convinced from the first moment I saw her that Mrs Tanios was the person I was looking for, but I had absolutely no *proof* of the fact. I had to proceed carefully. If Mrs Tanios had any idea I suspected her, I was afraid that she might proceed to a further crime. Furthermore, I believed that the idea of that crime had already occurred to her. Her one wish in life was to shake herself free of her husband.

'Her original murder had proved a bitter disappointment. The money, the wonderful all-intoxicating money, had all gone to Miss Lawson! It was a blow, but she set to work most intelligently. She began to work on Miss Lawson's conscience which, I suspect, was already not too comfortable.'

There was a sudden outburst of sobs. Miss Lawson took out her handkerchief and cried into it.

'It's been dreadful,' she sobbed. 'I've been wicked! Very wicked. You see, I was very curious about the will—why Miss Arundell had made a new one, I mean. And one day, when Miss Arundell was resting, I managed to unlock the drawer in the desk. And then I found she'd left it all to *me*! Of course, I never dreamed it was so *much*. Just a few thousand—that's all I thought it was. And why not? After all, her own relations didn't really *care* for her! But then, when she was so ill, she asked for the will. I could see—I felt sure—she was going to destroy it... And that's when I was so wicked. I told her she'd sent it back to Mr Purvis.

Poor dear, she was so forgetful. She never remembered what she'd done with things. She believed me. Said I must write for it and I said I would.

'Oh, dear—Oh, dear—and then she got worse and couldn't think of anything. And she died. And when the will was read and it was all that money I felt *dreadful*. Three hundred and seventy-five thousand pounds. I'd never dreamed for a minute it was anything like that or I wouldn't have done it.

'I felt just as though I'd *embezzled* the money—and I didn't know what to do. The other day, when Bella came to me, I told her that she should have half of it. I felt sure that then I would feel happy again.'

'You see?' said Poirot, 'Mrs Tanios was succeeding in her object. That is why she was so averse to any attempt to contest the will. She had her own plans and the last thing she wanted to do was to antagonize Miss Lawson. She pretended, of course, to fall in at once with her husband's wishes, but she made it quite clear what her real feelings were.

'She had at that time two objects, to detach herself and her children from Dr Tanios and to obtain her share of the money. Then she would have what she wanted—a rich contented life in England with her children.

'As time went on she could no longer conceal her dislike for her husband. In fact, she did not try to. He, poor man, was seriously upset and distressed. Her actions must have seemed quite incomprehensible to him. Really, they were logical enough. She was playing the part of the terrorized woman. If I had suspicions—and she was fairly sure that

that must be the case—she wished me to believe that her husband had committed the murder. And at any moment that second murder which I am convinced was already planned in her mind might occur. I knew that she had a lethal dose of chloral in her possession. I feared that she would stage a pretended suicide and confession on his part.

'And still I had no evidence against her! And then, when I was quite in despair, I got something at last! Miss Lawson told me that she had seen Theresa Arundell kneeling on the stairs on the night of Easter Monday. I soon discovered that Miss Lawson could not have seen Theresa at all clearly—not clearly enough to recognize her *features*. Yet she was quite positive in her identification. On being pressed she mentioned a brooch with Theresa's initials—T.A.

'On my request Miss Theresa Arundell showed me the brooch in question. At the same time she absolutely denied having been on the stairs at the time stated. At first I fancied someone else had borrowed her brooch, but when I looked at the brooch in the glass the truth leaped at me. Miss Lawson waking up had seen a dim figure with the initials T.A. flashing in the light. She had leapt to the conclusion it was Theresa.

'But if in the glass she had seen the initials T.A.—then the real initials must have been A.T. since the glass naturally reversed the order.

'Of course! Mrs Tanios' mother was Arabella Arundell. Bella is only a contraction. A.T. stood for Arabella Tanios. There was nothing odd in Mrs Tanios possessing a similar type of brooch. It had been exclusive last Christmas but by the spring they were all the rage, and I had already observed that Mrs Tanios copied her cousin Theresa's hats and clothes as far as she was able with her limited means.

'In my own mind, at any rate, my case was proved.

'Now—what was I to do? Obtain a Home Office order for the exhumation of the body? That could doubtless be managed. I *might* prove that Miss Arundell had been poisoned with phosphorus though there was a little doubt about that. The body had been buried two months, and I understand that there have been cases of phosphorus poisoning where no lesions have been found and where the post mortem appearances are very indecisive. Even then, could I connect Mrs Tanios with the purchase or possession of phosphorus? Very doubtful, since she had probably obtained it abroad.

'At this juncture Mrs Tanios took a decisive action. She left her husband, throwing herself on the pity of Miss Lawson. She also definitely accused her husband of the murder.

'Unless I acted I felt convinced that he would be her next victim. I took steps to isolate them one from the other on the pretext that it was for her safety. She could not very well contradict that. Really, it was *his* safety I had in mind. And then—and then—' He paused—a long pause. His face had gone rather white.

'But that was only a temporary measure. I had to make sure that the killer would kill no more. I had to assure the safety of the innocent.

'So I wrote out my construction of the case and gave it to Mrs Tanios.'

There was a long silence.

Dr Tanios cried out:

'Oh, my God, so that's why she killed herself.'

Poirot said gently:

'Was it not the best way? She thought so. There were, you see, the children to consider.'

Dr Tanios buried his face in his hands.

Poirot came forward and laid a hand on his shoulder.

'It had to be. Believe me it was necessary. There would have been more deaths. First yours—then possibly, under certain circumstances, Miss Lawson's. And so it goes on.'

He paused.

In a broken voice Tanios said:

'She wanted me—to take a sleeping draught one night... There was something in her face—I threw it away. That was when I began to believe her mind was going...'

'Think of it that way. It is indeed partly true. But not in the legal meaning of the term. She knew the meaning of her action...'

Dr Tanios said wistfully:

'She was much too good for me—always.'

A strange epitaph on a self-confessed murderess!

CHAPTER 30

The Last Word

There is very little more to tell.

Theresa married her doctor shortly afterwards. I know them fairly well now and I have learnt to appreciate Donaldson—his clarity of vision and the deep, underlying force and humanity of the man. His manner I may say is just as dry and precise as ever, Theresa often mimics him to his face. She is, I think, amazingly happy and absolutely wrapped up in her husband's career. He is already making a big name for himself and is an authority on the functions of ductless glands.

Miss Lawson, in an acute attack of conscience, had to be restrained forcibly from denuding herself of every penny. A settlement agreeable to all parties was drawn up by Mr Purvis whereby Miss Arundell's fortune was shared out between Miss Lawson, the two Arundells and the Tanios children.

Charles went through his share in a little over a year and is now, I believe, in British Columbia.

Just two incidents.

'You're a downy fellow, ain't you?' said Miss Peabody, stopping us as we emerged from the gate of Littlegreen House one day. 'Managed to hush everything up! No exhumation. Everything done decently.'

'There seems to be no doubt that Miss Arundell died of yellow atrophy of the liver,' said Poirot gently.

'That's very satisfactory,' said Miss Peabody. 'Bella Tanios took an overdose of sleeping stuff, I hear.'

'Yes, it was very sad.'

'She was a miserable kind of woman—always wanting what she hadn't got. People go a bit queer sometimes when they're like that. Had a kitchenmaid once. Same thing. Plain girl. Felt it. Started writing anonymous letters. Queer kinks people get. Ah, well, I dare say it's all for the best.'

'One hopes so, madame. One hopes so.'

'Well,' said Miss Peabody, preparing to resume her walk, 'I'll say this for you. You've hushed things up nicely. Very nicely indeed.' She walked on.

There was a plaintive 'Wuff' behind me.

I turned and opened the gate.

'Come on, old man.'

Bob bounced through. There was a ball in his mouth.

'You can't take that for a walk.'

Bob sighed, turned and slowly ejected the ball inside the gate. He looked at it anxiously then passed through.

He looked up at me.

'If you say so, master, I suppose it's all right.'

I drew a long breath.

'My word, Poirot, it's good to have a dog again.'

'The spoils of war,' said Poirot. 'But I would remind you, my friend, that it was to *me* that Miss Lawson presented Bob, not to *you*.'

'Possibly,' I said. 'But you're not really any good with a dog, Poirot. You don't understand dog psychology! Now Bob and I understand each other perfectly, don't we?'

'Woof,' said Bob in energetic assent.

Lightning Source UK Ltd.
Milton Keynes UK
UKHW020207280721
387846UK00006B/302